# A Matter of Blood

I watched the sheriff leave the park and I motioned for Dr. Yarrow to join me. "Any doubt about the cause of death?" I asked.

"Not that I know of now," he said. "Why?"

"No reason. You doing an autopsy?"

"Sure."

"Can I make a suggestion?" I went on.

"I suppose so."

"Look for a sign that Billy was unconscious before the rope went around his neck. Drugs, a blow to the head, something like that."

Yarrow frowned above his mustache, his black eyes hard and probing. "Have you some reason to think this wasn't suicide, Mr. Tanner?"

"Just one, so far."

"What's that?"

"It doesn't run in the family."

*Bantam Books by Stephen Greenleaf*

BOOK CASE
IMPACT
FATAL OBSESSION
STATE'S EVIDENCE
DEATH BED
GRAVE ERROR

Available from Bantam Crime Line Books

A JOHN MARSHALL TANNER MYSTERY

# FATAL OBSESSION

## STEPHEN GREENLEAF

BANTAM BOOKS
NEW YORK · TORONTO · LONDON · SYDNEY · AUCKLAND

FATAL OBSESSION

*A Bantam Crime Line Book / published by arrangement with the author.*

PRINTING HISTORY

*Dial Press edition published 1983
Bantam edition / January 1992*

ISBN 0-553-29350-8

*Published simultaneously in the United States and Canada*

PRINTED IN THE UNITED STATES OF AMERICA

RAD        0 9 8 7 6 5 4 3 2 1

*For Jon and Sue*

# Chapter
# 1

The plane descended over the heroic quilt of soil, bounced twice on the black and shiny tarmac, and taxied to the terminal unimpeded by other traffic. Except for a woman herding three children and two shopping bags down the aisle behind me, I was the last passenger to leave the plane.

The steep steel stairs creaked beneath my feet. The handrail was slick and damp from the thunderstorm that had crossed the airfield ahead of the plane and still sparked and rumbled in the eastern sky. I danced around the puddles that glowed in the ghostly twilight like the frozen eyes of madmen and pushed my way into the terminal behind a man wearing a houndstooth shirt and glen plaid slacks, glad to escape the heavy air, glad to be meeting someone I liked, glad, I decided finally, to be almost home.

She was waiting at the gate, my sister, on time as always, slim and sensibly attired as always, smiling as almost always. I hadn't been home for close to three decades and I hadn't seen Gail for three years, since she and her family had visited San Franciso for a week and me for a day three summers before. She looked the same now as she had then: tired. Gail had been weary since birth, the consequence of being too eager to please and to do right, too worried that something untoward might happen that she should have magically prevented, too good.

I liked Gail more than I liked my brothers. She was the next youngest to me, and was the only one I had really known growing up. She was the only Tanner I still communicated with outside the month of December and the only one I felt any debt to beyond the clinging debt that common blood begets, so when she had asked me to come back home to help resolve a family dispute I switched some appointments and begged off a new case from the biggest law firm in town and caught a United flight out of San Franciso with a stop in Omaha along the way.

"Marsh." The word bubbled, boiled by the heat of her eyes and her heart.

"Hi, Gail."

We hugged. When I tried to pull away she held me fast for several seconds longer. Through her cotton jacket her body felt small and frail, still a child's. When I finally saw her eyes again they had cooled beneath a spray of tears. "Hey," I said, and she found a smile, and I did, too, but mine was a shade uneasy and hers a shade afraid. The air was charged with more than the lightning that had recently ripped the sky. Gail had always believed I was more than I was, and I had disappointed her more than once as a result. I hoped it wasn't going to happen again.

"How are you, Marsh?" she asked finally, releasing her grip on my arm, swiping at her eyes with thin brown fingers capped by nibbled nails.

"Fine, Gail," I said. "You?"

"Oh, fine."

"Tom?"

"Fine, too."

"The kids?"

"Them, too."

"Good."

"Bruce joined the navy, did I tell you?"

"No. Why?"

"Oh, he didn't know what he wanted to do, I guess. He's at the Great Lakes Training Center. Likes it fine so far."

"Good," I said, then said it once again.

"As long as there's not a war."

"Right."

And then there seemed nothing left to say that could begin to span the years. As we walked to the baggage claim I wondered why Gail's answers to my questions had been so brief and standard, and then wondered why I was regarding her like a suspect or a reluctant witness. I took a deep breath, shook my profession out of my brain, slipped an arm around Gail's waist and a hand through the grips of my suitcase, and led Gail out of the terminal. By the time we were in her little Chevette heading south and east down Highway 5, I was relaxed and Gail was, too, and she was telling me some news about the town we were driving toward, about some people who lived in it now and about others who, like me, had lived there once but left, carrying a high school diploma and a one-way ticket to someplace else.

The thunderheads before us were thinning, scrambling the rays of the sun in abstract-watercolor smears. Now the air was cooler and less humid than the swelter at the airport. Beneath the sky the fields—straight squat rows of bean bushes and tassel-topped sprigs of corn—stretched over the rolling hills like a tufted shawl. I rolled down the car window and thought I could hear, even over the clicking engine and the slap of tires, the sound of growth, of magnificent hybridized fertility. Of course, the car was much too loud. And it was October, not July. You *can* hear corn growing in July, although the people where I live now don't believe it.

As she guided the little car down the narrow highway, waving to strangers in the cars she met and being waved at in return, Gail began telling me about a girl friend of hers, a girl my brother had dated long ago, just before he went to college, who now weighed three hundred pounds and at various times had had her jaws wired shut and her stomach surgically circumvented. And then about a boy who'd been killed in a car crash near Milwaukee, with a woman in the car who was not exactly a woman, and about another boy who'd gone bankrupt in the contracting business and fled to Mexico, where he'd died in prison of a beating, and about a girl who had gone off to an ashram in India and hadn't uttered a word since 1967. And on and on with tragic or comic histories until I asked her to tell me how things were with her, and why she'd been so insistent that I come home even though, with our parents long dead, there was no longer a home for me to come to.

"I just thought you should be here, Marsh," Gail said quietly. "So you can see how things are before you decide. So you can hear the way the rest feel, see what your decision will mean. Curt and Matt want to get the whole business over with once and for all, and I do, too."

"What whole business is that, exactly?"

"Why, what to do with the farm, of course. Like I said on the phone."

"How big is it again?"

"Half a section. Three hundred and twenty acres."

"Pretty big."

"For our part of the state it is."

"What's good farmland going for these days?"

"*Good* land, land like you're seeing out there right now, brings over three thousand dollars an acre."

"You're kidding."

"No, I'm not."

"Jesus. You mean the farm is worth close to a million dollars? That would be a quarter of a million apiece."

I was stunned. I hadn't thought about the farm for years, not until Gail had called. I hadn't kept track of it because the farm hadn't belonged to our father but to his childless brother, who had left it to us kids in four undivided shares when he'd died eight or so years before. Since then, the place had been farmed by a tenant, and most of the profits had gone back into fences and silos and similar improvements. The yearly check I got the week before Christmas was usually just enough to finance a weekend in Carmel and a bottle of Glenlivet. And suddenly this trifle had become a six-figure fortune, or so my calculations raced to tell me. But Gail was shaking her head against my dream.

"I said the *best* land brings that much, Marsh. *Our* place isn't near that good. A lot of clay in there, and the topsoil runs real thin. Even the best farms down home only bring twelve hundred or so."

"Even so," I said. "That's close to half a million."

"Not that much," Gail replied. "There's a lot of timber on the place. Lots of it's too steep to terrace, too. I doubt we could get more than seven, eight hundred an acre if we sell it as a farm. *If* we could find a buyer. That kind of money's hard to come by these days."

I put the mathematics to work again, then looked at Gail.

"You seem to know a lot about all this," I said. "I didn't know you were such an agrarian."

She smiled quickly. "Oh, I'm not. Not at all. But Karen, well, she and Paul, that's her husband, they're farming eighty acres out north of town on Paul's folks' place now, so I pick all this up when the kids come to Sunday dinner."

"You want to keep our place as a farm, I take it."

Gail nodded vigorously. "For Karen and Paul. Right."

"They're not making a go of it now?"

"Not on eighty acres, Marsh. No one could. Paul's the hardest worker you've ever seen," she added, imagining my doubt and opposing it.

"Could they make it if they could farm our place, too?"

"Sure they could."

"Can they buy it?"

"Outright? No. Not on a sixteen-percent mortgage."

"How about the others?" I asked, bringing images of my brothers to mind, faces I hadn't seen in the flesh for years. "What do they want to do?"

"Well, Curt is . . . I don't know, Marsh. He's just given up on life, it seems like. Stays out on that old place he bought over in Glory City, him and Laurel, never comes to town, never does anything. Poor Laurel's a prisoner out there, although she won't admit it. Has Curt talked to *you* at all, Marsh?"

"No."

"He hasn't to Matt, either."

"What's Curt's problem?" I asked, seeing him as I had known him once, strong, silent, sure of himself and his place in the world that so confused the rest of us.

"His boy, more than anything," Gail answered. "You remember how Curt loved that boy."

"Sure. Billy. Nice kid."

"He sure *was*."

"Was?"

"You haven't seen Billy since he was in high school, have you, Marsh?"

"No. Why? What's happened?"

"He went to war, that's what happened. Vietnam." Gail shook her head. "You wouldn't believe he's one of us, Marsh. Drugs. Liquor. Women. Fights. Half the time he walks right by me on the street like he's never laid eyes on me before. Then there's the stories . . . "

"What stories?"

"Oh, about his brawls and his wild antics and his hippie girl friend and, well, about him and some women in town who are old enough to know better. I'm sure some of the stories aren't true, but there's so many some of them *have* to be and that's bad enough. It's about taken everything that's good out of Curt, that's for sure. He just walks around in a gray daze."

"Where's Billy now?"

"Oh, he's still around town, at least he was a week ago. He comes and goes, dragging along some girl he says is his wife but probably isn't. I hear he's living in a shack he built out on the farm, down in a draw somewhere that doesn't even have a road to it. Don't know *what* he lives on, he's got no job. He's just real peculiar, Marsh, and Curt won't talk about it, so all I know is what I hear. Oh, it's so *sad*, Marsh. Billy won't have anything to *do* with Curt and it eats at him like a cancer, you can just see it."

"So how does Curt feel about the farm?"

"He wants to sell," Gail said sadly. "Mostly so Billy won't have a place to hide out, I think, as though there aren't a hundred other shacks around for him to hide out in. But Curt thinks if Billy had to leave the farm then he'd move home again and everything would be like it was, but he's wrong. Billy'll never be like he was."

"I'm sorry to hear that," I said. "I guess the war's still not over for some."

"Not for Curt, it's not."

We paused while we passed through a town that was little more than a wide spot in the road. I remembered playing basketball there once. The court had been on the stage in the school auditorium. One of our players had fallen off going after a loose ball. We'd changed into our uniforms in the school woodshop and after the game we found all our street clothes squeezed into the vises on the workbenches, mashed almost beyond utility. I smiled to myself at the memory. By the time the smile had vanished so had the little town.

"What about brother Matt?" I asked Gail as she accelerated back up to speed. "What does he think about the farm?"

Gail laughed. "Matt's really something these days, Marsh.

Big car, fancy clothes, big talk about this deal and that deal. Wears a gold chain around his neck, if you can believe it. He rolled through town last summer on his way from Chicago to Denver for some convention, driving a car as long as the town; people talked about it for weeks. He's on wife number three, you know. Going to bring her with him when he comes down to vote on the farm. Says she's the most beautiful woman in Chicago."

"Matt was always lucky with women."

"Matt's luck never lasted too long, though," Gail said as she slowed to let a combine cross from field to field in front of us.

"So Matt wants to sell?"

"Yes," Gail said, the word as stiff as a curse. "Probably so he can pay the keep on his new wife."

"Now, Gail." I reached over and patted her shoulder.

"I know," she said wearily. "I'm sorry. It's just that I've got some problems of my own, Marsh; one of them thanks to little Billy, as a matter of fact. And if we sell the farm, *one* of those problems won't go away."

"You mean Karen and her husband?"

Gail nodded. "It *kills* me to see them work so hard for so little, Marsh. Times are so tough. I feel if I could help them out just a *little* they could make it, but if I can't, well, I don't know *what* will happen. You won't believe how bad things have gotten back here, Marsh."

"So what's the bottom line?" I asked. "We're going to vote, is that it?"

"Yes. At least that's what the rest of us want. According to Uncle Raymond's will it takes three votes to change things. Matt and Curt want to sell. If you decide their way, then that's it. If you decide mine, then the farm stays in the family, the way it is now. So I'm hoping you won't give them the third vote, Marsh. I'm hoping real hard."

Gail took her eyes off the road and found mine. I had no doubt of the seriousness of her purpose and her plan. She had always been a girl of few but fervent passions which she pursued with all her energy and ability, which was as much energy and ability as there was in town. One Christmas she had single-handedly collected a garageful of toys for the needy kids in the county, and another time she had organized a boycott of the movie house until the management let her friend, a black girl, sit on the main floor instead of only in the balcony.

The farm was Gail's current project, and I was the means to its fulfillment. I squirmed in my seat and looked away from Gail and toward the vista that rolled to the dim horizon, a vista in which man was insignificant and thus more real. At times I had felt lost and helpless beneath that unedged sky, but now I felt comforted by its reach, by the absence of demand or threat in its aspect. "I'll do my best," I said to Gail.

"I don't expect you to decide right now, Marsh," Gail answered quietly. "Just keep an open mind while you listen to the others. I know in the end you'll do what's best. You always have," she added, uttering the expectant hell of families.

On the windshield of an approaching truck a plastic hand oscillated cheerily on its wire support, in indiscriminate hospitality. I looked at the driver to see if the sentiment was real but he was hidden behind mirrored glasses and a straw hat with a broken brim. I waved and was ignored by everything but the happy hand. "We're halfway there," Gail said. "Getting nervous?"

"About something," I said. "I'm not sure quite what."

# Chapter 2

Even in the new-moon dusk the land became progressively more familiar, its contours, swells, and vales arranging themselves into patterns that confirmed I was home. The highway was newer, straighter, flatter than it had been in my youth, thanks to a local businessman who had served a term on the state highway commission a while back. In contrast, the farmhouses seemed fewer, darker, sadder than before, doubtless because so many small farmers hadn't survived and had left their hollow homes and heritage behind to secure their debts. But the land itself, that furrowed sea of gray-black soil, the land seemed the same as always, at least to me, a city boy impervious to signs of topsoil loss and surface erosion and rootworm infestation and the thousand other imperceptible calamities that may one day render the Great Plains barren.

And soon there was the Chariton River Bridge, and the Dale Church hill, and the nursery and the Skinner place and the Chevy dealership and the Cooper Creek Bridge and then we were there. Home. Chaldea. Population 6,189, or so proclaimed the sign that greeted us from behind the scars of a fully-choked shotgun blast.

A rush of landmarks scrambled my memories, no single one able to leap forth and make itself fully known. But even at the edge of town I knew exactly where I was, the Dairy Queen and the scrapyard and the sale barn marking the place as firmly as a fingerprint. My general impression was that time had trod lightly on Chaldea, not fatally, but enough to stunt its growth. Almost all I saw was familiar and thus a part of me, for I had realized long ago that Chaldea had made me, more than anything except my parents, what I was and still was not.

Silent in our little car, we made turns and stops at predictable places, dodged the roaring cars of kids, and pulled to a stop in a sloping drive behind a big new Ford and beside a trim white house that lay beneath the drooping dying leaves of a Norwegian maple. "Here we are," Gail said, gaiety forced upon the words. "How does it feel to be back?"

"Strange," I said truthfully. "In a way it feels like I never left."

"Your hometown's like your first love, I think," Gail said. "You never quite forget it."

"Who was yours?" I asked.

"My first love?"

"Right."

"Scotty McDougall. Remember him?"

"Freckles. Drove a Merc with fender skirts. What's he doing now?"

"Drives a gravel truck."

"And he was the first?"

"You mean sex?"

"I guess."

"I don't think I'll tell you, Marsh. I don't think I want you to know."

I glanced at Gail. In the scramble of light and shadow her look was peculiar, a mixture of flirtation and righteousness. Sibling strangeness. I hauled my suitcase out of the trunk and followed her up the steps to the front porch.

Instead of opening the door Gail turned and leaned back against it, facing the town she lived in more than me. "I think you'll find it pretty much the same," she said softly. "Not much happens in Chaldea except births and deaths. Not much that's good, anyway."

It was a common sentiment but not exactly true. Whenever I talked to Gail on the phone she would regale me with news that was complex and vital and unending: acts of bigotry and hospice, comedy and courage, bankruptcy and philanthropy, slander and success. And among it all people like my parents and their friends had led lives of richness, highlighted by regular and substantial exercises in altruism, that eclipsed anything I knew or heard of since. Whenever I thought of my parents I inevitably thought of the things they did: hayrides and scavenger hunts and square dances and a hundred other things that seemed to bring them joy. But lives are least appreciated by those who live them, and so it was in Chaldea.

"Marsh?"

"Yes?"

"Have you changed? I mean, deep down?"

"I don't think so, Gail. A little, I suppose. Why?"

"I hope you haven't, Marsh. I couldn't stand it if you were different, too."

I breathed deeply and with dread in the wake of Gail's soft questions. I had probably lied to her about not changing, but since she would soon know better than I where the truth of it lay, I decided to let it go.

"You'll stay here with us, won't you, Marsh?" Gail asked.

"I don't know, Gail. I think a motel would be better."

"Don't be silly. We've got all kinds of room now that the kids are gone."

"I'm not used to living with other people, Gail. Plus you'd be better off if I was out of your hair for at least part of the day. Tom seems like a man who values privacy."

She yielded more quickly than I would have guessed. "Well, come in for coffee at least. Tom will be glad to see you. If he's home yet."

Gail fiddled with the lock on the door. The porch swing to my left purred quietly as it swayed on its chains, pushed by the evening breeze. Two dogs pranced purposefully down the walk and a street rod cut around its muffler a few blocks away, making the noise of battle. Then the evening sounds came not from the hum of busy streets but from trees and plants and the things that live in them. By the time Gail opened the door I was thinking how strange it was that it was locked at all.

The living room was dark, the air heavy and still. The lamp Gail turned on barely colored the blackness. I sensed the room was unused. The order was too permanent, the arrangement too formal, suited more to admiration than conversation. It was a place for visitors, company, callers, and it was also the place where my parents' furnishings had come to rest. The speckled couch and pouf, dad's threadbare club chair, the tile-topped coffee table listing slightly on a leg I had both broken and repaired, the glass-doored breakfront which had once housed china we never used and which then made room for schoolboy trophies. Even the *Book of Knowledge* and the *Harvard Classics* had found their way to Gail's front room.

These and other silent things beckoned me, but Gail slowed not at all so I followed her into the kitchen. It was a large, high-ceilinged room with walls of rough, undulating plaster, dominated by a six-foot white-pine pie saver and a thick black range. Various pieces of ironware hung on wooden pegs in the walls, as did prints of flying birds. The linoleum on the floor was as speckled as hash. The smells were of baked starches and canned fruits. The drop leaves of the round oak table had been raised to welcome me.

I sat at the table and looked at the ears of Indian corn in its center and at the platter of hazelnuts that surrounded them. The varicolored kernels had been polished to a pointillistic shine. I thought of holidays and snow and prayers of grace.

"Tom must be upstairs," Gail said. "I'll get him."

She started out of the room, then pivoted and walked to the counter beside the stove and pulled a heavy crockery jar off a shelf and carried it over to the table. Yellow birds and blue flowers were emblazoned on its bulbous flanks. "Here," she said. "I baked these this morning. I remembered you like them."

I reached into the jar and pulled one out. Gum-drop cookies. Soft yet gritty, as big as saucers. "Great," I said, around the crumbs. Gail went off to find her husband.

I ate a second cookie and walked around the kitchen, imagining the bounty that issued from it. Gail liked to cook, always had, great quantities of simple, wholesome fare. She was much better at it than our mother had been, and when they both realized it, during Gail's last year at home, the meal situation improved geometrically as did my weight: I gained twelve pounds and moved from halfback to full.

There were some snapshots taped to the refrigerator, each of them depicting a pretty, ash-blond girl who I knew was Gail's daughter Karen. She was alternately posed with her husband, a gangly, guileless boy, or her baby, a small and red and strange little package, like all babies. There were no pictures of Bruce, Tom and Gail's other child.

I pulled open a cupboard to see if there were any other goodies around but saw only canned goods and packaged staples and one thing more. Pills, bottles of them strung all along a bottom shelf, brown plastic cylinders with wide white lids. I lifted one and then another and found all of them were empty. I couldn't decipher the labels, but they were all made out to Gail's husband, Tom Notting. When I heard him trudging down the stairs I closed the cupboard.

Tom entered the kitchen with a hand outstretched. I took it in mine and we smiled the testing smiles of enemies and in-laws. I had met Tom Notting only once, when they'd come to visit. He had been quiet but pleasant, an observer rather than an initiator, agreeable to most everything that came his way. As I remembered, he held mildly liberal opinions about the events of the day and thought Gail was a divine presence on the earth. I hoped none of that had changed, but one thing certainly had. The hand that didn't hold mine held a gold-topped cane.

Within the folds of his red plaid robe, Tom seemed even thinner than his smile. His hair had dwindled along with his flesh, and his back bent thankfully toward his cane. The slippers on his feet were the type I associated with grandfathers. When I dropped his hand it trembled for an instant before sinking to his side.

In the bright fluorescence of the kitchen Gail seemed altered as well, her fatigue not a badge of Calvinist honor but the vestige of a plague. She had never worried about herself, her looks, her health, but always before she had been the better for it, her vitality making mockery of the beauty produced by bottles and oils and sprays. But now she appeared neglected, a plant in need of water, her hair straight and splayed, her brown eyes slow and overlidded, her shoulders slack and rounded, the whole of her beaten by something far more energetic than she had ever been.

Tom and I exchanged the basic greetings and then a silence swelled until Gail pricked it. "Marsh is talking about going to a motel. We won't hear of it, will we, Tom?"

"Of course not."

"See?"

"No," I said. "It's better to want to see people than to have to. I'll feel less guilty if I'm out of your way. Who knows? I may want to romp and stomp a little, as we used to say." I laughed uneasily.

"Please, Marsh. We've got a lot to talk about."

"We can talk all you want, Gail. But I'll make someone else listen to my snores."

Tom's failure to say anything beyond his ritual invitation made me all the more determined to override Gail's hospitality. I wanted to be free of family for at least a part of my stay, free to go wherever the dreadful thrill of being home again might take me, whether on nostalgic excursions or to the nearest bar. I looked at my watch. "Is the Welcome Stranger still in business?" I asked.

Gail laughed. "It's still there," she said. "A bit long in the tooth. There's a new place out Highway 60. And they've remodeled the hotel, Marsh. It's real nice. Why don't you try it?"

"The National?"

"Right. Some retired general from Kansas City bought it. Spent half a million fixing it up, so they say. There's a coffee shop and everything."

"Maybe I should give them a call."

"They aren't full," Tom said bluntly. "Never have been; never will."

"And you can take the Chevette whenever you want, Marsh. Just keep it while you're here. I can use the Ford."

"Tom'll need that at work, won't he?"

"Tom doesn't work anymore, Marsh. So don't worry."

I looked at Tom for some sort of explanation, but all he gave me was a blank and feckless stare. The last I heard Tom had been the county assessor. Now, apparently, he was not. I wondered if the reason was his illness, if he was too sick to work. I wondered what was wrong with him. But while I was wondering, no one said a thing. "Maybe I'd better get going, then," I said at last. "I'm kind of beat."

"Stay a little longer, Marsh," Gail said. "So we can talk. I want to tell you some more about Karen and Paul. And about the baby. Christine. Oh, she's just the cutest thing. Sleeps through the night already, never cries. They're all so sweet I could just cry."

She looked like she meant it, the crying part. Clearly Gail was concerned about her daughter and her family, about their future. As of course she should be. My problem was, that future seemed somehow bound up with me. "What about Bruce?" I asked. "What does he think of this farm thing?"

Gail looked at Tom. Tom frowned. "Bruce and I had a falling-out when he decided to waste four years of his life in the navy. We haven't talked to him about it, and I'm sure he couldn't care less in any event."

"Not even about the money?" I asked. "Assuming the place is sold?"

"Bruce won't get a penny of that money," Tom spat. "Not as long as I'm alive."

There was suddenly a lot of tension around, of a quality that seemed obscene in the placid room and town. I stood up to leave.

"Marsh?" Tom's smile was strange and crooked.

I waited for what he had to say.

"Thought you might want to read this," Tom went on. He walked to the counter and picked up a piece of paper and handed it to me. "Was on the front page of tonight's *Chaldean*."

I looked at the column of newsprint he had handed me and sat down at the table again and read it. The headline was "Decision Near on Tanner Plot," the byline was Mary Martha Gormley, editor and publisher, the text was long and somehow ominous:

After a lengthy period of speculation and conjecture, a decision is expected within a week on the future of the 320 acres on the southern edge of Chaldea known as the Tanner plot. For almost a year, various interests have made their desires for the future use of the land known to the heirs of Raymond Tanner, owners of the property. These interests include the environmental group WILD (Wilderness Is the Last Domain), which insists the property be dedicated as open space and a wildlife refuge; the Black Diamond Coal Company, which intends to strip-mine the property to reach a vein the company claims can be profitably extracted; and the Chariton Valley Oil Company, a subsidiary of Cosmos Petroleum, an independent wildcatting operation. Also expressing interest are various agribusiness concerns, most prominently an Illinois consortium represented locally by attorney Clark Jaspers. For its part, the city of Chaldea will reportedly seek to acquire the plot as an industrial park in an effort to attract small manufacturing concerns to replace the loss of payroll the city has recently experienced. The *Daily Chaldean* has learned that the four heirs to the Tanner plot are convening in Chaldea this week to vote on the ultimate disposition of the property, which is primarily grain farming on a share arrangement with the neighboring landowner. The Tanner heirs include local resident Gail Notting, wife of former Appanoose County Assessor Tom Notting, Curtis Tanner of Glory City, Matthew Tanner of Chicago, and John Marshall Tanner of San Franciso. Local sports fans will remember "Marsh" Tanner as an All-State football player at Chaldea High.

When I'd finished the article, I looked into the slanted smile of Tom Notting. "Thought you'd like to see what you're in for the next few days," he said. "Have fun."

I reached for another cookie and went out the door, my sister's eyes and hopes on me all the way to the car.

# Chapter 3

I parked in the alley behind the hotel, got a room and a key from a disheveled desk clerk who seemed nonplussed by the transaction, and went straight to bed. The building uttered groaning nightmares and all the plumbing seemed routed through the walls behind my head. Some people down the hall spent almost an hour performing stunts their bed was in no shape to endure. But some time after my travel alarm read one A.M. I fell asleep.

I got up early, or so I thought, but when I entered the coffee shop at seven-thirty it was already half full of an amazingly spry assortment of men. They were local business people rather than tourists, talking over the events of the previous day, filtering the world through the thin and biased fibers of Chaldea. I recognized a few faces, and matched names with about a quarter of those. As I moved to a table I attracted several stares, and a couple of them evolved into whispers. While I waited to see who would make the first move, I ordered a short stack of buckwheats from the buxom young waitress who was wearing what looked like a nurse's uniform. The hanky pinned to her waist bore the name Darlene.

A man sitting at the largest table in the room stood up and headed my way, a broad smile parting the thick flesh of his face, his walk the careless swagger of a man among friends. He stopped squarely in front of me and put his hands on the back of the empty chair. "Marsh Tanner, isn't it?" he asked cheerily, knowing the answer.

"Right," I said.

"I'm Norm Gladbrook, Marsh. Run the hardware store here on the square. Maybe you remember me. Your dad and I were real good friends, rest his soul. On the hospital board together. And you bought a ball glove off me once."

"Sure. How are you?"

"Real fine, Marsh. Real fine. And you?"

"Fine, too."

"Staying here at the hotel?"

I nodded.

"Fixed it up real nice, haven't they?"

"Sure have."

" 'Course, it's not like those places out in Frisco. Stayed in one once cost sixty bucks a night. Can you believe it? Sixty bucks. Bought a De Soto once for less than that."

I took a sip of coffee. My neck was beginning to stiffen from looking up into the sunny face of the hardware man. "Why don't you sit down, Mr. Gladbrook?" I asked, when it was obvious he had more on his mind than a greeting.

Gladbrook pulled back the chair. "Just for two shakes," he said. "Wouldn't want your buckwheats to get cold," he added, confirming my guess that any word I uttered could be heard throughout the room.

Gladbrook settled into the chair and the waitress brought my breakfast. I took a bite, uncomfortable under the heavy stare of my guest. With one more bite I gave up on the buckwheats and asked Gladbrook what he wanted to talk about.

"We heard you and the rest were coming to town about now," Gladbrook began. "You need anything while you're here, you just give me a call at the store. Anything at all."

"Thanks."

"You need a car? Marv Clemons, the Plymouth dealer, he's got a nice little loaner he'll let you have. Want me to give him a call?"

"No, thanks. I've got Gail's car, my sister's. It's no problem."

"Well, if you're sure." Without asking, Gladbrook sipped water from my glass. "Now, the thing is, your dad was a fine man, Marsh. Town lost one of its best when he went down."

"That's nice of you to say."

"Just the truth," Gladbrook said, his face suddenly losing sun and gaining shadow. I sensed the cause was more than his reference to the departed. "Your dad thought a lot of this town," Gladbrook went on. "Gave a lot of his time to it. Your mother, too," he added quickly. "Grace was a handsome woman. Real active in the community. Civic music. The Tri-T. Wednesday Club. PEO. She was up for Citizen of the Year at least twice, don't know if you knew it. Lem Fiddler beat her out one time, for his work on the bandstand. Don't recall the other. Might have been me," Gladbrook concluded with a chuckle.

I took another sip of coffee and eyed my soggy flapjacks, my mother's face alive and smiling in the space between us. I retained only a child's view of her, an unreal, romantic view, but one I wanted to keep. When I glanced around the room several eyes scurried away from mine.

Gladbrook seemed to be struggling over tactics. "Your brother here yet?" he asked. "Matt, I mean?"

"Not yet," I said.

He nodded. "You seen Curt?"

"No."

"Curt's changed."

"So I hear."

"Gail okay? Haven't seen her in a long time."

"Seems to be," I said.

"Haven't seen Tom much, either. Used to eat here of a morning, you know, but since he retired, well, he took it real hard when the party wouldn't back him. Real hard. Probably why the boy ran off so sudden, Tom tightening up that way."

"What boy?"

"Tom's boy. Bruce."

Because it seemed a betrayal of Gail to discuss her husband and her son, I stayed quiet, even though Gladbrook was poised to tell me more. Part of the mystery of Tom had been answered, but the part about his illness hadn't. I glanced at my watch and Gladbrook took the hint.

"Like to talk to you about this farm thing sometime, Marsh," he said. "I'm president of the Chamber this year, so the boys asked me to pass on the—what you might call the *business* community's thoughts on the thing. Not right now, necessarily. Maybe later today? You could stop by the store?"

I shifted in my chair. "I don't know my schedule yet, Mr. Gladbrook. I haven't talked to Gail today. I'll stop by if I can."

"Well, good. That's just fine. And if you can't make it, why I can catch you here at the hotel. Right?" The smile returned.

"Right."

"Matt going to be staying here, too?"

"I don't know."

"Bringing his new wife, I hear."

"So they say."

"Supposed to be a real looker."

"I imagine."

Gladbrook paused, evidently to remember if he'd forgotten any part of his gambit, then pushed his chair back. "Well, real good to talk to you, Marsh."

"You, too."

"Lots of things about the old town here you probably don't know about, being gone so long."

"I imagine."

"We need help, I don't mind telling you. Folks are hoping you feel about us the same way your daddy did, is what it comes down to, I guess."

Gladbrook's eyes probed my face. Since I didn't know what my reaction was, he didn't find the one he wanted. "Well, we can go into all that when you come by the store."

"Right."

"Well, that's real fine. Real fine. I'll be seeing you, Marsh. You have a good day."

"You, too."

Gladbrook stood over me, gazing down like a pachyderm. "Still remember that run you made against Bloomfield. Damnedest thing I ever saw on a football field. Still the record down at the high school, I think. Ninety-six yards."

I gave Gladbrook about half the smile he'd awarded me and watched him walk off, the fluff of a gray-white handkerchief sticking out of his pocket like the tail of a double-knit bunny.

My second cup of coffee came and went, as did some more diners. All of them spotted me, and a few nodded my way with a puzzled reflex. One or two looked like they wanted to say something, but none of them did until I stood up to pay the check.

The man who clasped me on the shoulder and shook my hand was one I knew and liked. Arnold Keene had been my high school history teacher. He was now superintendent of schools, or was the last I heard. He'd been the best teacher by far when I was in school, among other reasons because he had an approach to the Civil War that was both rapturous and mystical, of the stuff from which pacifists are made.

"Marsh."

"Hey, Arnie."

"It's great to see you."

"You, too."

"Heard you were in town, Marsh. Ann and I sure would like you to come to dinner while you're here."

"I will if I can, Arnie. Say hi to Ann for me, anyway."

Arnie nodded his balding head. He had to be over sixty-five but he looked a decade younger. His wife had been his student, and their courtship and marriage had been scandalous to many, as those things tend to be, but my knowledge of it was all hearsay. All I knew for sure was that they were both good people who'd taken a genuine interest in me when I was too young to be much of anything but irritating.

"How long you staying?" Arnie asked as I pocketed my change.

"I'm not sure. Probably only a day or two. How's Craig?" I asked, naming their son, a star miler in his time, which had been about five years after mine. Craig was a doctor in Texas, last I heard. The thought made me smile. Everything I knew about Chaldea's present was what I had learned through Gail. If she didn't deem it important enough to tell over the long-distance wire, it didn't exist.

"Craig died two years ago, Marsh," Arnie said, jolting my thoughts. "Car wreck. Down in Dallas."

"I'm sorry. I didn't know."

"It's okay. We're over it now. Took a while, I admit. Hard to understand a thing like that. Just like what happened to your folks."

He stopped, stabbed by the pointed blade of memory, and his gaunt face grew even longer, assuming an aspect that on another face would have been a caricature of grief. "Left a wife and three kids," he went on. "We never see them. She thinks we're too backward up here in the sticks. Big society woman. Married Craig's partner six weeks after he died. Thank God Ann has her church."

Arnie's eyes returned from the gruesome burden of the past. He rubbed them back to life and coughed while I searched for something to say. "Come see us, Marsh," he said, before I thought of anything.

Arnie slapped my shoulder again and walked away. I took some quarters back to my table and left them for the waitress. When she saw me she hurried up and asked if anything was wrong with the buckwheats. Her breasts bounced furiously within their sheaths. I told her I'd been too busy to eat, then hurried out into the street without meeting any of the eyes that sought out mine.

# Chapter 4

The Hotel National was in the center of town, on the east side of the city square. It faced, as did all the buildings on the square, the four-storied courthouse, whose Byzantine roofline and high clocked cupola and rough stone walls sheltered everything from municipal offices to the only public rest rooms in town. The clock was stopped at ten past twelve, and as far as I knew it had ever been thus.

On the lawn that stamped the center of the square were four Civil War cannon and the modernistic band shell that had garnered Lem Fiddler the Citizen of the Year award, but there were none of the giant trees I remembered climbing to view parades or peer in windows or show off for girls. I assumed they had fallen when Dutch elm disease savaged the state some years before. Without them, the square seemed meek and defenseless, open to plunder.

Between the hotel and the courtyard was traffic, two lanes of cars, one driving clockwise, the other counter, with parking in between. By day the drivers searched out places to park and shop, but by night they were looking and being looked at, with sex the ultimate medium of exchange. In my day a bargain was seldom struck, at least by me.

Like every other kid in town, I'd cruised the square as regularly as an electric motor, on Friday and Saturday nights and Sunday afternoons. One time, after a win in the big game, we had circled it one hundred and forty consecutive times in my father's Impala, checking the action, seeking brazen girls, finding none. At various times I'd been arrested on the square for shooting fireworks, gotten drunk on blackberry wine while circumnavigating it, necked in the shadow of the bandstand, and seen everything from knife fights to Estes Kefauver within its boundaries. Those times and others joined me as I began to walk, my dark glasses donned as black disguise, my stroll as brave as Lash LaRue's.

The Chaldea square. Never grand, it had dwindled further in the years I'd been away. Several storefronts were boarded up and many of the businesses I once patronized had been replaced by specialists in chiropractic or pictured shirts. It seemed less crowded, too, and so less prosperous. Times had never boomed in Chaldea, but I sensed depression, a hanging on. I didn't know precisely why or what had happened, but I had a feeling Norm Gladbrook, Chamber of Commerce president, would tell me all about it when and if I got around to stopping by his store. I left the east side and headed west.

It was only nine o'clock but already there was much activity. All the stores had opened, and most of the proprietors were sweeping off the walks in front of their establishments. I passed the Firestone outlet, where I'd earned my first paycheck patching tires; the pool hall where my brother Matt had spent every spare hour between the ages of twelve and eighteen; the old Ritz Theater, now a discount variety store, where I'd seen Gene and Roy and Johnny Mack Brown shoot it out for a dime and dreamed to strike it rich at Bank Night or to win a prize from Hadacol; and the Owl Drug, scene of my first date, tremulous words rasped across the top of a lemon Coke on a Sunday after church.

I went inside the drugstore but it had been remodeled in chrome and glass, with space for everything but a soda fountain and the kids it would attract. As a compromise I bought a roll of Necco wafers and went back outside to encounter Ziggy's, source of model airplanes and comics you could read without paying for or being urged to. And then the bank and the dimestore, the shoe store, clothing store, jewelry store, paint store, and Sears, Coast-to-Coast, Western Auto, Gamble's, Penney's, Woolworth's, Spurgeon's, and the Blackbird Café.

Not so different, really, from before, but not the same. Once I'd known and been known by every business on the square. Now the faces I saw were strangers, trying to weather the slings and arrows of economic fortune in a place that didn't have many things that anyone else in the world wanted very much.

I continued my stroll, noting other changes. There seemed to be a racial diversity that hadn't existed before—I noted several black faces and even an Oriental. And the farmers came to town in big cars instead of rattling pickups with hogs in the back. And the girls didn't seem quite as cute as the ones in my day, but they were sexier and knew it. And not as many people said hello to strangers like myself.

I'd almost made it all the way around when a man came out of the Blackbird and bumped into me before he saw me coming. We backed away and apologized routinely, then looked at each other a second time. "Marsh?" he said. "Marsh Tanner?"

"Hello, Chuck," I said, addressing my first and best friend.

"I'll be damned. Heard you were in town. Didn't know if I'd see you."

I laughed. "Everyone's already heard I'm in town and I didn't get here till last night."

"Yeah, well, you know how it is in Chaldea. Remember the time you took Bonnie Conway to the drive-in and wouldn't tell your mom who you went with? How long did it take her to find out?"

"Two hours. And I'd never been out with Bonnie before in my life."

"Know where she is now?"

"Where?"

"Vegas. Husband's a pit boss at the Sands. Look her up when you're there, she'll get you into any show in town, Sinatra included. You screw her that night, Marsh? You never said."

"Screw *you*, Chuck," I said, and laughed.

The smile dropped off Chuck's face. "Yeah. Screw me. Well, someone beat you to it."

I looked more closely at my friend. Like me he had added some pounds and lost some hair, but there was a further debilitation I didn't think we shared. His short jacket was frayed at the cuffs and collar and the front of his shirt was rumpled and puckered and in part unbuttoned. His skin had always been fair, as befit his reddish hair and blue eyes, but the flesh was waxen now, unpolished beneath a bristle of rosy beard. As the seconds drained away I thought I detected the smell of cheap booze.

At one time I would have died for Chuck Hasburg or at least have wanted the chance to, but when I'd gone off to the army our relationship had foundered after a couple of half-hearted letters full of facts and empty of feeling. Looking at him now, I wanted him to be the man he'd been at seventeen, but perhaps it was because I wanted to be who I'd been then as well. Chance meetings of former friends seldom work, but I owed Chuck something, a gesture at least, so I asked if he had time for coffee at the hotel.

He shook his head immediately. "I got to get going, Marsh. Thanks, anyway."

"Maybe we can have a drink before I leave."

"Sure. Give me a call." He started to walk away.

His lack of interest suddenly hurt me. "Say hi to Carol for me," I called out.

Chuck stopped and cocked his head and seemed to give my request more analysis than it deserved. "I will if I see her," he said after a minute, then teetered and almost fell. "We split up a while back. Guess you haven't heard."

"No. I'm sorry, Chuck. I . . . I'm sorry."

"Yeah. Well, people change. Carol, anyway."

Chuck's eyes left mine and found something behind me and he frowned, first with surprise and then with urgency. When he began to gesture oddly, I turned to see what he was seeing.

The only thing I saw was a man, walking along on the other side of the square. He was wrapped in a sort of cape and wore boots that came to his knees. His hair was long and tied in a braid behind his head. His walk was rapid, almost manic. He vanished quickly behind a building, perhaps fleeing from Chuck. "You want to know about Carol," Chuck said through clenched teeth, "you can ask that son of a bitch."

"Who is it?"

"You ought to know," Chuck said. "He and your nephew are big buddies. Two peas in a pod, the fucking double-crossing hippies." Chuck walked away, his hands balls of knuckled anger. I hurried after him and slowed him by putting a hand on his shoulder.

"I need to ask you something," I said when he stopped.

"Yeah? What?"

"People in town seem real involved in this business of what we're going to do with our farm. I mean, more than just idle curiosity. Or is it my imagination?"

"It's not imaginary," Chuck said.

"What's the deal, then?"

"The deal is the future of this burg, Marsh. At least that's the way some people see it."

"But how?"

"You've got big-timers interested in that place. Big money, big jobs, big boom. That's what people say. They look on the Tanner place as the salvation of the county."

"Are things that bad?"

"Worse. Look around. Square's half-empty. Only crowd in town's down at the unemployment office. Half the jobs have been taken by the niggers or them fucking boat people they brought in here. Hell, I'm out of work myself."

"No kidding?"

"Went with the box factory after we graduated. Then they went bust and I bought a fast-food franchise and that got squeezed out when the fucking Colonel came to town, and in the process I just about got myself wiped out. What little I had left Carol got, her and her fucking lawyer. Clark Jaspers, remember him? Remember how we all felt sorry for him, the crippled little bastard? Well, first he started getting fucking criminals off scott-free when they should have been hung and then he tried to make a mint in a real estate deal out by the country club and lost his shirt. And I let him get *me* into a deal that just went sour. The son of a bitch."

"I'm sorry, Chuck," I said again. "If I can help somehow, just let me know."

"Well, what you can do for me is think real hard about what you do with that farm of yours. About who gets it and what they'll do with it when they do."

"I will."

Chuck chuckled bitterly and shook his head. "Hell, don't let me get you down, Marsh. Other folks, either. There's lots of sob stories around, but they're not your problem. Take the money and run. It's what I'd do if I had the chance. Fuck the town. That's the way I see it. What'd it ever do for you?"

I could think of several things, but I didn't mention them just then.

"Hey," he said. "Know who's back in town?"

"Who?"

"Sally."

"Sally? Sally Stillings?"

"The one and only."

"Christ, Chuck. Sally? What's she doing here?"

"Same as the rest of us. Just trying to get through it."

"Through what?"

"Whatever it is between now and the day you die."

# Chapter
# 5

Back at the hotel I called Gail to check the schedule for the day. She told me to come for lunch, that Matt should be in town by then and that Curt was driving in from Glory City for a meeting and that I should stop at the South End Bakery for some rolls on the way. "Why didn't you tell me Sally Stillings was back in town?" I asked after Gail had stopped instructing me.

She laughed. "I was afraid you'd turn around and go back."

"I would have," I said. "And I still may."

"Not before we talk, Marsh. Please?"

I grumbled some more, then hung up and spent a few minutes thinking about Sally and deciding I wanted to see her again. After that I was bored, and I had a couple of hours to kill, so I got in the car and drove around town, doing what I'd always done in that condition.

I hadn't gone far before I began to sense again that ineffable freedom of a kid with a car and a Sunday afternoon and enough gas to get to the end of his world and back. The nip of autumn was in the air. Red and yellow leaves scampered frantically to avoid my wheels. My first forays as a detective had been on days like this, when I'd picked out other cars and followed them wherever they led me, for no other reason than my interest in other lives and how they were lived.

The town slipped past me like a winding river. There was less change in the residential areas than on the square, and as a result time collapsed around me. Some new developments, a rest home, a new grade school, even a new stoplight, bringing the town's total to two, were the only things that jarred me. But the major hallmarks of my youth, the high school, City Park and the pool, the library, the reservoir, the golf course, even the house I grew up in, were unchanged in every way but one: they were so much smaller than I remembered. I felt like Gulliver afoot in Lilliput, huge and unaware.

I kept driving. A thicket of memory thistles pricked at me relentlessly, some sticking, some jabbing me briefly but falling away, a few drawing blood. I passed the place where I'd fallen off a horse, where I'd fought in a rage over the rules to Red Rover, where I'd seen my first dead body, the result of an unwon race between a train and a car, and, down a little lane that led, ultimately, to a tiny Jewish cemetery, the place where I'd first touched a naked woman's breast. I passed the houses of friends and enemies and girls, and the gas stations and cafés where we'd hung out, and faded billboards that sang of Colonial Bread and Meadow Gold milk and Salada tea. I drove up the hill we'd slid down on snow and around the field we'd played football on in fall and past the grocery store I'd helped build and the office where my grandfather had practiced law and died, and more and more, clustered within a few square blocks, insignificant to anyone but me, and maybe by now to me as well, the way a bad poem is familiar but unimportant.

On a sudden impulse I stopped beside the high school and went through the door nearest the gym. There was no one around except a janitor pushing dust down an empty hall. I tried to peek inside the gym but the doors were locked. I made do with the trophy case instead.

I was still there, in the form of a photograph of me in my football uniform that had been carved into a little statue with my name and position printed on its base. But the statuette had been knocked onto its side, and the look on my face was more pathetic than heroic. A layer of dust dimmed both my features and my exploits. Wearing a number 30 on my chest and holding a ball, I looked absurdly young and well-groomed and almost pretty, silly and stupid and happy. I *hadn't* been particularly happy at that time in my life, partly because of

Sally Stillings and what we'd put each other through, but also because of my growing sense that I was not quite what everyone assumed me to be, that I was worse and I was less and I was blameworthy because of it.

But things are relative. If I had inflicted more punishment on myself than necessary I had also reaped more rewards than were deserved. It hadn't been enough, but it had been something—a time, the only time, when things I did were cheered. Somewhere a bell sounded and the hall filled with kids and I backed quickly out of the building, feeling like a trespasser who had glimpsed an ancient, cursed thing.

It was some time after that, after I'd passed the drive-in where we'd congregated after we were old enough to drive, when I realized I was being followed. It was nonsensical, this hint of big-city intrigue in little Chaldea, but after a few twists and turns through the dirt roads that wound among the impoverished shanties at the south end of town, I confirmed that it was real nonsense all the same. The car was blue and plain, the man within it thin and balding, his features blurred by the scrim of his windshield. I didn't think I had seen him before, but I was certain I would see him again.

I could have lost him—I retained a sense of the town's streets at least that good, acquired during those endless hours of cruising—but there seemed no point in doing it. Instead, I stopped at the bakery, then drove to Gail's and watched the blue Fairmont pull to the curb a half block away. A more precise identification of the driver was prevented by the shade from the huge sycamore that loomed like a parachute above him.

There was another car in Gail's drive—a pearl-gray Continental with Illinois plates—and its owner was the first to greet me as I entered the house. Matt had doubled in size since I'd seen him last, but it was a hard, sculpted poundage, the weight of power, not sloth. He squeezed my palm and pounded my back and blared his pleasure at seeing me again, and even though there wasn't an ounce of pure feeling in his words I smiled and patted him in return.

Matt was eight years older than I was, so he'd been more an icon to me than a brother, someone to observe and marvel at but not to know. For his part, Matt had ignored me entirely except for periodic production numbers he would stage, usually in the presence of a new girl friend, when I would be lavished with games and toys and stunts that usually ended with my being tossed to the ceiling or hung by my heels. Matt had been a promoter even then, a congenital salesman perpetually selling himself, and he must have gotten every single one of those genes our parents possessed because neither Curt nor I nor Gal had any at all. Matt was a bullshitter but he wasn't dull. Good bullshitters never are. Within a minute he'd told me a joke and a lie, and had me laughing.

Matt dragged me into the kitchen where Gail and another woman were standing beside the stove, talking in quiet tones. Between and around them was the smell of gingerbread. Gail was wearing a wool pants suit and some silly little boots and I knew she thought she was dressed up, but beside the other woman she looked like she was ready to slop the hogs. And the other woman knew it and was glad.

Matt pulled me within two feet of the strange tall woman and introduced us. She was Pilar, his wife. She was half Spanish. They'd been married in Mexico two months ago, and had honeymooned in Acapulco for three weeks afterward. They still had their tans. According to my brother, she was the best thing that ever happened to him, he still couldn't figure how he'd been lucky enough to snare her, and on and on like that.

For her part, Pilar smiled tolerantly and silently at both of us, looking bored by the words and the man who uttered them. I felt in the presence of the heir to a toppled throne and from his antics so did Matt. "Pilar's a singer, Marsh," Matt went on. "Earns three hundred a night or better. Has gigs in all the best clubs in Chicago—Palmer House, Playboy Club, you name it. You should hear her do 'Tangerine.' Man, oh man."

To her credit, Pilar seemed annoyed at the tout, and Matt finally wound to a quiet halt. It suddenly occurred to me that I had no idea what Matt was doing for a living.

"How was the hotel?" Gail asked me.

"Okay," I answered. "Met some people in the coffee shop this morning, then took a little stroll around the square."

"The square. Pilar, you've got to check that out," Matt said. "A real relic. You'll think you're on another planet."

Gail frowned. "It's not that bad. Really. It's not. We have some real nice shops, Matt."

I spoke quickly. "I bumped into Chuck Hasburg uptown."

Gail raised her brows. "Oh? How's Chuck? I haven't seen him for months."

"Not so hot. Lost his job. He and Carol split. He doesn't look too good. I think he'd been drinking."

"That's too bad. I heard he took it hard, the divorce I mean. I always liked Chuck," Gail said firmly. "I had a real crush on him once."

"I didn't know that."

"You weren't supposed to," Gail replied, and we both laughed. Then Gail's voice dropped. "They say Carol's changed a lot."

Carol and Chuck had been high school sweethearts. I don't think either of them had ever dated another person when they got married the day after graduation. Over the years of their courtship Chuck had told me everything about Carol, from the make of her shoes to the taste of her body. In some sense she had been, vicariously, the first girl I ever began to understand, even though I'd never had a conversation of more than ten words with her.

"They had a child, didn't they?" I asked Gail.

"A girl. Retarded. She's in a special school of some kind up in Cedar Rapids. They bring her home at Christmas, or they did before the divorce. She used to be a cute little thing, but she's almost thirty now. Kind of wild-looking. They say she won't live past forty."

My stomach began to ache during the story. Suddenly it seemed that Chaldeans bore more heartache than anyone should have to. Or was it just that I knew about it all, knew more of people here than I did in San Francisco, where so much life dances by dishonestly under a tent of gaiety and flash.

I turned and walked into the living room and sank onto the couch that had once been my parents', thinking of Chuck and Carol and of Sally and me. Chuck and Carol had been King and Queen of the Prom. They'd been solid and steady, confident, predictably betrothed, what Sally and I had struggled and failed to be, ending only in bitterness and tears. My tears, my bitterness. If Chuck and Carol hadn't made it, no one could expect to.

Matt came in and sat beside me and slapped my knee. "Hard to believe we spent eighteen years of our lives in this burg, isn't it?"

"I guess."

"People in Chicago don't believe it when I tell them where I'm from, that a guy like me came out of a place like this. Probably the same for you in Frisco, huh?"

"Not really."

Matt pushed his blue velour sleeves above his thick forearms. The bracelet on his wrist writhed like a viper.

"What you doing these days, Marsh? Still a gumshoe?" Matt's laugh was raw and slanderous.

"Still a gumshoe."

"I never understood why you quit being a lawyer. Hell, you were drawing down over thirty K, weren't you? That was decent money ten years ago."

"It wasn't decent enough," I said.

"Hell," Matt scoffed. "I bet you don't net that now."

"True, but that's not what I meant by decent."

Matt shook his head. "You always *were* weird, Marsh. But hell. To each his own. What you doing with your investment capital these days?"

"Spending it."

"I'm serious, Marsh."

"So am I."

Matt slapped me on the knee again. I had an urge to punch him in the face and dump him at Pilar's thin and perfumed feet. "You always were tight with a buck, Marsh," Matt went on. "I know you got something stashed away. And even if you don't, hell, when we unload this fucking farm we'll all be in clover."

"Will we?"

"Sure. Hundred grand apiece, minimum. And I got just the place for you to put your share."

"Where's that?"

"Oh, this little limited partnership I'm working up. Can't miss, Marsh. Immediate write-off of eighty percent, against a return of twelve points sure."

"What's the asset of this money machine?"

"Mobile-home parks. Ten of 'em, eventually. Hell, Marsh,

with the price of housing what it is, mortgage rates, your double-bottom mobile home is the only affordable habitation source for a whole hell of a lot of your middle-class. A hell of a lot. And I'm talking people earning twenty, twenty-five K a year, not some poor slob just swam across the Rio Grande looking for a pear to pick."

"Sounds swell," I said as Matt caught his breath. I worked to keep from laughing.

"These aren't your tacky roadside numbers, either, with a pickup and a bleached blonde beside each unit. I'm talking Caravan Towers, Marsh. Landscaped perimeters, semipermanent installation, foundation skirts, pool and rec center. The works. You know who got rich this same way?"

"Who?"

"Barbi Benton's husband."

"No kidding."

"Plus we go him one better," Matt said eagerly.

"How's that?"

"High rise. Build a steel frame with catwalks and lift two-thirds of those babies off the ground. Triple rent per space. It's revolutionary."

"It sounds it."

"You in? Not that I *need* you. Just doing you a favor."

"Sorry."

"Come on. Twenty units at a K apiece. Give yourself a break."

"Thanks anyway, Matt."

"Jesus," Matt spat. "No one ever *could* do anything for you, you simple shit."

I was silent, trying to think of something that would calm Matt down, when I was saved by the doorbell. Since Matt and I were the only ones in the living room, I hopped up to answer it.

The man standing on the porch was my brother Curt, but if I hadn't known he was coming I wouldn't have recognized him. "Hello, Marsh," he said, his voice almost inaudible.

"Curt. It's good to see you."

"You, too."

"Come on in. Matt's here."

"I heard."

I stepped back to let Curt enter, then involuntarily reached toward him because I thought he was going to fall. He was wearing work boots and bib overalls and a flannel-lined denim jacket, and from his manner it looked like he'd been performing convict labor since I had seen him last. Each movement seemed to occupy him entirely, all his muscle, all his mind. Curt was sick, and from what Gail had said it was a sickness of the heart. Someone should have cried for him.

Curt walked to the center of the room and stood there, gripping his hunting hat in his hands as though uncertain of what to do or even who we were.

"Jesus, Curt," Matt blurted from the couch. "You look like hell. You sick, or what?"

Curt's smile was feeble, though he tried to make it otherwise. I had a sudden urge to leave Chaldea, flee Curt and Matt and everything else I'd seen since I'd come back, so I could remember it all as it had been once, not as it was and would be for all time. There was the farm, of course, the money, but I didn't really need it. More than that, I probably shouldn't take it. Some of the most screwed-up people I knew were the ones that got rich quick.

Matt and Curt shook hands like a pair of fighters past their prime and fearful and addled because of it. Matt didn't even mention Pilar, or drag Curt off to meet her, or evidence anything but disgust for his younger brother. Curt seemed oblivious to everything but breathing and whatever it was that had damned him.

Eventually Gail brought Pilar in and made the introductions. Pilar and Curt looked at each other without comprehension, across an unspanned gulf. As the discomfort grew, Pilar finally pivoted on a pump and headed back to the kitchen, a glint of something close to terror in her eyes. Gail followed her out of the room.

Curt *was* fearsome, somehow, a man out on a ledge, beyond reason or entreaty. With all our eyes on him he walked to the couch and sat silently, still fingering his cap, an Okie at the palace of the prince. Above his socks his ankles were as white as bleached bone. "How's Laurel?" I asked, to give him something to do besides think.

"Not too well, Marsh. She wasn't up to coming in. She sent her best," Curt added lamely, as though her best would never be enough.

"You're living in Glory City, I hear. How is it out there?"

"Quiet."

"You farming?"

"No. Not anymore."

"Laurel still work at the bank?"

"No."

"I'd like to see her before I leave, if she's feeling better."

Curt simply nodded, his wife's health beyond words or cure. Matt kept glancing sideways at him, each time edging farther away. "How's Billy?" I asked, looking at Curt.

"Fine." Curt's word was barely audible, perhaps a plea that I say nothing more. If so, I didn't heed it.

"What's he doing now?"

"We don't see Billy anymore," Curt explained simply.

Matt chimed in. "Living out on the farm, isn't he? That's what Gail said."

"Gail would know better than I would," Curt mumbled. "Gail knows everything."

There was resentment in his words. And I was making matters worse because I had no idea how to make them otherwise. I grasped silently at straws but hadn't caught one by the time Gail came back into the room, this time alone.

"Pilar wants to rest awhile," she said to Matt. "She's gone upstairs. I thought this might be a good time to talk. Then maybe after we eat we can all go out to the grave. Can we? I bought a new wreath."

Three heads nodded slowly, eyes downcast, thoughts on the long-time dead.

# Chapter
# 6

We sat in silence for a time, we Tanners, more alien to each other than we had ever been. We had never been talkers, not at home, not about personal matters, matters of sex or rage or pain. There were things you did, and things you didn't do, and the distinction was unquestionably inherited, not taught. I tried for a moment to recall something intimate about any of the other three, something I knew that no one else did, and came up with nothing. The silence thickened and I floated on it, untethered to person or idea, depressed.

Matt would be the one to start it, and after a couple of minutes more he did. "Let's sell the damned thing," he said bluntly, his eyes shifting from one of us to the other.

"I agree," Curt murmured.

"Curt," Gail admonished sadly. "You don't *mean* that. You can't. You're a *farmer*, Curt."

"Not anymore." Whatever Curt was seeing was not in the room.

Matt stood and began to lumber from wall to wall. His white Italian footfalls caused the floor to tremble. "So it's two to one. Under the will it takes three to sell. Right?"

"Right," Gail said.

"So how about it, Marsh?" Matt challenged, his chest and his chain heaving high above me.

I took a deep breath. "Who do you plan to sell to?" I asked.

"The highest bidder," Matt shot back.

"Who's that likely to be? That newspaper article made it sound like everyone in town wants the place."

Matt looked at Gail. She looked at me. "I guess I know more of the answer to that than anyone," she said. "I'm here, where they can all get at me, and believe me, they have."

"Who?" I repeated.

"First, there's the city. They want an industrial park out there, so they can put up a building and offer the package cheap to this business they're courting."

"What business?"

"No one knows. It's a big secret, but supposedly they'll employ almost three hundred people. That's what the city's after, the jobs. We lost two factories in the past year."

"And the hardware man is the city's negotiator in the deal?"

"Norm Gladbrook. Right. He's chairman of the Chaldea Development Commmittee."

"What's the city willing to pay?" Matt asked.

"Not much, I don't think," Gail answered. "Since they're going to have to practically *give* the land away to entice this company to come in here, they can't afford much of a price. The figure I heard was a hundred an acre for a fifty-acre parcel."

"Five thousand bucks," Matt scoffed. "Peanuts."

"Maybe we could sell fifty acres to the city and the rest to someone else," I said.

"Possibly," Gail said, "but there are some problems with that. The fifty acres the city wants is some of the prime farmland, the flat part, and also the parcel with the best access to the highway and utilities and all that. If we sold that parcel off it would isolate the rest of the farm and leave whoever bought it vulnerable to the city's access requirements. Be sort of risky, I think."

I was impressed with Gail's analysis, unused to seeing her as more than a sister. I wondered what else she knew that I didn't.

"So much for the city," Matt growled. "Who else?"

"The man who farms next to us. The one who works it on shares now."

"How much?" Matt asked again, arms folded, eyes bright with the polished glint of greed.

"I don't know," Gail shrugged. "Not a lot, I would guess. He's been having a rough time. All farmers have."

"Shit," Matt said, "I been hearing how rough farmers have it since I was knee high. But they all manage to drive new cars and air-conditioned tractors and spend the winters in Texas. I should have it so bad."

"Would he share the farm with your daughter and her husband?" I asked Gail.

"I imagine. If he has to. Like everyone else he'll take anything he can get."

"Who else?" Matt prompted.

"The WILD people," Gail said.

"Who the fuck are they?" Matt said.

"An environmental group. They want the farm, at least the part down by the creek, made into a park, with the rest of it left as it is, as a wildlife refuge and wilderness area. Not even farmed. They claim there's some original prairie grass out there. I guess there's not much of the stuff left anywhere in the whole country."

"So what's in it for us?" Matt asked.

"The main benefit would be a tax deduction, as I understand it. Plus good will, as they put it. I think Billy works with WILD some, doesn't he, Curt? He could probably tell us more about it."

Curt didn't respond and Gail didn't seem surprised.

"Well, fuck 'em," Matt said. "Sound like radicals to me. Let's get to the big boys. The coal and oil and agribusiness."

"Well," Gail began, "Black Diamond Coal, they were here a long time ago, ran most of the mines around the county, them and Sunshine. But those were shaft mines, pony mines. Too expensive after natural gas came in, and the coal was too dirty, so they shut them all down. Now they're strictly strip miners."

"How do people feel about strip mining around here?" I asked.

"They don't like it much, but they like the unemployment rate even less. There'd be some bad feeling, but not much."

"What's their offer?" Matt asked.

"It's kind of complicated," Gail said. "I'm not sure I

understand it all, and they didn't waste much time explaining it to me."

"Are they looking at an outright purchase?" I asked. "Or just subsurface rights?"

"Just the rights," Gail said. "But all of them, not just coal."

"Is it a royalty arrangement, or what?" I asked.

"Royalty, plus a price per acre. Same kind of arrangement as the oil folks want, actually. The coal people will pay one hundred an acre plus two percent per ton extracted. The oil people will only pay thirty per acre and a four point six percent royalty per barrel on oil actually pumped out of there. Of course," Gail added, "they didn't sit down and haggle with me. I imagine both groups will go higher."

"If they hit oil out there we'll be shittin' in tall cotton," Matt said dreamily. "Millionaires, each of us."

"*If*," I said. "They've been looking for oil around here since we were kids. Is there any reason to think they'll find some now when they didn't before?" I looked at Gail.

"Not that I know of," she said. "But I imagine technology has improved in that time."

"So has gullibility," I answered with a glance at Matt. "Is there anyone else, or does that cover it?" I was eager to get it over, to steer the talk away from money. I glanced at Curt, to see if he was as ashamed as I was, but he seemed not to have heard a word. He still sat there, squeezing his cap, breathing through his mouth in whistling gasps, dying or giving a good imitation of it.

"The agribusiness people talk the best game in town," Matt said. "Outfit in Illinois, been buying up all kinds of farms around here lately. Clark Jaspers called me last week and told me all about it."

"How much?" I asked, conscious of aping Matt.

"Jaspers wouldn't quote me a figure. But he said they paid eleven hundred an acre for the Kenwood place six months ago. It's over in Wayne County. Can't be much better land than ours."

"Can we get that much?" I asked Gail.

"I doubt it," she said. "I'd say six hundred, tops. There's lots of timber out there."

"Which is still close to two hundred K," Matt pointed out.

"Split four ways," Gail countered, subdividing his greed.

"And a drop in the bucket compared to what we'd get if they find oil out there," I said.

"Isn't any oil," Curt said, speaking for the first time.

"How do you know?" Matt challenged.

"Just do," Curt said.

Matt thought for a minute. "I'm a tad cash-poor these days," he said finally. "Relatively speaking, I mean. The Towers. Other things. I say we take whoever puts the most money up front and get the hell out."

"Who would that most likely be?" I asked. "The Illinois people?"

"Looks that way to me," Matt said. "Let's wheel and deal with Jaspers, jack them up as far as they'll go, then give the figure to the oil and coal boys and see if they'll match it. As far as I'm concerned the city and those ecology nuts are out of it already." Matt began to pace at twice his previous speed. "I can handle the negotiations myself. I'll get hold of Jaspers right now. Should wrap it up by tomorrow, then we can all go home."

I held up a hand. "Not yet, Matt. I want to think this thing over. I may not want to sell to the Illinois people, or even sell at all."

Matt's face clouded. "Hell, Marsh. Don't be stupid, now. Take the money and run."

"Maybe I will," I said, "but don't rush me."

"Dammit. I can't keep that woman up there on the leavings of a fucking *sharecropper*, for God's sakes. I mean . . . well, you know what I mean."

I didn't say anything. Gail walked over and put her hand on my arm, her eyes grateful for what she assumed was our confederacy.

"Here's what I think," Gail said. "I think a strip mine is criminal, and I think the oil people are sleazy quick-money types that are trying to get something for nothing, and I think the city's problems aren't going to be solved by us practically donating our farm to the good citizens of Chaldea. The Tanner plot is family land, *farm*land. And my daughter and her husband want to farm it, want to keep it in the family, want to keep that land doing what it's been doing for a hundred years.

I think it's Karen's right, Marsh. Her birthright. Don't you? She and Bruce are the only Tanners who come after us."

"And Billy," I said.

"Oh. Billy. I forgot." Gail looked apologetically at Curt, but he didn't seem to have heard her. "What do you say, Marsh? Can I call Karen and Paul?"

I shook my head. "I don't know what I think yet, Gail. I want to consider it, maybe talk to some people. I'm not quite as willing to write off the town's needs as the rest of you seem to be. Chaldea was pretty good to all of us, all things considered. Maybe we should help it if we can."

"Bull poop," Matt muttered. "You got out of here as fast as you could and so did I and so did everyone else with brains. Gail stayed because her man was here and Curt, well, look what Chaldea's done to *him*. Fuck the town. Stick a fork in it. It's done."

I looked at Curt. His attitude puzzled me. From the time he was little he'd been the only one of us who'd truly loved the land, who learned what went on out there beyond the city limits, how corn was planted and beans were picked and lambs were sheared and cattle were slaughtered. He had joined the Future Farmers of America and the 4-H, run around with farm kids and spent a lot of time out at the farm we were now discussing, putting up hay, detasseling seed corn, mending fences, spreading manure, doing the chores that farm kids do. And now Curt claimed he wanted out. I was certain it had something to do with Billy and it was more complex than the reason Gail had suggested, but I wasn't sure quite what it was.

"What do you want the money for, Curt?" I asked him, half in jest but hoping he would answer. "Why are you so anxious to sell?"

I was smiling but Curt was not. He looked at me for the first time since we'd begun our debate. "I got some expenses coming up," he said simply.

"What expenses?"

Curt frowned. "Getting kind of nosy, aren't you, Marsh?"

"Just trying to do what's right, Curt."

"So am I," Curt countered. "And I don't need help."

"Well, I'm not going to sit around here for a week while you figure out how to turn this into a fucking *tithe*, Marsh," Matt blurted. "You think you're better than the rest of us, but you're not. Everyone thought you were going to be so great, big jock, big brain, but what are you? A *nothing*, that's what. A fucking gumshoe nothing."

Even Matt seemed shocked by his diatribe by the time he'd concluded. He turned away from me and retreated toward the kitchen. "Marsh," Gail began. "He doesn't mean it."

I held up a hand. "It's all right. Not everything he said was wrong, anyway."

And then there was silence again, broken only by the rumblings of someone upstairs, Pilar or Tom, I didn't know which. And then the phone rang once, and moments later Matt came in from the kitchen and looked at Curt. "It's for you," he said. "A Sheriff Eason, or something like that."

Curt frowned and pushed himself slowly off the couch, leaving the room without a sound. Matt went to a window and stared through it. Gail and I looked at each other. "Billy's probably in trouble again," she said softly. "He's been arrested at least three times. Poor Curt."

"Fucking kids," Matt said to the window. "Glad I don't got any."

When Curt came back into the room his hat was out of his hands and on his head. Some strong emotion had savaged his face and splashed his eyes. When he tried to speak nothing but a croak emerged, so he coughed and tried again. "They just found Billy. Hanging from a tree in the park. They say he's dead."

"Curt," Gail said. "Oh, no."

Curt nodded stupidly. "They want me down there." He started toward the door.

"I'll go with you," I said.

"Shall I go and sit with Laurel?" Gail asked, her voice shrill with urgency. "I think I should. Did you call her?"

"No. I . . . no. Would you do it?"

"Of course. Oh, Curt."

I put on my coat and went to the door. Matt went over to Curt and put a hand on his shoulder. "I better stay with Pilar. But if you need anything, just call. We'll be here or at the motel."

"Call. Sure." Curt stumbled toward me. I guided him through the door and off the porch, toward the body of his only child.

# Chapter 7

The park was near the high school. It was hilly and wooded, circumscribed by a narrow gravel road, with parking near the tennis courts and swimming pool. The old fire engine was still on blocks for kids to climb on, and the wooden shelter houses were there, too. In a vale across the road were the Boy Scout cabin and the VFW hut.

A sheriff's car and a city police car and a doctor's Chrysler were crowded into the parking area, and a group of men were huddled under a huge oak far down the slope toward the little caretaker's cabin. I didn't know what to say to Curt, so I didn't say anything. It seemed absurd for us to be walking through a forest of swings and merry-go-rounds, rolling barrels and twisting slides, on our way to see a corpse.

Curt was silent, his work boots crunching to dust the twigs and leaves and acorns in his path. The hands at his sides were more like maces than like fists. Once he muttered words I wasn't meant to hear.

As we approached the group of men one of them looked our way, said something to the others, then came to meet us. He was large and red-haired, and wore the Eisenhower jacket and khaki slacks of a law officer. When he reached us he stuck a giant hand toward Curt. Curt didn't notice or grip it, and the hand fell back. "He still hangin', Rex?" Curt asked, his words disembodied, his eyes afraid to search the branches beyond us.

The sheriff shook his head. "We cut him down. He's over by the tree. I'm sorry as hell about it, Curt. Real sorry."

Curt shouldered his way past the sheriff and the sheriff called out to another man, who hurried to Curt's side and guided him toward the shrouded lump that lay on the ground beneath the oak. "That's young Doc Yarrow," the sheriff said to me. "He's coroner this year. He'll watch to see if Curt needs help with it." The sheriff's eyes found mine. "Rex Eason," he said, and shoved the giant hand toward me.

"Marsh Tanner." The hand swallowed mine and chewed on it. "Curt's brother."

"From Frisco?"

"That's right."

"Heard you was in town. Hell of a way to welcome you home."

I nodded. "Any doubt it's Billy?"

"Nope. Had him in my car a dozen times or more. Know Billy better'n I know my own boy."

"Suicide?"

The sheriff shrugged. "Looks it. Drug that picnic table over under that low branch, there. Flipped the rope up over it and tied one end to the trunk, then made a little slip knot and stuck his head through and stepped off. Yep, he sure could have done it himself."

"But he could have had help."

The sheriff shrugged again. "I didn't figure Billy for the hangin' type, myself."

"Why not?"

"Too mad at things; too many demons he was tryin' to kill. Seemed like a man with a long list who wasn't about to quit till he'd gone through it."

"What kind of list, exactly?" I asked.

"You ask most any folks around town, they'll tell you what Billy Tanner worked at most was making people mad."

I wanted to question the sheriff some more but I heard the wordless noise of grief and looked toward the tree that muffled it. Curt was sobbing, leaning on the gnarled trunk, his back bent, one hand pressed to his face, clearly close to collapse. His torso arched stiffly over the shrouded body of his son as though mortised to shield it from further harm. I hurried to

Curt's side and took his arm and led him to the picnic table and sat him down. "Are you okay?" I asked.

He nodded but it was not an answer. A young man came over and sat on the bench beside Curt. "I can give you a tranquilizer, Mr. Tanner," he said smoothly. "It might make things easier the rest of the day."

Curt shook his head. "Don't want it easy," he said thickly. "Your boy dies, it should be hard; the hardest thing ever in your life."

The younger man nodded and looked at me. He had the clean confidence of a doctor, and the serenity of one who hadn't been in practice long. "I'm Mike Yarrow," he said. "Acting coroner."

"Are you Dan Yarrow's son?" I asked after I'd introduced myself.

He nodded. "Do you know Dad?"

"Used to. A hell of a shortstop, your dad."

Yarrow smiled. "That's what he tells me. Often." Yarrow's obvious affection for his father seemed almost a mockery of Curt and Billy.

I was thinking about Doctor Yarrow's father, and about how important it had been to be good at games when I was young, when I noticed the sheriff was about to leave. I hurried to where he was standing. "What you were saying before," I said, "about Billy and his demons and his list. You have any specific demon in mind that might have hooked Billy to that limb?"

The sheriff looked at me from beneath a heavy bush of brow. "You're a detective, is what I hear," he said calmly, passing the time of day.

I nodded.

"Been close to a lot of homicide investigations, I guess."

"A few," I acknowledged.

"Do it a little different here than in the big city. See that fellow over there by the body? Little feller in the Sunday suit?"

I looked and nodded.

"From the BCI. State Bureau of Criminal Investigation. Works out of the state capital, flew him down in their own plane after I called it in. Took him a half hour; would take three to drive it."

"If you think it was suicide, why did you call him in?"

The sheriff shrugged. "Hunch, I guess. Like I said, Billy didn't seem the type to mess with his own life. He was too busy messing with other folks'."

"Anything more tangible than that to go on, Sheriff?"

Eason smiled. "Nope. So suicide it is. For now." He turned to leave.

"Can you stick around awhile?" I asked him.

"Nope. Big fight out at Mickey's last night. I got a jail full of tough guys I got to get rid of."

"Can I come by and see you later? To talk some more about Billy?"

"Not today, you can't."

"See you tomorrow, then."

I watched the sheriff leave the park after saying a few words to the BCI man, then I motioned for Doctor Yarrow to join me. "Any doubt about the cause of death?" I asked when I saw we were out of Curt's hearing.

"Not that I know of now," he said. "Why?"

"No reason. You doing an autopsy?"

"Sure."

"Do it yourself?"

"Right."

"Done many?"

"Ten or so. Why?" His puzzled frown fit uncomfortably in his face. Doctors are used to knowing more than anyone about everything.

"Can I make a suggestion?" I went on.

"I suppose so."

"Look for a sign that Billy was unconscious before the rope went around his neck. Drugs, a blow to the head, something like that."

Yarrow frowned above his mustache, his black eyes hard and probing. "Have you some reason to think this wasn't suicide, Mr. Tanner?"

"Just one, so far."

"What's that?"

"It doesn't run in the family."

I left young Doctor Yarrow rolling his exasperated eyes and went back to where Curt was sitting. "I'm going to look at the body for a second," I told him. "You stay here. Then we'll go."

"Not till they take him."

"There's nothing you can do, Curt. The coroner will take the body as soon as the BCI's through, and that could take hours. Why don't we go?"

"Not till they take him," Curt repeated. I patted his shoulder and went over to the tree and bent down and pulled back the sheet of brown canvas that covered Billy's body.

The last time I'd seen Billy, even in photographs, was more than ten years ago, and I still pictured him in my mind the way he was then—late teens, handsome and strong, full of the spark and spirit of youth. But the body I saw beneath the shroud wasn't a boy at all and seemed never to have been one. It had been a man, thirty or almost so, emaciated and frightfully ascetic in appearance, with a long braid of greasy matted hair. Lividity wrapped his neck like a scarf. He had hollow sallow cheeks and a scruffy stubble of blue-black beard that crossed his face like the mask of an outlaw. He was wearing a faded field jacket and tattered fatigues, and I realized he looked something like the person I'd seen earlier in the day, the person who had suddenly angered Chuck Hasburg up on the square.

I looked again at the body. Billy seemed to have shrunk inside his clothes, as though his departed spirit had left behind a void and the flesh had reacted in abhorrence of it. He had the look of the wanderers I saw so often in San Francisco, the street people scavenging for food in trash cans, begging for change on corners, their homes the tattered bundles of rags upon their backs.

I moved Billy briefly, looking and feeling for signs of foul play, but the only thing I saw was a thin line of dried blood on the back of his neck. When the BCI man noticed me he headed my way with a frown on his face. I replaced the shroud quickly and was on my way back to the picnic table when he caught up with me. He was barely five feet tall and belligerent as a result. "Who are you, mister?" he challenged.

"Uncle of the deceased."

"Name?"

"John Marshall Tanner."

"Residence?"

"San Francisco."

That widened his eyes. "What brings you to Chaldea?"

I smiled. "First, who are you?"

"Agent Clarkson. BCI."

"Which is what?"

"Bureau of Criminal Investigation. State. Now. What brings you to town?"

"Family business."

"Where you staying?"

"Hotel National."

"How long you plan to be here?"

"Another day, at most."

"Let me know before you leave town. The sheriff will know how to reach me."

"Will do."

"You know anything about this?" he asked, gesturing toward the body.

"Nothing. I haven't seen Billy in ten years. Haven't been back here in longer than that."

"If anything comes to mind, you let me know. Pronto."

"Right. You calling it suicide, Agent Clarkson?"

"Not calling it anything till after the autopsy."

"Good."

"Why? You got doubts?"

"A few."

"Reasons?"

"Nothing specific."

"What do you do out there in Frisco, Mr. Tanner?"

"Private investigator."

"Yeah?"

"Yeah."

"Like Rockford?"

"Only not as clever."

"Not as cute, either."

"No, not as cute. And not as short."

Agent Clarkson swore. "Don't get in the way, Tanner. In this one you're just an observer. I see you touch the deceased again, I'll take you into custody. Now. That the father over there?" he asked, gesturing again.

"Right."

"Name?"

"Curtis Tanner."

"Residence?"

"Glory City."

"Yeah? What's he live out there for?"

"I don't know."

"He have any ideas why his kid ended up swinging from a tree?"

"Not that I know of."

"I'll want to talk to him."

"Can't it wait a day?"

The BCI man shrugged. "I'll get to him when I get to him. Meantime I got work to do. Why don't you clear on out?"

"He wants to wait till the body's taken away."

"Yeah, well, the coroner's called the hearse, so that won't be long."

"So you've about wrapped it up? No more evidence to gather?"

"Evidence of what?"

"Murder, maybe."

"Shit."

The BCI man turned away and went over near the body and said something to a man who was putting something into plastic bags. The man didn't stop doing what he was doing. Which meant the BCI man hadn't made up his mind about the cause of death, which was good. I went back to where my brother still sat.

"Are you okay?" I asked him again.

He nodded and pulled out a bandanna and blew his nose. The wind crackled the leaves overhead and sent a chill across my flesh. Up the slope behind us a child was pumping a rusty swing to life. "He's been dead a long time, Marsh," Curt said in a voice that became a whisper. "Dead for ten years. He just didn't know enough to fall down."

"What did it to him, Curt?"

"The war. That goddamned war. It killed Billy as surely as it killed the Heinz kid or any of the others they got out in the cemetery."

Small towns. If not for them there would be no one to man our wars. "What did it to him though, Curt? What did he do there that changed him so much?"

Curt shrugged wearily. "He never talked to me about it. Whatever it was, it turned him totally against me, and Laurel, and the town, the country, everyone but that group of hippies he hung out with."

"What group is that?"

"The WILD bunch. Run by a criminal who's walking free, thanks to Clark Jaspers."

"Where's their office?"

"Shack out on Elm Street that's about to fall down."

"Was Billy married, Curt?" I asked. "I heard he was."

"Had a girl. Don't know if they were married or not. Likely not."

"You ever meet her?"

"Not formal. Saw her once in a while. Kind of pretty but real sad."

"Where did they live?"

"Out at the farm, last I heard. They say Billy built a cabin for himself somewhere out there, but I didn't ever see it. Went out there once but couldn't find the place. Remember when we used to go out there for picnics, Marsh? The whole family, even grandpa? Remember grandpa and his gravy? And him always trying to catch a fish out of that little creek? He never did catch a one, I don't think."

A sudden sob forced its way out of Curt's throat, gagging him as he tried to keep it down. I put my arm across his shoulder, feeling helpless and stupid and somehow to blame for everything.

"It's all gone wrong, Marsh," Curt said through his sorrow. "You might as well put that rope around my neck and haul me up there, too."

And then Curt was crying openly, and so was I. For Billy and for grandpa and for the rest of us as well.

# Chapter
# 8

I took Curt back to Gail's house. There was no one there when we arrived, so Curt got in his car and drove off toward Glory City, refusing my offer of company. He was my brother, and it should have been a time for me to share his sorrow, but that's not quite how it was. Billy's death was already more of professional than personal interest to me. Had a crime been committed, and if so, by whom? That was all it was, though I tried to make it more. After Curt disappeared around a corner I went back to the hotel, absorbed by the foulness of greed and murder and my own hard heart.

There was no point in making assumptions about Billy until the results of the autopsy were in. And even then, well, boys like Billy, living on the outer husk of rationality, expose themselves to many similar minds and to the crazy, hallucinatory violence such minds find easy and perhaps require. Billy might simply have been killed by someone as universally hateful as Billy himself appeared to have become, by someone else beyond the sanction of morality or fear. If that's the way it looked, then I would probably leave it be. Such a case would be difficult for me to solve alone, and even if I did, no punishment would be worse than the madness already inflicted upon the guilty. But if it had been something else, an act more rational and self-serving, then I would have to do something about it.

I was in the bathroom of my hotel room getting ready to go out when someone knocked. I put on my jacket and tucked in my shirt, then opened the door and looked into the hazel eyes of the person who had convinced me, once, that everything was all right and would be.

"Sally," I said, my stiff throat a splint around the name.

"Marsh." A smile quivered, but for an instant only.

"How are you, Sally?"

"I'm fine. How are you?" She donned a new-moon smile this time. It glowed for seconds as I looked at her.

"I'm average or above, I guess," I said. "You look great."

"So do you."

"I don't, but thanks."

"Can I come in?"

"Sure. Sure. Sorry."

I backed away to let her enter, glad to be able to do something besides speak. And then I laughed.

Sally turned and frowned nervously. "What's so funny?" she asked, fingering her clothes, uneasy because humor had not been among the expectations that sent her to my room.

"I was just thinking of how many years I spent trying to get you alone in a hotel room. And here you are. Success at last, thirty years too late."

Sally relaxed and stretched her smile. "Here I am, all right. But not for the first time. Or maybe you forgot."

"I forgot almost everything, but not that."

"Good."

She was speaking of the first night we had allowed ourselves to do it right, the night before I was sent away for the summer to work on a ranch, the night we needed clean sheets and wide beds and safe harbors instead of cold car seats in crowded drive-ins or scratchy couches in the homes of parents. We'd driven in an awed silence to a nearby town, to a motel that lurked like a highwayman at its far end. I'd obtained a key and a smirk from a desk clerk who'd given lots of keys to lots of kids and liked it, signed Eugene Gant's name in the book, and led Sally into unit four with a hand as wet and hot as boiled clothes.

Perhaps because we had done it wrong so many times, it turned out just the way the songs and movies said it would, the ones with Rock and Doris or Perry and Patty. And though the place was more thrilling than the deed, somehow, the vision of Sally lying finally fully naked on a blue speckled bed below a white speckled ceiling, wearing blinking rays of neon and a blush, that vision had aroused me on many nights thereafter, college nights, army nights, lonely, hollow, seamless nights.

While I was away at the ranch that summer, Sally had dated someone else, as I had urged her to do but hoped she wouldn't. Even when my jealousy subsided, and we were allied once again, she had never allowed me to take her to such a place again. It was a perverse punishment, because we still groped and sweated in cars and parlors, shunning not biology but only the supernal beauty of romance.

Those memories were surprisingly hot, thirty years after they'd been lit, and they burned even brighter as I watched Sally Stillings move toward the only chair in the room, the chair beside the rumpled bed. Sally did look good, her vanity both a shield and a sword in her middle age. Her clothes were simple and flattering, her skirt and blouse pressed stylishly against her long legs and high breasts. The ponytail of old was now bobbed, its remnant a kind of knot at the base of her neck. Her skin was tan, the color of apple juice. Her eyes seemed bigger, her cheeks higher, her nose finer, but whether from a defect of memory or a triumph of makeup I couldn't say. When she was seated Sally looked at me with a flirting confidence and I felt like a kid again and vulnerable to the goblins that had plagued me then.

"I heard you were in town, Marsh," she began, "so I decided to come by and say hello. I hope you don't mind."

I shook my head. "I'm glad you did."

"Are you sure?" She raised one brow. "We didn't part on the best of terms, as I remember."

"No."

"But it wouldn't have worked out for us. Not then."

"I doubt it."

"But, well . . . I didn't mean to, well, you know. I had to do what seemed best."

"I know. It's all right."

"You never married, did you?"

"No."

"Was it because of me? Because I left you for Eric?"

"I don't think so," I said, trying to spike the hope in her

voice. It was like Sally to want to be a cause of pain, just a little, to have been a prickly presence in my life for thirty years, to have scarred me just a tiny bit. And she had.

Sally shifted her position and the subject. "I was sorry when your folks were killed in the accident, Marsh. I meant to write you but I never did. I liked them a lot."

"They liked you, too."

"Not always," she said with a wry smile. "Not your mom, anyway."

I laughed. "They liked you a lot better once I was safe in college and you were still unfertilized," I said.

"Do you think they knew what we were doing out there on the porch?"

"Sure."

"Did they ever say anything?"

"No. Not directly. Just some general discussion of abstinence and contraception, with emphasis on the former."

Sally frowned.

"That's a long time ago, Sally. No one's keeping track."

Nothing was said for a minute. She reached into her purse and brought out a cigarette and lit it. I fumbled with the knot on my tie, started to sit on the bed but then decided not to, and waited for Sally to speak.

"We're old, Marsh," she said suddenly. "Old."

"I know."

"Did you think it would turn out this way, Marsh?"

"What way?"

She frowned with thought, its burden wrinkling her upper lip the way it always had. "I don't know. Being so old so fast, before you had time to do the things you wanted to do . . . Being back here in Chaldea again . . . living our lives without each other." Sally's voice grew dry and crackled. I thought she was going to cry.

"It's not good to have regrets, Sally, if that's what you mean. It's too long a list. Once you get started you can never find a place to stop."

She sighed. "I know. It's being back here, I think. It seems like thirty years have passed and I haven't done a damn thing with them, except get old and worry about what menopause will do to me. And wish sometimes I'd married you."

"Why are you back, Sally?"

"Divorce," she said simply, then looked at me with eyes more defiant than shamed.

"I didn't know. I'm sorry."

"It's all right. For the best, really."

"Your husband was a dentist, right?"

"Orthodontist. Fell in love with his hygienist. The lack of imagination in that move is typical of his entire life."

"So are you back for good?"

She shook her head quickly. "God, no. I'm just spending my alimony, biding my time, giving Rachel some stability while I put myself back together. Plus letting Mom and Dad feel needed again."

"Rachel?"

"My daughter. Age sixteen, if you can believe it. Very beautiful."

"Like her mother."

"Thank you, sir. Luckily, Rachel's much smarter than her mother. About men, about money, about everything. She's been on the pill for two years."

"Is that what passes for smart these days?" I asked. It was automatic and mean. I still wasn't sure what I thought about Sally, it seemed, wasn't sure I forgave her.

"That stinks, Marsh. The things I could *tell* you about kids these days. About what they do, what they're *expected* to do. I . . ."

"Relax, Sally," I said. "I didn't mean it the way it sounded. I'm sure it is the smart thing."

"I'm a good mother, Marsh. Maybe not much else, but I'm a good mother. It doesn't count for much these days, I admit."

"It counts with Rachel. It counts with me."

Sally nodded, and some of the red left her face, but the pain stayed in her eyes. "So. How have *your* thirty years been?" she asked with a reluctant grin.

"Dull. Long. Quiet. At least the way they measure things these days."

"You're not a lawyer anymore, did I hear that right?"

"You did."

"Why not?"

"Lots of reasons."

"Like what?"

"Being a lawyer scared me."

"And being a, whatever you call it, doesn't?"

"Not as much."

"Why not? Don't people shoot at you and things?"

"Once in a while. But these days I know which direction the bullets will come from. When I was a lawyer I wasn't sure."

"Am I supposed to understand what you're talking about?"

"No. I don't understand it myself. What I've done for thirty years is find more reasons to stay alive than not, I guess. Not much else."

"Why *didn't* you get married, Marsh? Really." Sally's look was impish, her posture in the chair suddenly provocative.

"Marriage scared me, too, I guess."

"You sound like such a *coward*, Marsh."

I shrugged. "There's a lot around to be afraid of. More every day if you read the papers or walk the streets."

Sally stood and walked to the window. The pane was reinforced with chicken wire and the outer side was streaked with filth. The view as mostly brick, but through a crack you could see a portion of the square. "Remember where you first kissed me?" Sally asked.

"Where?"

"On the courthouse steps. On Pancake Day, right after the beauty contest. I still think I should have won."

"So do I. How was the kiss?"

"Off-center, as I remember. C-minus."

"And you were used to better?"

"You weren't the first, if that's what you mean," Sally said, and turned around and faced me. "To kiss me, that is."

There was a place to go with it then, but I hoped we wouldn't. I had the memories of those times and that emotion labeled and filed the way I wanted them, the way they were most useful to me. I didn't want them scrambled or even added to.

I reached into my suitcase for the flask of White Label I always carry when I travel and pulled it out and raised my brows. "A bit early, isn't it?" Sally asked.

"It's never too early; only too late."

Sally shrugged. "Why not?" I poured two drinks in cloudy glasses, added a dash of water to hers and handed it to her.

"Here's to nostalgia," I said, and drank mine down, then asked Sally about her parents.

"They still live on Maple Street," she answered. "Dad's retired, works the garden in summer and carves hunting dogs on hickory slabs in winter. Mom's still Mom. I'll tell them you asked."

"Do."

"How long will you be here, Marsh?" Sally asked softly.

"A couple of days, at most."

"Not long enough."

"For what?" I asked.

"To get to know you again."

A melancholy something in her face made me remember Billy. "You remember my brother, Curt?" I asked.

"Sure. A nice guy."

"You know anything about his son? Billy?"

Sally frowned. "I've heard some stories. Why?"

"Where'd you hear them?"

"Around."

"Where, Sally?" I repeated.

"Why, Marsh? What's happened?" The words were singed with alarm.

"Billy was found dead this morning. In City Park."

"How awful. What was it? An overdose?"

"Why do you ask that?"

"Well, that's what I heard. That Billy used drugs a lot. He acted like it, that's for sure. Talking to himself, stumbling around, sleeping all night on the square."

"What else did he do?"

"I heard he burned a flag during the Pancake Day parade a few years ago, for one thing. And then there was something about him and Tom."

"Tom who?"

"Tom Notting. Your brother-in-law."

"What about Billy and Tom?"

"I don't remember, exactly. Something about his job. The assessments or something."

"What else did you hear?"

Sally squirmed uncomfortably. "I don't know, Marsh. Why? What does it matter now that Billy's dead?"

"What, Sally? There's something on your mind."

"I . . . it's just something about Billy and some woman."

"What woman?"

"It must have been a lie, Marsh."

"What?"

Sally took a deep breath and looked at me. "I heard he and Carol were seeing each other. Carol Kline Hasburg. I heard Carol left Chuck for Billy Tanner."

I shook my head dumbly, my thoughts on my encounter with Chuck Hasburg that morning on the square. "That can't be," I said. "Carol's old enough to be Billy's mother."

"I know."

I was surprised, but not totally. In matters of sex anything is possible. "Have you seen Chuck since you got back?" I asked Sally.

"A few times. We went to dinner, once. He wanted to do more, but I didn't."

"He seems in pretty rough shape."

"He is. But so is everyone here, Marsh. You won't believe the stories you hear. Wife beatings and child abuse and muggings and all the other things that come with hard times. Chaldea's on edge, Marsh. They say it's worse than the Depression."

"You ever ask Chuck about Billy?"

"No. And he never mentioned him."

"Did you talk to Chuck about Carol?"

"A little. He just said she left him because he was drinking and because he lost his job."

"Have you seen Carol?"

"No. I called but she'd heard I'd been out with Chuck and refused to see me. You know, Marsh, all that time we double-dated Carol and I were never really friends."

"Why not?"

"Too much alike, I guess. Too dependent on the same things for survival."

I stood up. "Listen," I said. "I'm going out to the farm, Uncle Raymond's place, where we used to park. You want to come along?"

"I'll go wherever you want."

She gave me that look, the half-smile, the cocked head, the wide eyes, that always made me pleased to please her. I reached for Sally's hand and pulled her out of her chair and her touch warmed embers that had been cold for years. I flicked off the lights and we started down the hall. Not for the first time Sally Stillings linked her arm through mine.

# Chapter
## 9

The highway south of town ran to the Missouri border in just twelve miles. In my day, the stretch just past the city limits had doubled as the drag strip, where kids staged their chopped and raked machines, sounded their glass packs and Hollywoods, then strained the capacities of their Hookers and their Bardahl and their Wynn's. I had never been enthralled with either cars or combat, so the legend of Highway 5 was merely that to me. But there were a few blood spots down there on the pavement, and more than one Chaldean grave was occupied by a boy who'd blown a tire or a piston or a nerve trying to make himself the top street dragster in the county, or trying to prove he wasn't chicken.

Our farm lay across the highway east of the drive-in movie, just past the International Harvester dealer and Mickey's roadhouse and the new old-age home. I turned left onto the chalk-white gravel of a secondary road, rose over the first hill, and looked for the turn. As I slowed the car Sally reached over and rested her palm on my thigh, then scooted closer to me. It was the way we'd always ridden, flank to flank, flesh to flesh, over the thousand miles of youth.

The entrance strip was overgrown with milkweed and foxtail and goldenrod, but beneath the tousled weeds a faint track led off the county road and into the field, then up along its edge toward the old farmhouse and outbuildings, which rested atop the slope at the far end of a field of picked corn. The gate was hooked with a circle of barbed wire. I got out of the car and lifted it off the gatepost, then drove through the opening. As I went back to relatch the gate I noticed a curtain fall back across a window in the large white-frame farmhouse on the other side of the road. I waited a minute to see if anyone was coming out, but the screen door remained closed. I fastened the gate behind me, then drove toward the top of the hill.

Sally was humming an old song about fools and love as we wobbled up next to the abandoned farmhouse. I stopped the car and we got out. The sun was bright and warm. The ground was gnarled with acorns and walnuts and even hedgeballs, and the leaves on the trees on the far ridge were leaking color. Sally leaned back against a fender and raised her face to the sun. "Remember how we were, Marsh?"

"I remember."

"It was so crazy, what we went through. I used to go home from here and cry and cry and read the Bible and pray to be forgiven for what I'd done or let you do. Did you know that?"

"No."

"Did you feel it, too, though? The guilt?"

"Some."

"Were you afraid? Of getting me pregnant?"

"Sure."

"We were lucky, you know."

"I know."

"What would you have done if you had?"

"Married you, I suppose."

"You say that with such dread."

"It would have been much more dreadful for you, believe me."

I left Sally at the car and walked toward the farmhouse.

The corn crib was empty, waiting for the product of the dry drained stalks that rose out of the field behind the house. A dozen sparrows scratched and pecked for leavings among the wire and wood of the crib walls. Beyond the crib the barn listed eerily, its sides weathered the color of dead flesh, its doors gone, its rafters sagging from the weight of time and hay. An old manure spreader was parked beneath the mow, rubber tires flat, spiked spreader coated with the black waste of many springs. As for the house itself, the doors and windows were splintered and punctured, half the roof had collapsed, and the stucco walls crumbled like the sides of arid sand castles. The porch gave way perilously as I walked across it toward the door.

Inside, someone had removed much of the flooring, leaving only dirt and joists and framing-boards. Strips of wallpaper flapped like thirsty tongues down the walls. The cupboards were bare and dusty, the linoleum cracked and buckled, and over it all were bird droppings and cobwebs and the fine powder of crop dust. The northwest corner of the house was missing entirely, as though blown away by a bomb. The opposite corner was strangely clean, as though a nest for something large. I want back to Sally and the car.

"I thought maybe Billy had been living there," I said to Sally. "But it must be someplace else."

Sally nodded absently. "It's so pretty out here," she said, then came to my side and slipped her arm around my waist. I draped an arm over her shoulder and we started to walk, our city shoes slipping over weeds and clods, our city clothes gathering burrs and dust. "Are you going to sell this place, Marsh?" Sally asked as we strolled toward the barn.

"How do you know about that?"

"Everyone in Chaldea knows about that."

"I don't know what to do," I said. "Curt and Matt want to sell; Gail doesn't. I guess I'm the swing vote."

"Which way are you leaning?"

I shrugged. "I thought at first I'd sell, just take the money and sever all ties with Chaldea once and for all. But now that I'm here I'm not so sure. It would be nice to think that, come what may, there was always this place to run to."

"I know what you mean," Sally said. "When Eric moved out I came back here as quickly as I could. It's strange. I used to complain so much about Chaldea when I was young, and now here I am. Freudian, almost."

"Maybe just smart," I said. "Statistics say it's safer here than almost anywhere." And then I thought of Billy, who had not been safe at all.

We strolled in the sun and silence for a long time, kicking

clods, dodging cow pies, swatting flies, touching the soil and each other, afoot in a world that had no future, only past.

An engine throbbed behind us suddenly, too close to be a highway sound. A tractor was coming up the road we had driven in on, a big red one with an enclosed cab and tandem rear wheels and the pulsing sound of diesel strength. I couldn't see the driver behind the reflection off the isinglass, but when he got to where we were, he braked and climbed down, leaving the engine purring behind him, a cat behind its tamer.

He was tall and angular, wearing overalls and work boots and a brown work shirt. His cap read *Gooch's Best*.

"You're on private property, mister," he said as he approached. His teeth were brown and crooked behind the lipless tear of his mouth.

"I know I am," I said mildly.

"Going to have to ask you to leave then," the farmer said. "You ain't part of that oil outfit, are you?"

"Why?"

"Last time they was here they messed up part of the east eighty so bad with their Jeeps and such, I had to replant. Told them I'd get the twelve-gauge next time I seen 'em. *Did* take a shot at someone the other night. Don't know *who* it was, sneaking around that way."

"I'm not an oilman," I said. "My name's Tanner. My family owns this place."

The scowl on the farmer's sharp brown face fell away and his pose became extravagantly peaceable. "Well," he said, thrusting a big hand toward me. "Pleased to meet you. Name's Delbert Waiters. Own the place across the way. Farm this one on shares, as you likely know already."

I nodded and took the hand and felt like I'd grabbed a pine cone. "Gail's told me about you," I said to the man. "Says you do a good job."

"Mrs. Notting's a real fine lady. Knows her farming, too. She'd be your sister, now, am I right?"

"Right."

Waiters nodded now that the world was straight again, then looked curiously at Sally. I introduced them and Waiters bowed and actually tipped his cap. Sally blushed, and smiled, and Waiters turned back to me. "Used to watch you play ball," he said. "Thought maybe you'd turn pro."

"I wasn't nearly that good."

"Plenty good for Chaldea."

"That's not good enough."

Waiters frowned and shuffled in the dirt, as though my statement had brought him an unpleasant memory. "Guess that depends," he said, then looked again at Sally. "You used to do something at them games, too, didn't you?"

"Drum majorette," Sally said.

"Thought so. Used to throw that stick right out of the park there at the end, didn't you?"

"The baton. Thank you for remembering."

"There's not so much going on here I'd have trouble remembering *that*," Waiters said. "We ain't had a ball club worth spit since them days anyhow. Play like a bunch of girls. No offense, ma'am."

I laughed and waited for Waiters to go on his way but he made no move to leave. "Planned to look you up when I heard you was in town," he said. "Since you're here, maybe we could speak a bit." He glanced at Sally and she got his meaning. A stone would have gotten his meaning.

"I'll walk to the top of the hill," she said. "There aren't any snakes out here, are there?"

"Not any that'll kill you," Waiters said, his grin usable by a fiend.

"Marsh?" Sally said, her voice rising.

"It's okay. I'll come up there when we're through." I waited while she walked carefully up the hill, her eyes fixed on the ground as though it sprouted gold. When she was out of earshot I turned back to Waiters. He lifted his cap off his head and wiped his forehead on his sleeve and then replaced the cap. "That the lady you used to bring out here back when you was in school?" he asked suddenly.

"What?"

"You know. When you used to pull in here in that little Impala your daddy owned."

"You mean you saw us?"

Waiters smiled. "Only way I knew it was ten o'clock. The brood mare and me, we got a big kick out of it."

I scratched my head, amused at his reference to his wife, embarrassed at the ineptitude of my young scheming.

"We can go in the barn and set if you'd druther. Looks like you don't get much sun doin' whatever it is you do."

"I'm okay," I said. "What happened to the farmhouse, anyway? Looks like a bomb went off."

Waiters shrugged. "Just blew up one night. Lightning, I reckon. Don't know what else would of done it, other than a fallin' star."

I smiled. "My nephew Billy lives on the place, I heard."

"Don't know if he does or not. See him once in a while. He leaves me be and I return the favor."

I nodded. "What's on your mind then, Mr. Waiters?" I asked.

Waiters spat something into the weeds. "Well, sir, it's like this. I own a hundred and eighty acres over yonder," he said, pointing across the road, "with only a hundred and twenty tilled. Now, you know anything about grain farming in this part of the state, you know they ain't many farmers that size still operating. All them abandoned farmhouses you see, like this one here, they was mostly owned by men with less than half a section under plow."

"I know it's tough to make it," I said, not really knowing much of anything.

"When corn goes below three dollars and beans is less than six, like they is now and like they'll stay so long as the politicos keep on the way they have, why the only way to make it work is with more acreage. Elsewise, be better off to burn the crop in the field."

"And you've been making it work by what you got from your place plus farming this one on shares, is that right?"

"That's right exactly. And you'll sprout wings and fly before prices'll get back to where they should, what with us canceling a bunch of the food stamps and pissing off the Communists and all."

"The Communists?"

"Damn right. Those Reds can't grow a crop any more than they can yodel, so they got to buy from someone. Used to buy from us, gypping us in the process 'cause the folks in Washington are so damn dumb, but still we had a market. Now they go to Argentina and Canada, like we taught 'em to do during the embargo, and more and more men like me have to close the barn and move to town. Well, sir, it ain't gonna happen to me. Not without a fight. And that's what I wanted to say to you face to face. I got a hundred thousand worth of equipment to pay off, and ten thousand in fertilizer and almost as much in seed, and a note at the bank for more than you can count even with your shoes off, plus the brood mare and four kids still around home, though they're old enough to be somewheres else, but it's not gonna break me. Not if I can run my rig over here when I'm done workin' my place. Can I tell you something, Mr. Tanner?"

"Sure."

"When I started, this place of yours was all in corn. Yielded less than sixty bushels an acre in a good year. Well, I brought in some ammonia, and tried them herbicides till I found a preemergent that licked the pigweed and velvet leaf, and two years back I whipped the corn bores, too, and guess what my yield will be this year."

"What?"

"Close to ninety. Not much for them slick-land places up north, but around here, hell, that's a friggin' bin buster."

"I believe it."

"You and your kin will make some money, too, you know. The deal's half-and-half."

"I know."

"Okay. I ain't beggin' you, mister, but I'm tellin' you the only way I can survive is by farming this place along with my own. I just hope you understand that. I also hope you know that the only way you'll get me off here is at the point of a gun. And maybe not then if I see you coming."

"I understand," I said.

"Then I'll leave you and the lady be."

Without another word Waiters mounted his tractor and gunned the heavy engine and turned the rig around. Before he started out of the field he leaned out of the cab and shouted above the growling engine. "You ask around, you'll hear that Delbert Waiters never lost a fight. You might remember that when you're decidin' what to do with this place. Wouldn't want something bad to happen to anyone sent out here to drive me off. It's a long way from help."

With his final word Waiters gunned the engine and the

tractor leaped forward, belching a puff of defiant smoke toward the blue dome above us. I watched Waiters cross the road, then walked up the hill toward Sally over a strange soft street, threats and memories and an Indian Summer sun behind me.

# Chapter
# 10

Sally was waiting for me at the top of the hill, her skirt specked with burrs and thistle, her forehead glistening from the sweat of her climb. "Look at this," she said, lifting a shoe. "I've worn these exactly twice."

I looked. She had stepped squarely on a cow pie, and its moderately fresh filling rimmed her loafer like flakes of chocolate pastry. "Farming is not a pretty business," I said, drawing the smile I sought from her. "I'm going over to the next ridge," I continued. "Billy lived out here somewhere and I'm going to try to find out where. You want to come or stay here?"

"I think I'll go back to the car," Sally said. "Take off my sweater and soak up some sun. I'm not exactly dressed for hiking, as you may have noticed." She took two steps and looked back. "There really *aren't* any snakes out here, are there, Marsh?"

"Take off more than your sweater and they won't do anything but leer."

Sally shook her head. "Sex fiend," she said, and tromped back down the hill. I matched her stride going the other way, over the crest and down toward the creek that wound through the little valley on the other side, beneath a lid of crenelated leaves.

To my right, three white-faced heifers grazed lethargically, ripping dry grass away from its bed with thoughtless twists of their heavy heads. High above me a pair of hawks glided easily on the wind. Bursts of breeze sprinkled me with leaves. Somewhere a woodpecker rattled a tree. The high grass I waded through could have been just weeds or could have been the prairie grass that WILD wanted to preserve, a thin and final link to what the earth had been before man gouged it.

The little creek was almost dry, its water lying still in stagnant pools, its bed pitted by the hooves of thirsty beef. I skipped across it on the decaying trunk of a fallen tree. When I reached the other side I turned back, trying to spot the ring of rocks where we had built our picnic fires, but it was gone, like most of the people who had stoked the flames. I kicked a rock and tossed a stick and watched a squirrel scamper toward the dark clump of his nest, then climbed toward the top of the next ridge and plunged onward toward the next. When I reached it I could see nothing but the same rough nature I had come through. I walked on, and finally noticed something built by man.

They were curved pipes, two of them, emerging from the top of a hillock to my left, apropos of nothing I could see. I walked toward them, still mystified. Even when I was close enough to touch them I couldn't tell what they were for. I looked around. Below the rise on which I stood I saw some tools and firewood and other signs of life. I went down to where they were and finally saw what it was that Billy had done.

It was an underground house, cut deeply into the hillside, three of its sides and its top nothing but thick expanses of earth and sod. The pipes I had seen were vents for air and smoke. The front wall was built of heavy slabs of cedar, carefully wrought, the cracks between the boards laboriously chinked with clay. The only opening was a wide doorway completely draped with cloth. Warm in winter, cool in summer, hidden from prying eyes, Billy had fashioned a home that met his needs.

I called out and banged my fist on the rough frame of the curtained doorway. Through a gap in the curtain I could see the flicker of a lantern in the center of the room, but nothing else. I yelled again and a hand drew back the fabric that separated me from the aromatic darkness within the buried house.

She squinted in the sunlight, then raised her other hand to

shield her eyes. She was naked except for some handsewn shorts that were bunched around her waist by a knotted length of twine, and she was pregnant, many months along, so much so that her breasts swelled blue and tight with milk and seemed about to burst. Veins ran across her great belly in fine blue channels, like the marks of a careless scrivener. Her skin was red from the heat of her lantern or the magic of her fertility.

She beat me to speech. "You the man Billy went to see?" she asked.

I shook my head. "Which man is that?"

She shrugged, dribbling her fat breasts. "Just a man."

"What did Billy want to see him for?"

"Who knows?"

"What was his name?"

She shrugged again, and said nothing further. She was thin everywhere but around her middle. Straight brown hair hung from the crown of her head and from the pits beneath her arms as well. Her eyes were large, as bright and brown as belt leather. Barefoot, she almost matched my height. "I'm Marsh Tanner," I said finally. "I'm Billy's uncle. From San Francisco."

She nodded. "I think I heard him say something about you once. Aren't you into something weird?" Her blatant question startled me.

"You mean being a detective?" I asked.

"That's it. A detective. Like Sherlock Holmes."

"Roughly."

She nodded again. "San Franciso. I wish I lived there, sometimes."

"Why?"

"I don't know. It's a groovy place to say you're from, I guess."

"Do you mind if I ask you your name?" I asked.

"Starbright."

I looked again at the arrogant expanse of stomach. "Is Billy the father of your child?"

"Sure," she said simply. "Billy's not around, though. Been gone since yesterday. Not that you have to leave or anything."

The invitation wasn't flirtatious, it was just fact. I didn't have to do anything I didn't want to. A common definition of freedom, and a meaningless one. "How long have you lived out here?" I asked.

She frowned, no friend of time. "I don't know. Three winters, I guess."

"Anyone else live here but you and Billy?"

She glanced down. "Not yet."

"Are you okay? I mean, is the pregnancy going all right? No complications?"

"I'm real fine. Billy made me a birthing stool and everything. We're all ready for him."

"Him?"

"Giap. The baby. It's going to be a boy. Definitely. You can tell from the color of the urine."

"Whose urine?"

"Mine, silly." She giggled and plucked some strands of her hair from her mouth.

"What's his name again?"

"Giap," she said, and spelled it. "Billy named him. After someone he knew in the war, I think."

The someone was the commanding general of the North Vietnamese Army, the architect of their victory over the South and us. Starbright didn't know that, but Billy had.

Starbright reached into the darkness behind her and brought out a bowl, shaped from thick red clay, irregular in form and not attractive. "Billy made this. Fired it himself. For the placenta."

"What?"

"The placenta. The afterbirth. You cook it and feed some to the baby and eat the rest yourself. Prevents cancer."

I looked into her eyes and saw no sign of wit, though some sign of strayed intelligence. She was one of those who will spend most of their lives believing nonsense, perhaps because she was raised on it.

"Do you have any friends in Chaldea?" I asked, after the image of french fried placenta had evaporated, or almost.

"Not here on the farm. I know some people at WILD."

"The environmental group?"

She nodded.

"Can you go into town and stay with them for a while?"

"Why would I want to do that? Billy will be back tonight for sure. Or tomorrow. I'm all right here. No one bothers me, no one would dare, that knows Billy. Besides, Billy doesn't like me to go to WILD anymore."

I didn't want to tell her what I knew, but I couldn't leave her the way she was, so I blurted it out. "Billy's dead," I said. "He died last night."

Her eyes stopped fluttering and found my face and searched it. When she saw I had told the truth she wrapped her arms across her breasts and nodded. "I just didn't think it would happen so soon," she said calmly. "We thought he'd have more time."

# Chapter
# 11

Her apathy drove me from her like a shove. "You sound as though you knew he was going to die," I said.

"I did," Starbright answered simply. "Billy did, too."

"Are you saying it was suicide?"

She shook her head quickly. "Billy would never do that. Not with the baby coming."

"Then why did he die?"

"He was sick. Sick so bad we knew it was going to kill him, eventually. But we thought it would be later."

Billy hadn't died from anything that medicine could treat, but I didn't tell Starbright that. Instead, I asked her how long Billy had been sick.

"Since the war, is what he said. Ever since I knew him, for sure."

"What exactly was wrong with him?"

"All kinds of things. He was weak, mostly; weaker all the time. Couldn't sleep; had these terrible nightmares. And there was, like, this *rash* all down his legs, even on his cock. Blisters and everything. I wouldn't give him head, finally, it got so bad. I mean, he understood, you know; it was just too gross."

"Anything else wrong with him?"

"Only *everything*. His chest hurt, like a heart attack, only that wasn't it. Plus, he couldn't breathe right, and got nose-bleeds all the time. And stomach cramps. He was wiped out, and it made him mad, so he was always raging out about something or other. He even hit me once, but he was real sorry afterward."

"Did he see a doctor?" I asked, after the catalogue of doom had ended.

"Once. The doctor couldn't figure it out, either. Gave Billy penicillin and Valium and told him to come back if they didn't help. They didn't help, but Billy didn't go back."

"Which doctor?"

She shrugged absently. I decided to shift gears. "Did Billy have any enemies?" I asked. "Anyone he fought or argued with recently?"

She thought a moment. "Not really. I mean, Billy pissed lots of people off. He said what was on his mind, you know? He wouldn't take any shit, and sometimes, well, it seemed like he just had to let off steam, let his temper go before he blew himself up. He got in lots of fights, but I wouldn't say he had enemies."

"Did he have any fights recently?"

"Not that I heard of. Why?"

I took a deep breath. "Whatever sickness Billy had, he didn't die from it, Starbright. They found him hanging from a tree with a rope around his neck. He either hung himself or someone did it to him."

"A *tree*? Billy was hanging from a *tree*?" For the first time a gasp of dismay occupied her face. She hugged her stomach as though to shield its occupant from the knowledge.

"That's what happened," I said. "Do you think Billy hung himself? Do you think maybe the sickness got so bad he couldn't take it anymore?"

Starbright shook her head, her long hair lashing her bare shoulders. "He wouldn't do that to himself. Not that way; not alone. If he wanted to die, I would have helped him. He knew I would. We talked about it once."

"What brought it up, the talk of dying?"

"The sickness."

"Then maybe that's what it was. It was just too much for him to handle."

"No. *No*. That wasn't it. All that kind of talk was before the baby. He wanted to see his baby in the worst way. Nothing could have kept him from doing that, *nothing*. You don't *know* Billy." Her words were shrieks.

It made sense, as much as anything does when it comes to flipping a coin between life and death. "Did you ever hear Billy talk about something called Agent Orange?" I asked after Starbright seemed calm.

"What?"

"Agent Orange. Or dioxin? Did he talk about anything like that?"

"Is that some kind of organic fruit? We buy lots of stuff like that from a place down in Missouri."

I shook my head. "It's not important."

It wasn't important, not now, because Billy was dead and because the government that had sprayed Agent Orange over its own soldiers and caused thousands of them to suffer exactly the kinds of things that Starbright had said Billy suffered from, that same government was denying responsibility for any of it. It was refusing to pay for the suffering or the treatment, even though the spray it had used to kill all that jungle foliage was full of dioxin, one of the most toxic substances known to man. But there were hearings going on, and studies, and lawsuits, and maybe someday it would be different, treatment would be rendered, compensation paid, and if so, someone should know that Billy was a victim. I made a note to find out who had treated Billy, then looked again at Starbright.

She looked helpless, confused, the whites of her eyes twin badges of uncertainty. "I think I should take you into town," I said to her. "To stay with your friends for a while. Till you get used to Billy being gone."

She thought it over quietly, then nodded. "I'll have to get some things," she said.

"I'll wait here." She ducked out of sight into the cabin, carrying within her a baby who, if Billy had the disease I thought he had, might be born without toes or fingers, arms or legs, might be born a freak.

I kicked at the nearest thing to me and walked up a path that led to the top of the next hill, anxious to get my mind off Billy and his family and onto something less damned, planning a return to the house in Starbright's absence to see what Billy might have had that would lead me to his killer. Because

Starbright had convinced me that's what it had been. A killing. The murder of a boy named Tanner.

I was still thinking of Billy as I walked, and of other boys I knew for whom there had been no difference between war and peace, who had returned from Vietnam so scarred within and without that they couldn't fit into the society they'd been sent to defend, boys wounded more by sights and deeds than bullets. At the top of the hill I sat beneath a sycamore and stared idly across the next valley at the trees and scrub brush on the opposite slope, my thoughts on the folly and inevitability of war. Then, gradually, something about the scene jarred me.

The vegetation was wrong, somehow. There were not only trees and grass and weeds and brush but an undergrowth of some kind, a crop, in fact, staked and tended and arranged in rows that snaked around the trees that rose above it. As I looked more closely at the stalks and their oddly tropical leaves I knew with certainty what they were, and added another possible cause of Billy's death to my list.

The marijuana was carefully cultivated. The stalks were as thick as broomsticks, rising eight feet or more, replete with the pointed leaves of dopers' joy. There were at least a hundred plants, many times too much for Billy's personal use, so it was a cash crop, raised for profit, ready for harvest. I wasn't current on drug prices in the Midwest, but I guessed the street value of the leaves and seeds arrayed before me would approach a hundred thousand bucks or maybe more.

From the lay of the ground and the health of the plants, this wasn't the first such crop grown in this lost valley. Which meant Billy could have died in a drug sale that went sour, in one of those seamy little infamies that mean nothing to anyone, just another victim of the stampede to avoid the way we were. I suddenly felt a little less damaged by what had been done to the nephew I had so seldom seen.

I got up and followed the path back to the cabin. Starbright hadn't emerged, so she didn't know I had discovered their new system of crop rotation. I decided not to mention it just yet.

When Starbright came outside she wore a loose peasant blouse and a long skirt and carried a bulging bag of clothes and shoes and jars and stuff. She still seemed serene, as though untouched or at least undaunted by Billy's death. It was a natural way to react for anyone who believes, as many profess to, that a more exalted form of existence begins on the other side of death, but it is uncommon all the same. As uncommon as true belief. I took Starbright's arm and her bag and helped her up the hill.

Along the way she told me she had grown up in Dubuque, as a cheerleading, churchgoing Catholic, and at the first chance had run off to a commune in Taos with the bass player in a rock band called Hemp. She'd lived around Taos for five years, moving out on the bass player and in with a one-legged potter, then returned to Dubuque after a scary experience with LSD. She waited tables and wrote poems for two years after that, living at home with disapproving parents, waiting for something to happen that would change her life.

What happened was Billy. She met him at a Led Zeppelin concert and came back with him to Chaldea and eventually conceived his child. She was into natural foods and herbs, was a vegetarian and a sort-of Sufi. When we got to the car I introduced her to Sally.

They were as opposite as coal and diamonds. Both at first drew back from presumed attack. But Starbright's swollen belly and Sally's rumpled attire were common bonds sufficient to unite them for the time it took to drive back to town. By the time I stopped in front of a dilapidated bungalow on West Elm Street, Sally had passed on a few tips on childbirth and care and Starbright in return had counseled Sally on the regenerative powers of tofu.

The bungalow was ostensibly the headquarters of WILD, but it looked like just another blighted residence to me, on a street where they grew like dandelions. The house was square and battered and featureless except for the shiny Cyclone fence that circled both the house and the scraggly lawn around it. The windows were masked with black curtains, the chimney had collapsed atop the roof in heavy hunks of brick. The van in the driveway was painted with a portrait of a wild-eyed warrior mounted on a fire-breathing steed that had carried him to the clouds. Beside the door someone had painted the word WILD in red block letters and decorated them with lacy vines. Other than the acrylic vines and warrior there was no sign of life about the place.

Starbright thanked me for the ride and shouldered her bag and started to leave the car. I asked her to wait. "Who runs this WILD organization?" I asked her.

"Zedda," she said.

"What's his last name?"

She shrugged. "He's just Zedda."

"Were he and Billy friends?"

She nodded. "Till lately. They were in the war, I think."

"Is that where they met? Vietnam?"

"I guess so."

"Does Zedda live here?"

"Him and some others."

"What does WILD do, exactly?"

"Protects the environment."

The grandeur of her statement was ridiculously undermined by the decay of the sad little house on the other side of the crumbling walk. I asked her how they went about it.

Starbright widened her eyes and took a deep breath and began a litany. "By opposing urban sprawl. By demanding soil conservation programs. By pushing for herbicide and pesticide controls and the elimination of nitrates in pork, so we won't all be killed by chemicals." Starbright's voice grew firm. "I mean, this is the *country* and all," she went on dramatically, "but you wouldn't *believe* the kinds of things that go on out here, things that threaten us all, especially babies." She wrapped her arms around her belly once again.

"Is WILD part of a national group?"

"I don't think so. I never heard anyone say anything about it."

"So this Zedda is the head man?"

Starbright nodded. "His old lady is my best friend. Sort of. She's pregnant, too. We meditate together twice a week. If you touch the womb when you say your mantra, it prevents crib death."

I decided to let Starbright go and look up this Zedda another time, to talk about Billy and maybe about the crop he had apparently planted.

As Starbright got out of the car the door of the house opened and a man walked toward us. He was tall and thin, Billy's age or a bit older. He wore his hair in a black mane that hung to the nape of his neck. His shirt had been made from sackcloth and was gathered at the neck and wrists. Above his tight black slacks and high black boots it gave him the aspect of a swashbuckler just in off the seven seas. His eyes had the sharp edges of intelligence or cruelty. He was the man I'd seen on the square while I was talking with Chuck.

"Who're they?" he asked Starbright as his easy saunter brought him toward the car.

"He's Billy's uncle," Starbright said quickly. "Billy's dead, Zedda. Hanged."

"I know," Zedda replied, the words flat, his face unreadable.

"Billy wouldn't hang himself, would he, Zedda?" Starbright asked, as though what Zedda answered would be the one and only truth.

"Who knows? Billy was weird lately." Zedda came close to the car and looked through the window, across Sally at me. "Which one are you?" he asked. "The salesman or the private eye?"

"Guess."

He smiled peaceably. "Not the salesman."

"We have a winner."

"I was a winner before you came along," he said.

I looked over his shoulder at the house. "Is that the prize?"

He followed my glance, then smiled again. "Among other things, Mister Detective. Among other things." His glance made Sally look away.

We were silent for a minute, measuring the extent of our dislike of each other. "We should talk," Zedda said finally.

"I agree. When?"

"Not now. Tonight. Late."

"How late?"

"Midnight."

"Where?"

"Here."

I nodded. "I'll try to make it," I said, and slipped the car in gear. "Take care of Starbright. That's my kin in there."

"Like one of our own," Zedda said, smiling still. I wasn't comforted.

Starbright got out of the car without his help and lugged her baby and her bag toward the little house. I almost called her back, to put her someplace else. Zedda stayed where he was, making Sally squirm in his presence. As I drove away the hot ray of his black-eyed stare climbed my neck like a bug. "He gives me the creeps," Sally said.

# Chapter
# 12

When I got back to the square I asked Sally where I could drop her. She looked at her watch. "It's dinner time, Marsh," she said. "Want to join me?" Her voice was high and lilting, her face wide with bogus innocence. The lack of subtlety depressed me a little, as did my inability to refuse her.

"Pick the spot," I said.

"There's a new Italian place over in Seymour," she said. "And a steakhouse in Bloomfield."

"I don't want to drive that far."

"Want to try the Blue Star? It's still going strong."

"Okay."

I drove to the rear of my hotel and parked. "Let me run in and call Gail," I said to Sally. "I'll be right with you."

"Can I go freshen up in your room, Marsh?" she responded. "I feel like I've just come in from a hayride."

I considered quickly whether there was anything in the room I didn't want Sally to see, then flipped her the key. "Meet you back at the car," I said.

Sally hesitated, started to say something, then stopped and got out of the car slowly. I interpreted it all to mean she was hoping I would go to the room with her. Once she had been the best and worst of my life and now she was becoming the threat of change and one thing worse: the threat of reliving my bungled youth.

I directed Sally toward the stairs to the second floor, then checked at the desk for messages. There was one, a call from a Mary Martha Gormley. I juggled the name and caught it. She was the editor of the paper, the one who'd written the article Tom Notting had given me. I threw away the message slip and called Gail.

Her husband answered after eight rings. "Gail isn't back yet," Tom said, after I told him who it was. "She's still over in Glory City with Curt and Laurel. She called a while back, said she might spend the night. Hell of a thing," Tom added, without emotion.

"It is that," I said.

"Of course, he was asking for it for a long time," Tom went on carefully.

"How was he doing that?"

"The drugs. The people he hung around with. The crazy way he acted, the things he said. Made lots of people mad."

"Exactly what things was he saying?"

"Oh, he was always making these, these *charges,* outlandish accusations with no proof at all. I mean, he made these wild statements and then got enraged when no one took him seriously."

"What kind of accusations?"

"He accused the best lawyer in town of malpractice, for one thing. And claimed the agricultural extension man didn't know his business." Tom paused and chuckled dryly. "He even went after me. Claimed I played favorites with the assessments. No one took him seriously, of course, but that kind of gossip can hurt you. After the party decided to run young Wilton for assessor instead of me I had a chance to go in with a bunch over in Ottumwa as a consultant. Your little Billy took care of *that.* But hell." Tom laughed. "This retirement thing beats work any day."

There was nothing humorous in the tone Tom used, and nothing truthful in his praise of early retirement. I asked Tom why Billy had gone after him that way. He said he didn't know. The way he said it made me think he did.

Billy had evidently been Chaldea's gadfly, if not its scourge. There are a thousand secrets in a small town, secrets that only stay secret because of the studied and belligerent posture of unawareness that people choose to adopt. Billy seemed to have made it difficult to maintain that stance, which meant there could be a thousand motives for killing him. I told Tom I'd see him the next day.

"Funeral's tomorrow," he said. "I was supposed to tell you."

"What time?"

"One."

"Where?"

"Cemetery. They're not doing anything at the church. Curt wouldn't let them. Said Billy had betrayed his faith."

I shook my head wordlessly, told Tom good-bye, and went out to wait for Sally.

She came out ten minutes later, gave me back my key, pressed a brief kiss to my cheek, and settled in for the ride, angled so she could study me. Her glossy lips left a stripe of grease on my cheek. She smelled of lilacs. "Can I ask you something, Marsh?" she said as we reached the edge of town.

"I guess."

"You don't make much money, do you?"

"What makes you say that?"

"Your things. Your suitcase. You don't have anything very . . . new."

I didn't say anything.

"Do you need money?"

I still didn't say anything.

"I have some. It's yours if you want it."

"Leave it alone, Sally. I make as much money as I need; probably more than is good for me."

"Well," Sally concluded sweetly, "I'm always here if you need me."

I wanted to push her out of the car.

Ten minutes later we pulled into the parking lot at the Blue Star, a restaurant a few miles out of town, a place that used to serve great steaks and I hoped still did. "Rudy and Madge still here?" I asked.

"Can't you tell? A new owner would have done something about that sign. Their daughter June does most of the cooking now."

"June? Jesus. I remember when she was born. Rudy showed movies of the birth on the walls. Complete with sound track."

Sally smiled. "June's married and has four kids of her own. Rudy's got heart trouble and Madge has an ulcer. They spend the winters in Florida and the summers on the lake. Rudy loses all their profits betting the horses at Ak-Sar-Ben."

"What's that mean again? I forget."

"It's just Nebraska spelled backward."

I pulled off the highway and onto the gravel bed of the parking area beside the squat block building behind the winking star-shaped sign with a dozen bulbs blown out. Rudy and Madge weren't in evidence when we got inside. A young girl with an old beehive showed us to a table with a plastic tulip in the center and a rack of napkins on the side, next to a cruet of curdled cream. We ordered drinks. The room was full of people wearing clothes they didn't like. The jukebox was playing the Oak Ridge Boys. The menus had been glued to boards shaped like paddles and the prices had been erased a lot.

A T-bone cost five times what it had the last time I'd been there. I changed my mind and ordered a sandwich. A breaded pork tenderloin. We marked time munching celery and removing melba toast from cellophane shells. We had two drinks before the meals arrived. The meat in mine was twice the circumference of its bun.

"I've tried to find these in California for twenty years," I said after the first bite. "Sometimes I have dreams about them."

"It's good you still like them," Sally said. "When you get our age it seems like nothing's as good as it was or as you thought it would be."

"You're even more cynical than I am, Sally."

"Eric would make the Pope a cynic."

We ate awhile in silence, amid the convivial buzz of the room. "Can I say something?" Sally asked suddenly.

"Sure," I said, not so sure.

"Now don't let me frighten you, Marsh. I mean, what I'm going to say is just talk. Nothing definite."

"Okay," I said, more leery by the second.

Sally shifted and squirmed and got ready for a speech. "Like I said, I'm in Chaldea to get my feet on the ground, to decide where to go and what to do."

I nodded.

"Eric makes lots of money. I have a good alimony

arrangement and he's generous to Rachel. He's agreed to pay for her education, as far as she wants to go."

"Good."

"And I can work. My secretarial skills are good. I worked in an insurance office for a year before I got married. I'm not afraid to hold a job."

"Good."

She paused, arranging her thoughts in a pattern I was increasingly certain I didn't want to hear. "What it all means," she said finally, "is that I'm free to do what I want. Go where I want to go. So one place I could go is San Francisco, Marsh. Rachel and I could move out there. We could be there by Christmas."

What she saw on my face after her breathy rush of words made her hurry with an elaboration. "I don't mean move *in* with you or anything, Marsh. I mean I could get an apartment, put Rachel in a nice school, then get a good job. But take my time, you know? Find the right thing."

Sally paused again, wanting me to help her in a way that would imply both aid and encouragement. "What do you want me to say, Sally?"

The question was the best I could do and it irritated her. "I guess what I want you to *say*, Marsh, is that you *like* that idea. I mean, that you would, I don't know, be my *friend* when we got out there. Something. Help me, Marsh, for God's sake. This isn't easy, you know."

"I know it isn't," I said, and reached out and placed my palm over the hand that was rubbing the sheen off her swizzle stick. It's always silly when people who have been lovers start talking about being friends. What they are is something more and less than friends, something sadly worse, and there's no other way about it. I knew enough about myself to know that if Sally did what she had just described we would quickly become lovers or enemies, but nothing in between. I think Sally knew it, too: it was why she was so scared. She had one enemy like that already.

Sally still waited for me to say something, and I did, but it wasn't the yes or no she wanted. "I can't promise you anything, Sally. I mean, what with Billy and all I haven't really been able to think about you—us, that much. And I have to warn you, my relationships with women have been pretty rough for the past few years. I'm getting real hard to put up with. Everything seems to be so much *trouble*. So, I mean, you shouldn't count on anything. Not anything you want from me."

She smiled, with a hint of rue and shame, then forced a laugh, and her resilient humor reminded me why I had loved her so much for so long, reminded me how often she had propped me up when my life seemed to have gone so mysteriously awry, reminded me that for a lot of early years there was one thing I had always known for sure, that I was the most important thing in the world to Sally Stillings.

Sally reversed our hands and grasped mine firmly. "Forget what I just said, okay, Marsh? I'm not going to haunt you. It's just that I've been so *lonely* since Eric; hell, even *before* Eric. There's been just Rachel and me for so *long*. I love her more than anything, but that's not enough. I need someone to talk to the way *we* used to talk about things. Remember?"

"Sure."

"No one wants to do that anymore, talk about important things. I wonder why not."

"Maybe it's just that the important things have changed."

"Not for me, they haven't."

"That's good," I said, not knowing whether it was or not.

"How about you? Have they changed for you?" Sally asked.

"I don't know. I guess I don't think about what's important much anymore. Not in the abstract, at least."

Sally smiled that smile again. "I was always asking you what you were thinking and you were always trying not to tell me. Actually, I think I only asked you what you were thinking so you would ask me what *I* was thinking. At least that's the way it usually worked out. Then I could tell you all my problems. There seemed so many then; now those days seem like heaven."

Sally grasped my hand with both of hers and squeezed it. She leaned toward me and the lilacs made my nostrils twitch. "Can we go back to your room now, Marsh? Please?"

"Sally . . ."

"Please? You don't know how many times I've thought of this, of us meeting again. Not just since I came back here, but for years and years. I need this to happen to me, Marsh. I need something *nice* to happen to me."

Her eyes swam in pleading tears. I knew what she was talking about because I had thought of it often, too, seeing Sally once again. My fantasy usually placed us in some large city where neither of us was known. I would take her to bed in a fit of the passion that absence and betrayal breeds, then listen to her tell me I was the best there ever was. This wasn't that, but it was as close as I ever get to seizing fantasy. And I had it within me to make Sally's dream come true as well, or so she thought. But reality never quite swells up to dreams—it's the reason for both monks and drunks—and I would fail her. Which was why I finally decided to go ahead.

I paid the check and helped Sally on with her coat and we started to leave the restaurant. Suddenly my way was blocked by a swarthy, stocky man wearing a shiny exercise suit and white running shoes. His hair was as thick as a mop in tar and his face was glistening as though his flesh were mirrored. If he ran anything it was the numbers. "Your name Tanner?" he growled. His tone implied I should be punished for it.

I acknowledged that I was.

"You got a brother name of Curt?"

"I do."

"I been trying to reach him. You tell him that. You tell him we had a deal, and I want my dough."

"What kind of deal?"

"That's between him and me. You just tell him what I said."

"Who are you?"

"Pantley. Rufus Pantley. I'm at the Tall Corn Motel. I'll expect the dough tomorrow. I don't get it, I come after."

The thick man turned away, heading for the door. I grabbed his arm. "What's this all about? What did you do that Curt owes you money?"

He swore and ripped his arm away. "It ain't what I did, it's what I'm gonna do. Now back off, pal."

He looked dumb or crazy enough to go to the limit of violence if I tried to stop him, so I let him go. Sally hurried to my side and asked me what it was all about. I told her truthfully that I didn't know, then went out into the parking lot and found my car. I picked Sally up at the entrance and drove back to town.

The Christmas decorations on the square were already up, or maybe they had never been taken down. The only lights in the stores came through the oily windows of saloons. I asked Sally if she wanted to go in for a drink. She shook her head and shivered. I turned on the car heater. "Want to ride around?" I asked.

"You mean cruise the square? Go out and park?"

"Sure."

"What kind of a girl do you think I am?"

"That kind."

"Let's go."

I fell in line with the pickups and sedans and sheepishly joined the parade. We attracted many stares and several smirks, but mostly we were welcomed. I pointed to a window above a clothing store. "The woman who lived up there was a whore. When there was a coffee cup in the window she was open for business. For ten bucks you got everything she knew or had read about, which wasn't much."

"You ever visit her, Marsh?"

"No."

"Why not?"

"Scared I'd get caught or catch something."

We turned two more laps.

"Christina Batchelor used to do it for money, did you know that?"

"Christina Batchelor? You're kidding. She was Rainbow Queen, for God's sakes."

"She told me one night when we were selling popcorn at a basketball game. She charged five. She told me after I sold a bag of popcorn to one of her customers."

"Who?"

"I can't tell."

"Who?"

"Carol's father."

"Carol Hasburg?"

"Yes."

"Jesus."

We both were silent and then we both laughed, at the ridiculous conversation and its distance from the way we had tiptoed around such earthy matters thirty years before. I turned off the square and headed for the reservoir.

"How many women have you slept with, Marsh?"

"Not many."

"Really. How many? More than a hundred?"

"No. Christ. I haven't even *talked* to a hundred."

"More than twenty?"

"Maybe."

"I was the first, wasn't I?"

"You were. How about you?"

"Six, counting you."

"Any while you were married?"

"Two. But not till it was over. Not till Eric did it first and told me the gory details. If I tell you something, will you promise not to get mad?"

"What?"

"You weren't the first for me."

"Who was?"

"Chuck."

"Chuck Hasburg?"

"He came by one night after he and Carol had had a fight. He had some beer. We went out behind the foundry. I'd never been drunk before. He had his way with me, as they say. Then I threw up."

"My old buddy Chuck."

"It was my fault as much as his."

"No, it wasn't."

Chuck and Sally. I thought of how careful I had been of her, how slowly I had inched toward her virginity, how leery I had been of piercing her psyche as I pierced her hymen. The inevitable pathos of ignorance made me laugh.

"I thought you'd be mad," Sally said.

"I am, a little."

"If I'd told you about it when it happened, you'd have never spoken to me again, would you?"

"No."

We left the town and bounced along an abandoned stretch of highway and turned onto the dirt road to the reservoir. The night was black and cold. The windshield frosted crisply behind the hot powder of our breaths. I drove to the top of the dam and stopped. We looked out over the black water of the lake, divided by a creamy stripe of moonlight. The only sound was the faint splash of water coursing down the spillway, as peaceful as the sound of my erased illusions.

"My father built a sailboat once," I said after a while.

"I didn't know that."

"It was before we started going together. He got a kit, spent hours and hours on it every night after work. Broke champagne over it when we launched it and everything. Chuck and I brought it out here one Sunday and sank it."

"Clear to the bottom?"

"Yep. Still down there as far as I know."

"On purpose?"

"No. Jesus. Why would I do it on purpose?"

"I don't know. I thought maybe you were mad at him."

"I was never mad enough to do that."

"Your father must have been upset."

"Sad was more like it. As far as I know he never built another thing in his life."

"And you blame yourself."

"Not really, I guess."

The spillway splashed some more, unused and useless liquid trickling off to nowhere.

"Remember when we went skinny-dipping?" Sally asked.

"Yeah."

"I was so afraid."

"Of getting caught?"

"Of you being disappointed in how I looked next to Carol."

"As I recall you looked just fine."

"Her breasts were bigger."

"That's true."

"You liked big breasts. I know you did."

"Yours were big enough."

"They're bigger now."

"What?"

"Eric made me get an implant."

"Is it . . . does it work?"

"Here."

She took my hand and put it on her breast. What I felt excited me. "Feels the same," I said, and tried to laugh.

"Not to me."

I dropped my hand away.

"Carol looks good, have you seen her?" Sally said.

"No."

"She's changed a lot, I hear."

"How?"

"I don't know. She's bitter, and angry. They say she sleeps around a lot." There might have been a hint of triumph in the last. "With more than Billy, I mean."

"Did you ever hear anything more about Carol and Billy? Besides what you told me?"

"No."

"They're burying Billy tomorrow," I said after a while.

"Do you want me to go with you?"

"I'd better stick with the family."

"I'm family, Marsh. I'm more family to you than Matt."

"I guess you are."

I drove back to town and parked behind the hotel. "Are you sure you want to do this?" I asked as we sat in the quiet darkness.

"I'm sure."

"Okay."

Some time during the evening it had become easier to do what she wanted. I didn't know why and didn't want to. We got out and entered the hotel and climbed wordlessly to the room, past the sleeping eyes of the desk clerk.

The room suddenly seemed tawdry, as tawdry as what we were about to do. "Just don't say anything, Marsh," Sally said as I turned to her. "Nothing at all. Let me do what I want."

Sally went into the bathroom and shut the door. I found the pint of Scotch and poured myself a drink and downed it in two gulps. Then I started to take off my clothes and then I stopped. Sex seemed suddenly unmanageable. I poured another drink, then picked up the book I was reading and lay on the bed and cast my eyes over senseless words.

"Marsh?"

The call from behind the door interrupted my nervous fit.

"What?"

"Turn out the light."

I went to the wall and did what she asked. The bathroom door opened on a squeaking hinge.

She was naked, her pose burlesque—arm overhead, hip

cocked, leg thrust forward, back arched—the final bump at the end of the act as the lights go out and the patrons cheer for more. Her flanks aflame from the light behind her, Sally saw where I was looking. "You like them?"

"Very nice."

"I'm glad. Now don't say anything else, Marsh. Just take off your clothes. No. Come here. Let me."

I walked as near to her as I could get, still carrying my book as though it made me immune to fault. Sally began unbuttoning my shirt. I began to help her. She brushed my hands away.

She removed my clothing and my reluctance. I let her go ahead, uncertain whether as reward or punishment, certain only of desire, remembering how terribly she'd cried the first time I touched her breast.

"Put down that stupid book," she said, and then said nothing.

# Chapter
## 13

When we were finished Sally nodded off, making herself cozy beside me, silence becoming sleep. I looked at the cracked and sagging plaster in the ceiling, its slight disrepair comparing favorably with my sense of honor.

I had enjoyed it more than I thought I would, but part of the reason was that, someplace along in there, I had tried to make Sally pay for what she had done to me thirty years ago. To make matters worse, Sally seemed to understand and assent to what I was doing, to endure my roughness as her due. Or maybe it was how she got her kicks. Sex is so terribly wonderful, it becomes too easy to make it the converse. I rolled to my side and slipped out of bed and got dressed. Sally murmured a question and I told her to stay where she was. I had a date with a WILD man.

The streets of Chaldea were empty of all but strays. Swaddled in the buzz of sleep and drink, I felt like one myself. A single light burned in the window of the WILD bungalow. Sounds of Eastern music crept out of the blackened windows, tickling my ears with the strains of sitars. The fragrance wafting through the air was sandalwood and beneath that, something more biting, more familiar; something that had, I guessed, begun its life on the secret slopes of the Tanner farm. I crossed the porch and knocked on the sagging screen door.

Zedda opened the door and beckoned me inside. Both the music and the smell intensified in the entryway, which was lit to a golden hue by two large candles that rose off some sort of altar at the far end. The object of worship seemed to be a picture of John Lennon. From rooms at the back of the house came giggles and halting song fragments. I sensed many people, mostly female—a harem for the dashing Zedda. I followed him into the living room.

The floors were bare, the wax finish worn to the hardwood where traffic was heaviest. Mounds of tasseled satin pillows were scattered about, as were bits of clothing, ashtrays, books, and empty cans of food. In the corner a three-foot hookah rose off the floor like a cobra being charmed.

Zedda sat on a pillow and urged me to do the same. On the wall behind him, the intricate mix of colors in an Oriental rug seemed to ebb and flow, evolve and subside, in the prismatic haze. The room had a warm and muffled aspect, cozy in a dingy sort of way. I had to glance around two times, through the smoky glow and to the umbra beyond it, to make sure Zedda and I were alone.

As I struggled for comfort in the pillows Zedda asked if I wanted some tea. I shook my head. "Grass?" His smile was mocking.

"No, thanks."

"We have alternatives, if you have a drug of choice."

"Only alcohol."

"We have wine, is all. Hard liquor reduces sexual function."

"I'm fine, thanks."

"Swell."

I started to lean back, then realized there was nothing behind me to lean back on. The incense made me work to stifle a sneeze. My shoes felt suddenly the size of coffins. Zedda stood suddenly and left the room through a door at the end of the entryway. The candles and I both trembled from the draft that blew through the room like the leavings of a ghost.

When he came back, Zedda was puffing on a meerschaum that contained cannabis instead of Prince Albert. The bowl was carved into the shape of a dragon. He wore the same leather pants I had seen earlier in the day, but now his shirt was ribbed and fluffy, as though fashioned from a bedspread or a drape. A clear crystal amulet hung from his neck. From time to time it caught the candlelight, which turned it blue and icy, the color of slow death. A red bandanna pressed his long hair to his temples. At the center of the bandanna was a silver star. I gestured toward it. "Military?"

He nodded once. "I'm a certified genuine American hero." His grin was more maniacal then heroic.

Zedda inhaled deeply the smoke from his pipe, held it in his lungs for long seconds, then exhaled and leaned back against the wall and clasped his hands behind his head. He seemed prepared to be expansive. I asked him what he did before he went into the army.

"Nothing." The smile was broad again, but late. "Everything."

"Drafted?"

"Is there another way?"

"When?"

"Sixty-eight."

"Where'd you take basic?"

"Fort Knox."

"How about AIT?"

"Fort Polk."

"Nice place, I hear."

"If you get off on swamp."

"Is that where you met Billy?"

He shook his head. "Nam. I met Billy-boy in the Southeast Asian Republic of Vietnam. He was quite the boy."

"How do you mean?"

"Why Billy, now, he was one of those *special* souls. They'd given him the best they had—jump school, ranger training, even some time at a counter-fucking-insurgency school in the Philippines that only three people in the Western world know about. Oh, yes. Billy-boy was quite the troop by the time I caught his act."

"Where was that?"

Zedda ignored my question. "These farm boys, see, they make number-fucking-one killers, man. They been killing pigs and chickens and shit since the day they were born, see, so they get real used to it. I mean, taking life ain't such a big *deal* to them, not like to city boys, *white* city boys, at least. The only thing is, you got to make sure your basic plowboy is convinced that killing what you want him to kill is the American *way*. I mean, he's got to think God *wants* him to kill gooks, just like God wants him to kill pigs and shit. When you get that job done, you got yourself one hell of a weapon. Just point the fucker in the right direction and stand back."

Zedda laughed to himself and drew deeply from the pipe and looked at me through shiny, sleepy eyes. "Who are you again, man?" he asked carelessly.

"Billy's uncle."

"Oh, yeah. Right. Billy. Hell of a dude, man. Sorry he's gone. Even if he did fuck me over."

"How did he do that?"

"What?"

"Fuck you over."

Zedda inhaled again. "None of your business, man. Billy's dead. I loved the dude. He did what he thought he had to do and I respect him for it. R.I.P., man. R. fucking I.P."

I let the borrowed black patois float to the ceiling with the smoke, then tried to get Zedda back on the beam. "Where'd you meet Billy?" I asked him again.

"Nam. I thought I said that already."

"Where in Nam?"

"Base camp outside Tay Ninh. We'd both been in-country about nine months, but Billy, he'd started out down in the delta someplace, wading around in the slime paddies, slitting gook throats, and he was so fucking good at it they attached him to us as some kind of special scout or some such shit. See, Billy was so fucking slick at killing gooks every swinging dick *over* there wanted him in his unit. The body count, you know, man."

I started to say something but Zedda started his soliloquy again. He was on a reefer roll and I let him go. Since I didn't know what I wanted, I decided to take it all.

"See, what I learned later was, when I met him Billy was just back from Cambodia. Now at that time Cambodia was a sovereign fucking *nation*, man. I mean, we weren't supposed to be *in* there, if you know what I mean, so you can imagine the kind of undercover shit Billy must have been into to get there. I mean, when I saw him first his fucking jungle boots were worn down to the slick and his tiger suit was so faded you couldn't see the fucking *stripes*, and his *eyes*, man, you could have roasted wienies on *those* baby blues. The poor fucker was *insane*. And he loved it, was the thing, *needed* it, even. I mean, he was fucking *into* killing Cong, man. And it was all hand-to-hand. Fucking knife-in-the-teeth, crawl-on-your-belly, *sneaky* shit. Oh, yeah, Billy-boy was one lethal son of a bitch till I straightened him out." Zedda's smile was oiled with smugness.

"How'd you do that?"

"See, the command group up at division, they finally figured out that Billy-boy was getting off a little *too* much on this counterinsurgency shit, figured maybe he'd start practicing on *white* ass, you know, so they made him stay in the rear for a week with the rest of us REMFs."

"REMFs?"

"Rear Echelon Mother-Fuckers. I served Uncle by tending bar and dealing dope in the EM club. That's where I first saw Billy. He was on his twentieth beer or so one night, looking like he wanted to waste every troop in the place with a smile on his face, so I went over and bought him a few more brews. We started rapping and over the next couple of days Billy-boy started to get real interested in what I had to say."

"Which was?"

Zedda's lazy smile narrowed. "Just some *facts*, man. Facts that related to the military-industrial complex in this country. Facts that related to exactly who was doing the *dying* over there in terms of the socioeconomic structure of society; facts that related to how the war was being fought in its *racial* aspects; facts that related to the corruption of everything from the Thieu regime to the army club system. Facts like *that*. Before the week was out I laid out the whole fucking *picture* for Billy-boy."

"And Billy came to oppose the war."

"That's affirmative. Billy-boy came to oppose that fucking war in every corner of his Anglo-Saxon soul."

"What happened then?"

"When the week was up they tried to send him back out in the boonies with his knife strapped to his leg and a grenade in his teeth, but he told them to get *fucked*. He *about* slit some bird colonel's *throat*, is what I heard. They talked some about court-martialing him, but Billy-boy knew some shit they didn't want coming out in no fucking courtroom so they sent him to a shrink for about six minutes and then sent him home.

Like to have been there when mom and dad laid eyes on the boy. Anyway, I came along a couple of months later, and eventually ended up down here."

"What brought you to this area?" I asked.

Zedda took another puff, sucking smoke to his toes. I was afraid he was going to pass out. "The land, man," he murmured. "All this fucking *dirt*. I'd seen so much land ripped up over in Nam I decided to do something to save what was left of it over *here*, you know, man?"

"There's land in Michigan, land in Nevada, even land in Jersey. Why here?"

"Because this is the *pro*totype. American Gothic and all that. There's shit growing all *over* this state. Ain't nothing *but* land here."

"Then why Chaldea? The soil here's only marginal at best. Why not up north, where the good stuff is?"

"Well, Billy was here, and I knew his old man had some kind of spread. And this place needs help more than up north. I mean, they ain't got soil to waste down in this neck of the woods. If the good folks don't wake up and fly right, the dirt around here won't be fit to grow weeds. They *need* WILD, man. We can show them the *way*."

Zedda had drifted out of his drug daze into the ritualistic, messianic fervor of his public pose. His chatter, though possibly true, was mostly slogans, and his life-style belied a serious interest in the kinds of things he was talking about. I waited till Zedda's eyes seemed focused again, then asked him what Billy had been doing for WILD.

"Whatever the fuck he *wanted* to do. Messing with people's minds, mostly."

"Why?"

"Well, these are the folks that sent him over there, right? These are the friends and neighbors who said sure, go ahead and *teach* our little Billy just exactly how to *slit* a slant-eyed throat. Well, Billy made sure they knew exactly what they'd done to him, see. He told them what he was and what that made *them*."

"How, exactly?"

"Oh, he'd be sitting in a bar and some polyester dude would come up and start to rap with him, just being polite, you know, they all liked little Billy Tanner. And the conversation would swing around to the war, eventually, and sooner or later the poor bastard would ask Billy what he *did* over there, you know. How things *were*. And Billy would tell him, man. I mean, the *details*, you know? And just before the poor fucker puked his Bud all over the floor Billy would pull out this ear, this fucking gook *ear*, man, and set it on the bar. Fucking thing looked like a dried *turd* laying there or something, and Billy would smile and the polyester bastard would ask him what it was and Billy would lay it out for him real soft and polite, with just those baby blues rolling a little too much for comfort, is all, and that usually took care of things. Yeah, they liked the Billy they sent *off* to war, but they didn't much care for the one that came *back*."

Zedda sucked more dope into his system. I was getting a contact high myself.

"Starbright told me Billy was sick. Any idea what it was?"

"Poison, man. Genuine American-made poison."

"Agent Orange?"

"The one and only."

"Was he doing anything about it?"

"What's to do? The dude was dying. Someone just accelerated the program."

"Who?"

"Who killed Billy?"

"Right."

He shrugged. "I hear the police call it suicide."

Zedda's smile was a calibrated insult.

"I don't care what they call it," I said roughly. "Billy was murdered. I'll prove it before I leave town. So. Again. Any idea who killed him?"

"Nope."

"None at all?"

"Oh, I got a *thousand* ideas, man. I just ain't got *one*. You see what I'm saying?"

I saw. Zedda didn't much give a damn who killed Billy. Zedda had been a guru to Billy and, as usual with gurus, the benefit ran only one way. "I hear Billy dug up some dirt on a few of the locals," I said, still determined to mine Zedda's well-stoned mind.

"If he did it's got nothing to do with me."

"Who-all did he go after?"

Zedda shrugged, his lids drooping even lower across his eyes, giving him an Oriental aspect to match the décor and the history he had just described. "The town lawyer. The assessor. The extension man. I don't know who-all. That was Billy's private fight."

"What about Carol Hasburg?"

"What about her?"

"She's a woman here in town. I heard she and Billy were an item."

Zedda laughed and sucked his pipe. "Starbright was Billy's chick. I don't know about the others. Some chicks like to play with fire, man, and that's what Billy was."

"How is Starbright?"

"Fine and dandy."

"She here?"

Zedda shrugged. "Comes and goes."

"Will you see her in the morning?"

"I suppose."

"Tell her Billy's funeral is at one. Tell her I'll come by here and pick her up at a quarter till. If she wants to go."

"Funerals are a drag, man."

I pushed myself up off the pillows. "Just tell her," I said, and headed for the door.

"Hey," Zedda called out. "You and your people decide what you're going to do with that farm out there?"

"Not yet."

"Be a big mistake to cave in to the developers or the strip miners, man."

"Maybe. Seems to depend on who you talk to."

"It's the *land*, man. Should stay the way it is. Grass and birds and animals, man. Nature."

"Some people don't see it that way."

"How about you? How do you see it?"

"I don't know yet."

Zedda leaned forward and got his feet under him and stood up. The crystal amulet darted across his naked throat like Tinker Bell in transit. "It would do a lot for the movement for us to be able to say we put a stop to mining or development out there, man. So much so that WILD is willing to make a financial contribution to encourage you to dedicate the place to public use. You dig?"

"How much of a contribution?"

"Fifty thousand dollars. For a deed of the Tanner plot to WILD."

I looked to see if he was serious. He seemed to be. "That's a lot of money," I said.

"Our fund drives are a bitch."

"Bullshit."

"What?"

"I said bullshit, Zedda. Let me tell you what I think. I think WILD isn't an environmental group at all. It's a cover for a wholesale marijuana operation, maybe other drugs as well. You came down here because Billy Tanner had access to a half section of farmland and because marijuana would thrive on it with a modicum of cultivation. You came down here to make a killing in the drug trade, Zedda. That's what I think. And you used Billy to guard the crop."

"Well, well," Zedda said, his pipe in his hand instead of his mouth, his eyes broken and scrambled by the flickering candlelight. "So that's what you think."

"It is."

"You tell anyone about this crap you been talking, man?"

"Not yet."

"You going to?"

"If it helps me find the man who killed Billy, I will. Was a drug deal going down, Zedda? Did it go sour? Is that why someone strung him up?"

Zedda shook his head. I realized I had been screaming at him on some unnatural high of my own. "Billy didn't have anything to do with drugs, man. Not after they came in off the farm. Nothing going down involving *Billy*-boy. Nothing at all."

"If I find out different, I'll have the law out in that field in about three seconds," I said.

"Be cool, man. I'm telling you, we weren't *dealing* this week. Now, we got a deal for the farm? Fifty grand, man. All cash. Uncle don't ever have to know."

"No deal," I said. "And if you were a REMF, how'd you get the Silver Star?"

Zedda smiled his evil smile. "Traded an ounce of righteous smack for it, man. How else?"

When I left him he was laughing.

# Chapter
# 14

When I got back to the hotel there was a note on the pillow: "Let's do it again sometime. All it takes is a call. S." I got undressed and lay down on sheets still warm from her body, still wet from our sex, and struggled to find sleep.

I felt rough the next morning, as though I'd absorbed a beating or a binge. I stayed in bed with my book until I was sure the locals had left the coffee shop to ply their various trades, then wandered down and ate some toast and eggs. Afterward, I wandered back to my room with the morning paper. After I finished reading of Hawkeyes and Cyclones and Bulldogs, I called Gail. She sounded for a moment as if she didn't know me from a crank. Then she told me Curt and Laurel were taking Billy's death as well as could be expected. "They seem relieved, Marsh, if you want to know the truth. Billy was like a yoke for them, I think; a sin. They felt responsible for what he was."

"From what I hear it was the war that changed him," I said. "Curt and Laurel didn't get us into Vietnam."

"In a way they did, though. In a way we all did. I mean, we supported it, we said nasty things about the ones who went to Canada and the ones who burned their cards. He made us realize that we were prepared for war to *kill* a boy like Billy, but we weren't prepared for it to send him back to us so different. We weren't prepared for him to hate so much, or worse, to tell us why."

I didn't speak until the echo of Gail's words had died away. Then I asked if Tom was home.

"No. Why?"

"What happened between Tom and Billy, Gail? The thing about the assessments?"

Gail's sigh stretched slowly across the wire. "Oh, it was so bad, Marsh. First, the party decided not to back Tom for reelection. He took it hard, being abandoned after all those years. But he came out of it, gradually, and had another job lined up, when all of a sudden Billy made these *charges* against him. Billy went down to the courthouse and looked through all the assessments on our house and the mayor's house and the sheriff's house and people like that, and some of our neighbors, too, and then compared those assessments with those of people who weren't in city government and people who didn't know Tom, and he made it look like Tom had been doing favors for his friends and his political allies over the years. The newspaper printed the figures—not the local paper but the one in the state capital—and reporters came down and it made Tom look like such a *crook*, Marsh. They called it the Little Watergate and everything. He lost the job opportunity, of course, but what's worse, he lost his will to live, almost. He's like he was when the party kicked him out."

"What's wrong with him, exactly?"

"No one knows. I mean, Doctor Yarrow told me once he thought it was psychosomatic. Some kind of defense mechanism Tom created to lessen his responsibility for the things Billy said he did. But I don't know. It's too complicated. All I know is that Tom and I, well, there's not much left there, Marsh."

"I'm sorry, Gail."

"We all have our burdens, Marsh. I'm just thankful mine didn't come along earlier."

"That's nonsense, Gail. If it's all over between you two, then you should leave him."

"I couldn't do that."

"Sure, you could. Divorce isn't always a mistake."

"In Chaldea it is."

For the first time in my life I felt Gail needed something

abstract from me, felt that whatever had sustained her over all these years, her faith, her friends, her town, had failed her when she needed them most. The problem was, I didn't have anything to give but platitudes, the same thing she got from all the rest. Instead I asked a question. "Why do you think Billy did this to Tom?"

"That's what no one knows, Marsh. We asked Curt about it and he didn't know, and I even tried to talk to Billy about it once, but he wouldn't say. Just smiled that crazy smile of his. It's a mystery."

"Was Tom involved in the war in any way?"

"No. How could he have been?"

"I don't know. It just seems that everything Billy did was connected to the war somehow, that Vietnam was his obsession."

"I guess maybe that's right, but I don't see how that would have involved Tom more than anyone else in town."

"I don't either," I admitted. "The funeral is at one, right?"

"Yes. We're supposed to go out to Curt's afterward, for cake and coffee. Laurel's been working like mad making food. It keeps her mind off Billy, I guess. And Matt wants us to meet then and decide about the farm one way or another. He wants to leave town tonight."

"I don't know if I'll be ready to decide by then."

"Why not, Marsh? What have you been doing, anyway? I tried to call you last night and you weren't there. I'll bet you were with Sally."

I didn't tell Gail about the marijuana field, or about the threat from her share farmer, but I did admit to dinner with Sally. "I'm bringing someone to the funeral," I said, after I'd lied about the way Sally and I spent the evening's end.

"Sally?"

"Billy's wife."

Gail gasped. "You mean that girl with the hair down her back?"

"That's the one."

"Were they really married, Marsh? No one seemed to know for sure."

I didn't know either, and I told Gail so.

"Then do you think it's right to bring her? I mean, Curt and Laurel have enough people picking at them as it is."

"The girl's carrying Billy's child," I said, a bit angrily. "That should be a sufficient ticket to the show, don't you think? Even in Chaldea?"

"Are you sure it's Billy's baby? I mean, you know how they are."

Gail's primness worked like an auger in my stomach. "How *are* they, Gail? Fertile?"

"Oh, never mind. Do what you think is right."

"I will," I said. "And I suggest you do the same."

"I don't need lessons from *you* on how to act, Marsh Tanner."

"I didn't think so up to now," I countered, and then I asked a question more with anger than with sense. "Where was your husband last night, Gail? Did he go out at all?"

"He goes out every night. Explorer Scouts. That's the only thing he ever does anymore, meet with his precious scouts. But what does that have to do with anything? Oh. I see. You think Tom might have done something to Billy because of the assessment thing, don't you? Oh, Marsh."

Gail began to cry and hung up before my apology reached her ear. I brandished the receiver like a cudgel and trained it on myself, then replaced it.

I had taken advantage of a vulnerable time for Gail, and by springing my surprise had forced her to act like something she was not—a personification of Midwestern religiosity, the pseudopiety that finds Bible-quoting, teetotaling deacons ranting against niggers and hippies and bemoaning welfare and cheating the tax man all the while. I dialed Gail's number again. When she answered I told her I was sorry.

"Me, too."

"Should I come over?"

"No. I'm okay. It's just that so much is happening. Life is upside down. I can't deal with it all, sometimes. Bring the girl, Marsh."

"Good. See you at the cemetery."

"Okay."

"I am sorry, Gail."

"I know." The words were tired and sad and I had made them so.

I hung up again and looked up the number for young Doctor Yarrow. His nurse said he was with a patient but he would call me back shortly. I gave her my number and name and dialed again. The sheriff picked up the phone himself.

"Well, Mr. Tanner. How you doing today? Hear you sampled the local steakhouse last night."

"You hear pretty good, Sheriff. Pretty fast, too."

"Enjoy your loin?"

"Very tasty."

"Better than a steak these days," the sheriff said. "Can't get good beef anywhere. People in these parts get too willing to sacrifice quality for quantity."

"Happens everywhere, Sheriff."

"Seems like folks don't think for themselves anymore, you notice that out where you live? Just stand around and wait for someone on the TV at breakfast time to tell them what's good and what ain't."

I told the sheriff what he said was true. "You ever hear of a man named Rufus Pantley?" I asked when the philosophy had ended.

"Nope. Any reason I should?"

"I hope not."

"That all then, Tanner?"

"Just wondering if you had any further thoughts about Billy Tanner's death."

"Thoughts? You mean other than that he was too damn young to die, and that a rope around the neck sure plays havoc with the circulation? You mean thoughts other than those? Not any worth breath."

"Still calling it suicide?"

"Yep. Hoping it was, too."

"I think I can convince you that's not what happened."

"That so? Well, why don't you hold your convincing till I see the autopsy report. Then I'll know more how bad I want to be convinced."

"The report's not in?"

"Doc Yarrow's supposed to bring it by any minute."

"Then maybe I'll talk to you later."

"You're welcome to talk, Mr. Tanner. Can't promise I'll listen."

"Let me ask you one more thing, Sheriff," I said quickly. "Do you have much of a drug problem here in Chaldea? I mean something more than a few kids smoking grass to show off?"

"Well, I'd say it was a little more serious than that. We got a lot of marijuana around, and it's not just kids using it, neither. You'd be surprised the smells come out of some of those big houses in Conklin Heights. We got more than marijuana around, too. More than one runny nose in town wasn't caused by ragweed. Pills, too. What makes you ask?"

"Just curious. People say Billy used drugs. I was just wondering where he got them."

"Don't know for sure," the sheriff said. "Plenty of times I saw him I knew he was high on something. But I never busted him, never caught him dealing, and I figured what he did to his mind and body was his own business. I mean, he had a rough time of it over there in Vietnam. I figured I owed him something."

"You a vet, Sheriff?"

"Korea."

"Me, too."

"What outfit?"

"Big Red One."

"First Marines," the sheriff said. "A lousy war."

"They don't make them any other way."

"Lately, for sure."

We both stopped there, experiencing a fresh fix of war for an instant, hating a lot of it but not quite all. "Sheriff," I said finally, "what I'm getting at is, if Billy was a big drug user, then maybe he was a dealer, too. Maybe this was just a deal that went sour. Hell, the streets of San Francisco are littered with kids who got burned trying to rip off the big one. It could happen here."

"It could, but I don't think it did."

"Why not?"

"No evidence of it, for one thing. No drugs, no money, no nothing. But mostly the way it was done. Hanging's not that common, you know. Not in a murder case."

"I know. That bothers me, too. Any strangers in town lately, Sheriff?"

"You mean besides yourself?" The sheriff's laugh was uneasy. "Hell, there's always strangers in town, and these days you can't tell the dope dealers from the priests. Campers going to the lake, hell, most of *them* look like they just blew out of the state pen. Eyes ain't worth a damn in law enforcement anymore, not since folks quit getting haircuts."

"You're not much help, Sheriff," I said.

"Maybe you need more help than I can give you, Mr. Tanner. Maybe you're trying to make this something it's not. Maybe the boy just got tired of living in the body God gave him. It happens."

"I know it does," I said. "I just don't want to think it happened to one of us."

I hung up and took a shower and got dressed and picked up my book again, determined to hole up until the funeral. Which reminded me to check to see if Starbright wanted to go. I looked WILD up in the phone book and was surprised to find a listing. The phone rang a long time before it was answered.

The voice on the other end was thick and indistinct. I asked to speak to Starbright. When she came on the line she told me she'd just gotten up. "We had a service for Billy last night," she said. "We watched his spiritual core ascend. The trail was really pure."

"The trail?"

"The path of transubstantiation. The spirit dwells in this kind of husk, see; sort of a shell. And when it leaves the body it casts off the husk, bit by bit, and if you're tuned in, I mean, if your mind is locked onto the cosmic fact and is open to the oneness of the life and the death of the person, you know, well, you can see the path of the ascension. It's kind of like a space shot, you know?"

"And you saw Billy ascend?"

"I sure did. It was far out."

I believed it. "Want to go with me to the funeral, Starbright?"

"I told you, we already had our service."

"I know, but maybe you should go to this one, too."

"Why?"

"Because that's Billy's child in your belly. Because his people ought to know you're carrying it."

"Why?" she repeated.

"I don't know. So they can help you out if you ever need it. So they know the line's being carried on. So they know the newest limb on the family tree."

"Well," she said dubiously, "if you think so."

"I think so."

"What should I wear? The only clothes I got are . . . well . . ."

"It doesn't matter. I'll see you a little before one."

"Okay."

"Starbright?"

"Yes?"

"Was anyone else at WILD real close to Billy? Anyone except you and Zedda?"

"I don't think so. Mostly it's just women here."

"Were there any women he used to see?"

"You mean sex?"

"Yes."

"Well, Billy wasn't, we didn't, I mean, he was *free*, you know. We gave each other space. So he got it on with other women sometimes. I knew about it, you know. He was always up front with me."

"Is there anyone there now who Billy got it on with?"

"Tamara."

"Who's she?"

"Zedda's old lady."

"Does Zedda know she and Billy had an . . . got it on?"

"I don't know for sure, but I doubt it. Zedda's kind of into possession, you know?"

"Anyone else?"

"No one that's here now. People come and go, you know. I mean, it's sort of a crash pad here. There aren't that many in this part of the country, so we get lots of visitors."

"Billy get into fights with any of those people? Fights over women, or drugs, or anything else?"

"Well, sometimes. But Billy fought with lots of people. That's just the way he was."

"How about Zedda? Did he and Billy fight?"

"Sometimes."

"What about?"

"Things. But it wasn't serious. I mean, Billy and Zedda were scared of each other, I think."

"How do you mean?"

"Well, Zedda was afraid of Billy because he was so violent sometimes and because he knew so much about killing, and

Billy was afraid of Zedda because, I don't know, I think he was afraid Zedda knew something he didn't."

"About what?"

"I don't know. Life. Death. You know, *big* things. Zedda's real deep sometimes."

"So what did they fight about, exactly?" I asked.

"I don't think I should tell you any more about it. People might get in trouble, maybe. Like, I don't really *know* you, you know?"

"I'm Billy's people, Starbright."

"I know that. That's why I'm going out there with you to watch them put him in the ground. They should burn his vessel, you know. So it can't be occupied by another spirit."

She paused and I heard noises in the background. When she spoke again she said she had to go, that Zedda was mad and had called a meeting, that he wanted to know if the people had found jobs yet, like he told them to. I wanted to talk to her some more but I had to be content with our date for the funeral. A few seconds after I hung up the phone it rang. It was Doctor Yarrow. I asked if he'd finished the autopsy on Billy's body.

"Just wrapped it up. Body's been released for burial."

"What was the cause of death?"

"Strangulation. Just the way it looked."

"Any possibility he was strangled before the rope was put around his neck?"

"Unlikely." Yarrow's voice grew cautious.

"Was he drunk, or drugged? Any sign of poisons? Anything you couldn't identify in his system?"

"Hold on, now, Mr. Tanner. One at a time. Now I *think* the answer to all that is no. There was some alcohol in his blood, but not much. Not enough to kill him, that's for sure."

"How about make him unconscious?"

"Nope. Not unless he had some unusual sensitivity. A few beers at most."

"How about signs of a blow to the head?"

"No. His trachea and larynx were crushed and he was asphyxiated. Now, does that take care of it?" The doctor was annoyed.

"Not unless you're telling me that there was nothing at all unusual about Billy's body. Is that what you found? Because I don't believe it."

"The only thing I *found*, other than strangulation and its indices, and other than a certain medical condition that Billy suffered from that is not germane to his death, was that Billy had engaged in sexual intercourse a short time before he died. And it must have been a hell of a fuck."

In the middle of the medical jargon the expletive was jarring. "What makes you say that?" I asked. "Are you a connoisseur?"

"Sorry. I shouldn't have put it that way, of course. It's just that whoever the woman was, she left her handprints all over him. She must have tried milking the semen out of him, he was contused so badly."

"Were there traces of semen on the body?"

"Of course."

"Any unidentified pubic hair or fiber particles that might lead to the woman in question, if that becomes necessary?"

"Yes, I've collected some material like that. It's available if the police request it. Now, I've got a waiting room full of complaints, so I'll say good-by. My nurse is taking the report over to Sheriff Eason in a few minutes. If the sheriff wants you to see it, I assume he'll let you know."

"One more thing, Doctor," I said. "The medical condition you referred to. Did Billy consult you for that? The sores and lesions and all?"

"I don't reveal patient records, Mr. Tanner."

"The patient is dead, Doctor. Plus, the fact of consultation itself isn't privileged, so you can tell me that at least. Did Billy ever consult you?"

"Yes. Once."

"When?"

"Several years ago."

"For the sores, and the chest pains, difficulty breathing and sleeping, that kind of thing?"

"I can't say."

"Tell me this. Did you make a diagnosis?"

"Not at the time, I didn't."

"Subsequently?"

"I reached a conclusion, yes. But Billy never returned for treatment. I tried to get word to him several times but he never responded."

"Could this condition have altered his mental state, Doctor? Could it have made him do some of the crazy things he did around town?"

Doctor Yarrow paused. "If my diagnosis was correct, it's very possible. There's a degree of cellular alteration involved, and that always opens up the possibility of a personality change. Now, I really have to go."

"One more thing. What's wrong with Tom Notting?"

"*That* patient is very much alive, Mr. Tanner. I'm not at liberty to tell you anything at all about *him*."

# Chapter 15

There had to be more to it than Doctor Yarrow had told me, more than he had found or more than he had disclosed. But Billy would be in the ground in about two hours and whatever else there was about his body that might reveal any facts about his killing or his killer would be buried with him. There are ways to stop a burial, temporarily at least, but there aren't any ways to do it without inflicting pain on the survivors. Since I didn't want to add to Curt and Laurel's anguish, I was going to have to solve the case without the help of forensic pathology.

The only thing the coroner had given me to go on was the unnamed woman who had left her bruising handprints all over Billy's body. I only knew of three possibilities: Starbright, Zedda's girl Tamara, and my old friend Carol, former wife of my old friend Chuck. I was pretty sure Starbright hadn't seen Billy that night, so that left two. In the middle of my planning how to get to each of them, my telephone rang. "Marsh." The hearty voice didn't give me time to acknowledge my name. "Norm Gladbrook here. Been expecting you to drop by the store."

"I've been kind of busy. My nephew died the other day."

"I know. A terrible thing. Always hard to believe when someone decides they'd be better off dead than alive. Believe me, I know." His voice was as grave as a prophet's. "Curt and Laurel holding up okay?"

"Well enough, I guess."

"Kind of relieved, I imagine, what with the way Billy's been since he came back."

"How is that?"

"Well, you probably heard the stories by now. The way he ran around with that devil from WILD, not that Billy was as evil as him. But acting crazy, like he was out to punish us for something."

"I think maybe he was."

"But what?"

"I guess that's for you people to decide."

Gladbrook paused, and when he spoke again it was in the liquid tones of salesmen, in which truth and fiction sound the same. "I'm down here in the coffee shop, Marsh, getting my midmorning Sanka, and I thought maybe we might talk some about that farm of yours. Or I can come up to the room, whichever."

"You don't need to come up," I said quickly. "I'll be down in a minute. But I can't stay long. Funeral's in an hour."

"Sure, sure. I'll be waiting. Want me to order up something for you? Marjean bakes a great coffee cake on Thursdays."

"No, thanks."

"Be waiting on you, then," Gladbrook warned, then hung up on anything that might pass for an excuse.

One way out of it would have been to climb down the fire escape, but even that wouldn't have worked for long. Guys like Gladbrook make their way in the world doing the things no one else wants to do, and they get used to getting the scut work done whatever the obstacles. They're irritating but necessary, and every town has one or wishes it did. I put on a tie and locked my room and tromped down to the coffee shop, bearing a reluctance that weighed a ton.

Gladbrook stood up when he saw me and thrust out a hand that was red to the wrist from sun. "Good to see you, good to see you. How about some Sanka?"

"No, thanks."

"Sweet roll? Tang? American fries?"

"Nothing, thanks."

As I took the seat across from him Gladbrook took a giant bite of fluff and icing. "The wife hates it when I bring this stuff home, so I have to feed my face in public," he said around a mouthful of bleached flour. "Got to have *some* vices, right, Marsh?"

"Right."

Gladbrook gnawed at the roll again, and gulped some Sanka laced with cream, dissolving the icing in the coffee in his mouth. His cheeks ballooned, then shrank, his gullet jumped once to accommodate the sweet, then Gladbrook licked the tips of his fingers, one by one, inspecting his work at the end of the operation as though he were a philatelist and his fingers were stamps. When he had them cleaned to his satisfaction he looked again at me. "Want to tell you a little about the town, Marsh," he said, quietly. "Want to tell you how things are in Chaldea these days. That okay with you? Good enough. Now, back when you were making all those touchdowns for CHS, we weren't in real good shape. Remember?"

"That was what I understood. Yes."

"The coal mines had closed, the farms around here never *were* that profitable, and no industry had come along to take up the slack when the mines turned everybody out. We were just hanging on, waiting for someone to help us out, someone meaning the government, I guess. Well, finally your dad and I, and some other men in town, we decided not to go down without a fight. Your dad and mom were born here, and I was, too, and well, we didn't want to see Chaldea die, 'cause if it did, why we'd die with it. We decided to follow what we heard in church and begin to help ourselves. So we flat went out and got us some industry in here. A hundred other towns like Chaldea were trying to do the same, but we were bound and determined to succeed no matter *what* it took, determined to provide a payroll that would put some life back in the place. Worked our butts off, too, your dad as much as anyone. I bet he spent four nights a week at meetings back in those days, trying to convince one business or another to locate here. He probably missed a few of your ball games because of it."

"A lot of my ball games," I said, voicing a resentment I didn't know I had.

"Sure. Well, all that work eventually paid off. By the mid-sixties, we had six new businesses here in town, over twelve hundred new jobs. We'd turned the corner, or so we thought. People were building new houses or painting the old ones up, all the stores on the square were filled, Chaldea looked like a city with a future. That's our motto, you know. Thought it up myself. You'd have been real pleased to see the way the place came back. Only too bad your dad and mom didn't live to see what we'd all accomplished."

Gladbrook looked at me mournfully, whether for my parents or the town I wasn't sure. After another gulp of Sanka he went on. "We got—complacent, maybe, is the word. Things were going so well, and we'd worked so hard, we just quit keeping watch. And it didn't last. In seventy-four, the recession, we lost the button factory and the box plant. The appliance company shut down but only temporarily that time, so we thought we'd be all right. But all it took was another recession, the one we've been in for a year or more, to shove us off the cliff. I'd like to tell you exactly how it is around here now."

Gladbrook finished off his Sanka and beckoned for the waitress to bring him another. While she poured, he rested a proprietary hand on her ample hip, next to the frilly handkerchief that was pinned there. The waitress didn't seem to mind or notice. When she walked off Gladbrook winked at me. "If I was a day or two younger I'd try to get me a piece of that," he said, loud enough to indicate he was hoping to be heard. "Know what I mean?"

"Sure."

"Her old man's in town only one week a month. Works construction in Wyoming. She's got to need it sooner or later, right, Marsh?"

"Right."

Then, as if his expressions were activated electronically, Gladbrook clicked off his leer. "Like I was saying, first we lost the appliance business. For good, this time. Shut her down in a week. Two hundred jobs gone, building still sits there empty as a Ping-Pong ball and about as valuable. No taxes, no rents, no nothing. We gave them such a sweet deal—tax breaks, special utility rates, zoning variances, hell, we even told them the names of the men who'd try to unionize their plant if they hired them on—and now we got nothing but four walls and a roof. Then the car battery place shut down, what with the depression in the auto industry. They say they'll come back on line in six months, but they won't unless they start making batteries for Datsuns. Then the fireplace manufacturer closed up because of the housing problems. Then the fucking city council let some slicker out of St. Louis put up a mall on the north end of town and half the businesses on the square moved out there and now there's empty storefronts on all four sides and the place looks like a movie set after the movie's over. No one's doing good but the doctors and the lawyers. No one at all."

"Sounds bad."

"It's as bad as a goat's breath and there's more on top of it. Just last week we lost the railroad. I mean, the train's flat not going to run *through* here anymore. Remember how we all used to go out and watch the train come in of an evening? Put pennies on the rails? Good times, right, Marsh?"

"Right."

"Well, they're going to tear up them rails and sell them for scrap. Which means the plants that *are* still open won't be able to ship to Chicago by rail. Which also means farmers will have to pay truck rates to ship grain. Which means two bits more per bushel in transportation on top of costs that have sucked away all the profit already. Which means farmland values will start to fall. Which means the bank will be calling some notes. Which means farmers will move away, and businesses in town will be stuck with a lot of bad paper. Hell, it about makes me puke to think about it." Gladbrook paused for breath. "Are you getting the picture, son?"

"I guess I am. And I'm sorry to hear about it, Mr. Gladbrook, but what exactly is it you want from me?"

Gladbrook pushed back his chair. "We want that farm of yours, Marsh. Want to see something go in there that will put people to work, *lots* of people, something that will mean money paid out here in Chaldea will stay here. We want you to save this town, Marsh. It's as simple as that."

I fidgeted under the heat of his stare. "It's a tall order, Mr. Gladbrook. I'm not sure I can fill it."

"Your daddy *gave* a damn about this town, Marsh. We hope you'll give a damn, too. Folks around here were pretty good to you when you were young."

"I know that. And I'll give what you say some serious consideration. But I can't promise anything. I can just tell you that I do care about the town, Mr. Gladbrook. But there are three other people involved in this, too. I'm only one vote."

"Way I hear it, you'll make the difference."

"Maybe, maybe not. But just so I'm clear, what you want mostly is long-term employment. Something in there that will create jobs."

"Right. That's exactly right."

"You got any project in particular in mind?"

"What I got in mind is flexibility, Marsh. Which means you folks selling to the city and letting us play it the best way for everyone."

"But you're not willing to pay top dollar."

"Can't."

"So we just pass up a big chunk of profit out of the goodness of our hearts?"

"We can structure it so you can get a nice tax break."

"I've got as much use for a tax break as I do for a valet, Mr. Gladbrook."

"Well, we could extend the payout, then. Maybe plug you into a portion of the rents when we lease it out."

"If there are any rents."

"Well, yes. Or maybe a joint venture? Something tricky like that?"

"I'll think about it. That's all I can say." I looked at my watch. "Time for the funeral," I said, and stood up.

Norm Gladbrook's face was as dark as the dregs in his cup. "If something don't happen around here soon, you can bury this whole town alongside Billy," he said. "And that's a fact." I left him with his Sanka and his crumbs.

I had time to put in a call to my office in San Francisco before it was time to pick up Starbright. When Peggy answered I asked her how she was.

"Pretty good, Marsh. Spent the weekend at Stinson with friends. Got enough tan to get me through the winter, I think. So how about you? Romping through the cornfields and skipping rocks in ponds and all that rural stuff?"

"Not quite. My nephew died the other day. Kind of complicated matters."

"I'm sorry, Marsh. How old was he?"

"Thirty or so. Never quite grew up, though, it seems. Or

maybe he grew up too much. Had a tough time in the war and never got over it."

"When will you be back? You sound so down."

"I don't know. Not long, I hope. Funeral's today, so maybe I can get out of here tomorrow."

"Did you sell your farm?"

"Not yet. There's something you can do for me along that line, though. Call Clay Oerter, the stockbroker, and ask him to dig up some data on Black Diamond Coal Company and also on Cosmos Petroleum. Just if they're legitimate enterprises, how they look financially, that kind of thing. Tell him I'll call tonight and see what he has."

"Anything else?"

"Not on this end. How about you? Any problems at the office?"

"Nothing that your checkbook and I can't handle."

"New clients?"

"Not unless you call someone who wants you to track down the man who sold her sixty-five different aluminum cooking pans a client."

"I don't think so."

"Marsh, I'm really sorry about your nephew. What was it, a traffic accident?"

"I'm trying real hard to avoid it, Peggy, but I think the only sensible answer is that it was murder."

"There?"

"Here."

We talked some more and said good-bye.

I was splashing water on my face and wondering if I could wear a plaid sports shirt to the cemetery when the phone rang again. "Mr. Tanner?"

"Yes?"

"Mary Martha Gormley speaking. Editor and publisher of the *Chaldean*. Like to interview you today. About the Tanner plot."

"I saw your article," I said, her officious assault filling my ear like a cork.

"Good. Norm Gladbrook, president of the Chamber, was supposed to see you."

"I just left him."

"Excellent. So you know the situation."

"I know yours; do you know mine?"

"How's that?"

"They're burying my nephew in half an hour, Ms. Gormley. I intend to be there."

"I see. This evening then?"

"Maybe. Why don't you call me?"

"I've *been* calling you, Mr. Tanner. You don't seem to get my messages."

"I get them."

"I see. You seem quite reticent, Mr. Tanner."

"I am."

"But why?"

"I don't know. Maybe it's because a member of my family's just been murdered. Maybe it's because of all the ridiculous plans you people seem to have for our farm."

"Murder, Mr. Tanner?" For the first time she sounded like something other than a drill sergeant. "I've heard nothing about a murder."

"You haven't been talking to the right people, Ms. Gormley."

"Whom should I talk to?"

"Me, for one. His wife, for another."

"Wife?"

"Starbright is her name. She's at least Billy's common-law spouse and maybe more. These days it doesn't make that much difference."

"I see. Perhaps this does bear some investigation. Sheriff Eason seems to have been holding something back."

"Sheriff Eason seems like a cautious man. Not a bad thing in a sheriff."

"Perhaps at most times."

"Maybe I'll see you around then, Ms. Gormley. I'll be doing a little investigating myself."

"Do you feel you're qualified?"

"Both personally and professionally."

She considered my boast. "We must definitely speak again, Mr. Tanner. In the meantime, I hope you won't do anything rash. A murder scare would *not* be good for us. The city fathers are in the middle of sensitive negotiations with a major East Coast business. If they bear fruit, it will be a substantial boon for Chaldea. It could all fall apart if they receive the impression, false though it may be, that this is a violent community. I hope you understand."

"I do. But my nephew's been hung. I intend to learn who did it and why. I hope you understand that."

"I do. But I warn you. If you make rash accusations, I can't be responsible for what might happen."

"A threat, Ms. Gormley?"

She ignored the question. "I'll be talking to you again, Mr. Tanner. We haven't gotten to the purpose of my call."

"Which was?"

"To learn what you intend to do with your farm."

"I'll tell you what I've told a thousand others, Ms. Gormley. I haven't the faintest idea."

"Good day, Mr. Tanner."

"Not so far," I said.

# Chapter
# 16

By the time Starbright came out of the WILD bungalow and climbed into the car we were running late. She was silent, stiff, and scared. I told her to relax.

"Can I stay with you the whole time?" she asked.

"If you want to."

"I won't have to say anything, will I? Scriptures or anything? I don't remember much of that."

"Not if you don't want to."

"I don't. I said what I wanted to say while he was alive. That was one good thing about his sickness. He knew how I felt."

"Lots of people never seem to get that done. Say what should be said." Me included.

"They'll hassle me, won't they?" Starbright said a few blocks later.

"Why do you say that?"

"Because Billy and I weren't married. Not in the way *they* mean."

"Happens a lot these days," I said.

"Not in this town," Starbright said simply. "Not after the parents get wind of it."

"Maybe Billy's death will make people more tolerant."

"What if it makes them worse?"

I had no answer because I had no real sense of the girl. I

didn't know whether she lived on the outside because she chose to or because she had been forced out there, exiled by minds who saw diversity as threat. I drove awhile longer, then asked Starbright a question. "The night Billy died, he was gone the whole evening, is that right?"

"Right."

"You hadn't seen him since that morning?"

"No."

"Did you make love before he left?"

"What? Why do you need to know that?"

"Just curious."

"My old man was curious like that. Always wanted to know what I did with boys. All the details. What a pervert."

I could sense her eyes on my face, probing my own perversion. "I guess this is different," she said finally. "No, we didn't screw that morning. We weren't doing that much anymore."

"Where was Billy going when he left you?"

Starbright shrugged. "He was just going. He came and went all the time. I never asked where or why. If he wanted me to know he'd tell me."

"What about the man he was going to meet? Who was it?"

"I don't know."

"What was Billy doing that morning? Anything special?"

She shrugged. "He spent some time out in the garden. Came back all dirty. Then he was fiddling with some wires inside the house. Rigging something, I don't know what. Billy was real handy that way. Then he went outside for a while, and then he ran back in and said he had to see some guy, and kissed me on my stomach and ran off up the hill."

"You mean it happened all of a sudden? Like he'd just remembered the appointment or something?"

"Sort of. Yeah."

"Did he seem frightened at all?"

"Billy? No. Intense, though, you know? Like he had something real important to do."

"Anything else?"

"I don't think so. He seemed kind of spaced, you know. Wild, I mean. But he was like that a lot," she added, making sure I knew her Billy.

"Did he do a lot of drugs?"

"Yeah. Sometimes."

"What kind?"

"Grass, mostly. Speed a lot, to keep him up. He didn't sleep for days, sometimes. Said it hurt too much."

"The sickness, you mean?"

"Yeah."

"Where'd he get the drugs?"

Her eyes hardened. "Around," she said.

"I'd like to talk to Tamara about Billy," I said.

"What for?"

"Just to see what she thought about him."

"She thought he was crazy," Starbright blurted, suddenly fierce. "That's why she got off on him. Tamara's crazy, too."

"When do you think I could see her?" I asked.

"Anytime, I suppose."

"I mean without Zedda around."

"I don't know," Starbright said petulantly. "At the Laundromat maybe. She does the wash on Fridays. That's tomorrow, isn't it?"

"That's tomorrow," I agreed, marveling at her displaced sense of time, wishing mine were as neglected. "Which Laundromat does she use?"

"The place next to the DX station. You know where that is?"

"Near the lumberyard. I pumped gas there one summer."

Starbright wasn't interested in my past. I was starting to be less interested in it myself.

Just ahead of us the gates to the cemetery were open wide and I entered them, not for the first time, to see a member of my family interred within the enclosure. My parents were there, and one set of grandparents, and now a nephew, the reaper skipping my generation for the moment but not for long.

Two high slopes rose out of a winding creek bed, their tops sprinkled with pine trees, their edges fringed by forsythia and laced by a white rock road, their sides lined with graves and grass. The sky was mostly clear, though lightly sugared with clouds. A warm harvest breeze blew out of the southwest, rustling the flowers and evergreens atop the graves. It was almost lovely enough to make me wish I was dead myself.

On the far hill a small group of people had gathered beneath a canvas tent, beside a freshly dug grave. I drove across the wooden bridge that spanned the creek, its planks rumbling beneath my wheels like dice in a velvet cup, then followed the narrow road up the other side, surrounded by obelisks and crosses, doves and angels, urns and scrolls, all crafted of stone and faith.

The dates on the graves reached back to early in the previous century. Many were majestic, some were ludicrous, all were tended, even the precise row of short pine boards that marked the home of paupers, perhaps the most hallowed ground of all. I drove as close to the tent as I could, then parked and helped Starbright out of the car. We crossed to the tent, stepping carefully as though to avoid disturbing a dead man or a god, and joined the others. Ribs were nudged, whispers exchanged, and soon all knew we had arrived. Before us were a black-suited minister and a flag-draped coffin and a six-foot hole flanked by heavy chunks of moist red clay.

No one greeted us with words, but many eyes swept quickly over our faces, then less quickly over Starbright's patchwork skirt and the swollen belly that was under it. A murmur swelled, then died. I looked at Curt and nodded. He looked through me at something else, perhaps at Starbright, perhaps at a friendless future.

The only smile I saw was on the face of the minister. He was short and blond and seemed too young to know much about life and anything at all about death. I took Starbright's hand and squeezed it. The closest I had come to what she was going through was one afternoon I had spent with Sally's father, just the two of us in the house, watching a baseball game on television, enduring three hours of unuttered disapproval.

Starbright squeezed back, then refused to release my hand. Beyond the casket and the grave I saw two gravediggers, swathed in layers of heavy comic clothes, shod in rubber boots, leaning on hoes and rakes, sucking impatient puffs of smoke from stubby cigars. Anything can be a job. Sex. Death. God.

The mourners grew quiet, the minister said a prayer and read a psalm, and we were floating toward the predictable end of the rite when the minister turned a page in his Bible and began another psalm, this one not predictable or even, given what Billy had been, particularly comforting to those of us that heard it. Suddenly it seemed that the speaker was not the young blond minister, or even the biblical David, but Billy himself, casting one last shadow upon us all:

> "Have mercy upon me, O Lord, for I am in trouble; mine eye is consumed with grief, yea, my soul and my belly. For my life is spent with grief, and my years with sighing; my strength faileth because of mine iniquity, and my bones are consumed. I was a reproach among all mine enemies, but especially among my neighbours, and a fear to mine acquaintance; they that did see me without fled from me. I am forgotten as a dead man out of mind; I am like a broken vessel. For I have heard the slander of many; fear was on every side; while they took counsel together against me, they devised to take away my life. But I trusted in thee, O Lord; I said, Thou art my God. My times are in thy hand; deliver me from the hand of mine enemies, and from them that persecute me. Make thy face to shine upon thy servant; save me for thy mercies' sake. Let me not be ashamed, O Lord; for I have called upon thee; let the wicked be ashamed, and let them be silent in the grave."

There was a new silence under the awning, a stilling of the nervous shuffling that had rustled before the psalm was read. The crowd had absorbed the words in spite of itself, applying them to Billy and then to themselves, wondering. It was one of those times when religion is not the worst there is, but rather better than anything else, more consoling and revealing than you thought it ever could be. I looked again at the blond minister. He seemed to have aged during the scripture, to have become infinitely wiser and more aware. I wondered if he'd known Billy, wondered if he had any idea how close the psalm came to being what Billy was or, perhaps, to what he wanted to be.

The closing prayer was brief and hopeful, a sail for Billy's spirit, and in the quiet that followed I looked at faces. The family was there, down in front. Curt and Laurel were rigid, afraid that movement would bring tears and shame. Tom and

Gail clasped hands. Matt stood alone, his striking Pilar somewhere else, too variously programmed for rural grief. Gladbrook was there, too, along with some other men I'd seen in the coffee shop the day before, including Arnie Keene. And other faces I knew but couldn't match with names.

And then I saw Carol Hasburg. She stood alone at the rear of the group, separated from the other mourners by both distance and the depth of her emotion. She was wearing a gray suit and hat and clutching a handkerchief to her cheek as though bandaging a wound. The dark glasses over her eyes were an inadequate mask, for her body was shuddering visibly beneath her tears. I was about to walk to her when I heard the unmistakable chatter of rifle rounds being quickly chambered.

They were somewhere behind us, and their volleys seemed to rearrange the ground we stood on. A military funeral had doubtless been Curt's idea, and as doubtlessly Billy was raging against it, wherever and whatever he was.

The third volley rang out and then, from the hill on the other side of the wandering creek, came the hollow bugle tones of taps. As the balloons of sound crossed slowly to us, I wondered which kid they had hauled out of school to play it; in my day I'd been the one, summoned by men with stiff hats and expressions, driven to a secret place where I would hide behind a tree or stone, rub my mouthpiece and flex my lips, and hope and pray that I would play it through without sounding a clinker that would mar the day for good. As the final note drifted away from the dead and toward the town behind us, two American Legionnaires folded the flag that draped the coffin and handed the triangular result to Laurel. She clutched it to her bosom like a suckling babe.

The Legionnaires saluted and moved back and the crowd began to file away, a few stopping to shake the minister's hand, others pausing to say a word to Curt and Laurel. I let most of them move on before I told Starbright to wait for me and walked to Carol's side. When she saw me coming she started to hurry away, then stopped, more afraid of notice than of me. "Hi, Carol," I said.

With the hand that held the hanky, she pressed her dark glasses closer to her eyes, shielding as much as they could shield. She lifted her other hand then, and I took it in mine.

"It's been a long time, Marsh," she said, her voice low and flat, expectant.

"It's been that," I said. "How are you?"

"Fine. You?"

"Fine. You look good, Carol."

"You, too."

We stood in silence then, surrounded by the dead and by our memories. Carol was leery, wondering what I was up to. I didn't quite know myself. "Is that your wife with you?" Carol asked finally, glancing quickly at Starbright.

"I'm not married. That's Billy's friend. Her name's Starbright."

Carol jerked her hand away from mine, then realized the gesture was revealing and gripped my arm to disguise whatever it was she felt and thought. "I know about you and Billy, Carol," I said quietly. "At least I know what people say. And I know you and Chuck have split. I saw Chuck yesterday."

Carol looked at me closely, trying to read my attitude, then glanced around to see if we were being watched. "How did he die, Marsh?" she asked in a whisper. "I have to know. Did someone kill him?"

"I think so," I said.

"Oh, my God."

"Do you have any idea who might have done it, Carol?"

"I . . . no. Of course not."

"Come on, Carol. You were thinking of someone. Who was it?"

"Is there any evidence, Marsh? Do the police have suspects?"

"No. They're calling it suicide."

"It wasn't suicide. That wasn't Billy."

"I don't think so, either. Do you think it was Chuck, Carol? Did Chuck know about you and Billy?"

Carol glanced wildly about her again, looking for help or lies. "Not here, Marsh. I can't talk here," she said finally.

"Where?"

"My place, I guess."

"When?"

"Tonight? Ten or so?"

"Fine. Where are you living?"

"Six twelve Jefferson. Across from the drive-in bank."

"I'll be there."

Carol started to move away, then looked at something behind me. I followed her stare and saw Starbright's swollen profile. "So that's her," Carol said softly. "She's pregnant, isn't she?"

"Yes."

"He told me about her. He loved her a lot, actually."

"That's good," I said. "I hope someone will love their child."

"I will," Carol said. "If she stays in Chaldea I'll look out for it. I really will."

I bent and kissed her above her glasses and below her bangs. "See you later, Carol."

"See you Marsh. I'm glad you're back, but you're not going to like some of the things I have to tell you."

"I haven't liked anything I've heard since the minute I hit town."

I left Carol and walked through mourners back to Starbright. "Who was that?" she asked me.

"A woman named Carol Hasburg."

"Oh. Her. Billy knew her."

"I know."

"She's real nice-looking. For someone that old."

I smiled. "I've known Carol a long time," I said. "We were classmates."

"Billy was using her," Starbright said abruptly.

"For what?"

"I don't know. He just said he was using her, that's all. Can we go now?"

"I want you to meet the family, first. Your child's grandparents. I want them to know who you are."

"Do I have to?"

"I wish you would. For the child, if nothing else."

"Well, I'll do it, but they won't be happy about it. I know what they think. Billy told me."

"Let's just see, shall we? Maybe they're not that bad."

I took her hand again and pulled her to where Curt and Laurel were standing, talking quietly with Tom and Gail. The four of them looked at me and then at her and then at me again, then collectively retreated a single step. Their expressions ranged from Tom's amusement to Laurel's fright. I realized what I was doing might be the wrong thing for everyone but me, but I plunged ahead. "This is Starbright," I said. "She lived out at the farm with Billy. Starbright, these are Billy's parents, Curt and Laurel Tanner, and his aunt and uncle, Tom and Gail Notting."

"Hi," Starbright said.

Gail was the only one who returned the greeting.

"Starbright is pregnant," I went on, as bland as bouillon. "She's going to have Billy's child in, what, two months?"

"Three."

"She's sure it's a boy. A Tanner boy. I thought you all should know."

Curt's face was as dark as the dirt Billy would soon be wrapped in; I thought for a moment he was going to hit me. Laurel hid behind his heavy shoulder as though to avoid contamination. Gail wore a smile that could have meant peace or war. When someone finally spoke it was Tom. "Were you and Billy married, Starbright?" he asked with false bonhomie.

"No," she said. "Not like you mean."

"So we don't *have* to treat it like a Tanner, do we?" Tom's eyes and rhetoric were trained on me.

"Why wouldn't you want to?" I asked.

"Oh, I'm just getting the options straight," Tom said. "I think that's all we need do just now, don't you?"

"You might have options," I said to Tom. "I don't think Curt and Laurel do. This is their grandchild. The only one they'll have."

I had hoped Curt would go along with me, would indicate he was willing to embrace Starbright and her baby, or at least not shun them. But he didn't. He just looked stricken, impossibly wounded by what had happened to him over the past days, including the dilemma I had just presented him. And then I remembered Billy's disease, and what the dioxin might have done to the fetus, and I could think of nothing to do except retreat.

I guided Starbright away. Somewhere to the left of me I heard Matt telling someone about asphalt pads and covered lanais. "See you at Curt's, Marsh?" Gail called out. I turned and nodded and then walked on, hoping to hear more from someone in my family but hearing not a word.

Starbright hurried to keep pace, then gripped my arm and

stopped me. "I don't need them for anything, Mr. Tanner," she said fiercely. "I can take care of my baby just fine."

"You might not need them, but I think they're going to need you," I said, and then walked on.

When we reached the car I helped Starbright inside, then told her I'd be back in a second. For three long minutes I walked through the cemetery, searching for the grave of my parents and finally finding it, one section east of where I thought it was.

The stone was simple, the flowers fresh, Dad's American Legion marker slightly tilted and tarnished, a charred daisy, its face twisted toward the sun. They'd been dead more than a quarter of a century, dead before I really knew them, before I realized how much they had and could have taught me. People said nice things about them, and I believed the words, but they were probably better or worse than the image I carried in my bag of childhood memories, ever different from what I thought they were.

I gazed at the mound of grass, at the earth that bore our roots. Matt's viral materialism was down there, and Gail's obstinacy, Curt's martyrdom, my own befuddlement, all our traits growing from the union of those bodies, and from the bodies that bore them. I waited a while longer, said hello and then good-bye, then felt a hand fall on my shoulder. It was Arnie Keene, my old teacher and my parents' old friend. He seemed to have aged since I'd seen him in the coffee shop. I began to wonder how well he'd known Billy.

"They've been gone a long time," he said softly, looking where I had been looking, thinking private thoughts.

"Forever, in a way," I said.

"It seems like yesterday to me," he replied.

No one said anything for a moment. The murmurs of the people at the gravesite floated toward us like a muffled motor. "Do you remember her well?" Arnie asked at last.

"Mom? Sure. At least I think I do, but it may be more from pictures than from life. She had a lisp. And always said 'gosh darn.' And made peach cobbler all the time."

"She was a wonderful woman."

"So they say."

"The accident was so ridiculous, you know. They just drove right off the road and into a tree. Right on the edge of town, by the new supermarket. Your dad probably drove down there at least once a week. It's almost as though it was a divine punishment. Craig, too. I feel the same way about my son's death."

I'd thought as much about divinity as I cared to for one day. "It does seem weird," I said. "What time of night was it when they crashed?"

"Eight. Dusk."

"He didn't drink, did he?" I asked. "I don't remember him as a boozer."

"No. She didn't, either."

"Hard to figure," I mused, ready to leave. But Arnie Keene still lingered, his eyes transfixed by the granite marker that rose before us.

"I think they must have been fighting," he said slowly. "Arguing about something. And your dad looked away from the road for a moment, perhaps to make a point, and ran off the road. That's what I think must have happened."

He looked at me for confirmation. "Sounds plausible," I agreed. "I'm sure they fought, like every couple does. I can't remember that much about it, though. I know he'd get mad if dinner wasn't ready on time."

Arnie Keene smiled thinly. "Yes. She felt he was too demanding about household matters. And other things. He could be quite stern, at times."

"You must have known them well."

He nodded. "This is such a small town. We see our friends several times a week. Almost daily in the summertime. You learn a lot over the years." He paused. "Enough to think that if things had turned out differently they'd still be alive. That's what I can't . . . I mean, well . . ."

I looked at him. He seemed gripped by something far more powerful than nostalgia. "What is it, Arnie?" I asked. "Is there something about them I don't know? Something about their death?"

He shook his head quickly. "No. Nothing. I'm sorry, Marsh. It's just that they, well, they were very special to me. Even after all these years I still miss them terribly. It's never been the same since that day; I've never been as happy. Does that seem strange?"

"A bit."

"Maybe when you're older you'll understand."

"Maybe," I said, then said I had to leave. "Are you coming out to Curt's?"

"No, I don't think so. Please express my condolences. Billy was a complex young man, but I enjoyed him. I think he would have contributed a lot."

"I'll see you, Arnie," I said. "Give my best to Ann."

"Of course."

Arnie Keene looked down at the gravestone one more time and closed his eyes for a long moment, then opened them and walked toward the other departing mourners. I went back to the car and drove Starbright back to WILD. When we got there I told her I would call her before I left town, to give her my address and telephone number in case she ever needed to reach me or decided to go to California. Then I drove west out of Chaldea, over the twelve miles between me and Glory City, my mind as dead as Billy and my mom and dad.

# Chapter
# 17

It had never been a city, and whatever glory it had once suggested to its founder had surely vanished unattained. The majority of houses were either boarded up or stripped to the foundations, which peeked above the earth like fortifications for a private war. Except for the highway that split the town, the streets were neither paved nor peopled. Commerce was confined to a gas pump, a feed store, and a tavern. There had once been a bank and a drugstore, but they were closed—the town profiting from neither money nor neuralgia. Why Curt lived in Glory City was a mystery. The obvious guess was that he had wanted to surround himself with desolation, to do some painful penance. Perhaps with Billy's death the need for suffering would vanish, or at least evolve.

I found the house easily—it was the only one in the block that appeared inhabited. The plastic sheets stapled over the windows rattled in the wind like regimental guidons. Hay bales ringed the brick foundation to fend off winter winds. The roof seemed too low to allow people to stand with pride beneath it.

As I walked to the door an old couple drove by in a rusted Dynaflow, inspecting me the way they would inspect a Martian. I waved and they waved back. The big car was as incongruous as a pterodactyl. Except for the Buick the entire town seemed still, in mourning for Curt's loss, in awe of his shame.

No one answered my knock, so I let myself inside. Tom and Gail sat in the front room, surrounded by antique trappings splashed with doilies, looking at everything but each other. The couch they were sitting on was draped with a pale wool blanket. The floor beneath their feet was planks of painted wood. The paper on the walls was the color of blood and water and was decorated with even rows of roses. The only book in sight was a Bible. The way its spine was bent, it was clear it had borne too great a burden for too great a time.

As I was about to say something to Gail, Curt came lumbering into the room, still dazed by the day. When he saw me, his face and eyes turned immediately away. I walked to Curt's side, still conscious that in trying to help him I had hurt him more. "If I was wrong to bring Starbright to the cemetery, I apologize," I said to him. "Maybe it wasn't my place."

"Maybe it wasn't," Curt agreed flatly.

"She's a fact, though. She and the baby. I just thought you ought to know."

"Me and the whole town."

"For God's sake, Curt. Haven't you stopped worrying what people are going to say?"

"If you live *here*, you can't ever stop worrying about that."

"The hell you can't. Besides, from what I've learned, people have said everything they could think of to say about Billy already. Why don't you just decide what's right and do it?"

"I don't need you to tell me what's right, Marsh. I never did."

"I know you don't, Curt. I always learned those things from you."

It was far past time for me to let Curt win. "Maybe I got a little overwhelmed by family obligations," I went on. "Easy for me, I guess, since I don't have a family of my own to worry about. So I'll shut up. And I don't think you'll hear from Starbright unless you ask for it. She's not the type to beg."

"Billy wouldn't have been with her if she was," Curt said, and rubbed his huge hand over his face and sighed from under it. The hand was scarred, its surface was gnarled as a gourd. "It's just too soon, Marsh. We'll do right by the baby. If the girl lets us. But don't expect too much right now, okay?

There's been so much . . . so much . . ." His voice broke like rotted timbers.

"I know, Curt." I hesitated then, unsure of whether to say what I thought I had to. But I'd made so many mistakes with Curt already, I finally decided I might as well make another. "There's a good chance Billy was murdered, Curt," I said quietly. "In fact, I'm sure he was."

He only half heard me. "What was that?"

"I said I think Billy was murdered."

"You *think*," Tom chimed in from the couch. Gail admonished him with a frown he didn't see.

"Then who did it?" Curt asked me.

"I don't know. I'm trying to find out."

"How?"

"By talking to people."

"About what? How will that help?"

"If I learn enough about Billy, I'll also learn who had a reason to kill him. If I take a strong enough motive to the sheriff, maybe he'll take the investigation the rest of the way."

"Everyone had a reason to want Billy dead," Tom said, again the curmudgeon. "You can start with me."

There was a time to go into that with Tom, but the time wasn't now. I ignored him and looked at Curt. "Murder," Curt said, and made the word itself a sin.

"The sheriff says suicide," Tom pointed out. "Why don't you let him handle it? I don't think we need a big-city detective in on this. Not even the great Marsh Tanner."

"Would you rather it was suicide, Curt? Does that make it easier, to think Billy took his own life?"

"No. No. How could it?" Curt started out of the room, then stopped. "I just don't want to talk about it anymore, Marsh. What good will it do, thrashing around after the killer? I mean, we all know the kind of people Billy hung around with. That girl and her like. That guy Zedda, who ought to be in jail. If he *was* killed, one of those hippies did it. Maybe we should just leave it lay. Let him die, Marsh. That's what I think. We should just *let him die*."

Curt turned toward the kitchen again and my final words were to his back. "He's already dead, Curt. He'll stay that way no matter what we do. The question is, will life be easier for *you* knowing Billy's killer is walking around loose?"

"Compared to other things, it just might," Curt said over his shoulder.

"What other things?"

"Learning something about Billy that will hurt us more than we're hurt already. Hurt us more than we can stand."

Curt rushed from the room and the next eyes I saw were Gail's. "It's not your business, Marsh," she said sadly. "Curt's the one who has to live with it. Not you."

"I've been around families that have suffered a loss like this before, Gail. If the last chapter is never written, the book is never closed, the uncertainty does more damage than the original deed."

I stood up and went to the door. "I'm going to walk around the block," I said, then went outside and did it.

The Dynaflow sailed past me once again. A dog thought about accosting me but decided not to. From the house behind Curt's came the threats of a radio preacher who was picking the pockets of his audience. By the time I got back to Curt's house Matt's car was sitting like a beached whale in the center of the driveway.

I went inside. There were two or three other guests as well, neighbors expressing condolences and bringing food. Their somber words echoed through the house like the chants of monks.

Matt and Pilar stood in the center of the room, displaying themselves. Pilar wore some kind of fur on her back and some kind of feathers on her head and some kind of leather on her legs and feet that had to move when she did. For an instant I found myself alone with her. "Anxious to get back to the big city?" I asked, making conversation as well as I can make it.

"Aren't you?" Her voice was bored and bloodless.

"Not completely."

"You actually *like* it here?"

"In some ways."

"Like what?"

"I like the land. The way it rolls on and on, with room enough for everything. The way you can watch the weather come toward you like a train."

"But the *people*."

"What about them?"

"There's no style, no flash."

"If that's your thing, then you're definitely in the wrong place. But to me it's kind of nice to be in a room for twenty minutes without hearing about real estate or wine."

Pilar shook her head at my hapless naiveté. A feather flew off her head and attached itself to my sleeve. I plucked it off and pocketed it. "And it's a hell of a lot quieter than Telegraph Hill," I said, wrapping it up or so I thought.

"Telegraph Hill," Pilar mused absently. "Isn't that where they have that giant penis sticking up off the ground?"

"Coit Tower. Right."

"How bizarre."

Pilar left me where I was, which pleased us both. I began to think of how I could leave. Then Gail came up to me and with one look knew what I was planning and took hold of an arm to stop me. "Oh, no you don't. You're not leaving, Marsh. Not yet."

"I'm trying."

"We have to talk about the farm."

"Then let's get to it."

"What have you decided, Marsh?" Gail asked in a whisper. "You're not going to make us sell, are you?"

"I don't know, Gail. I really don't. I see some merit on all sides."

"It's our heritage, Marsh. With Mom and Dad dead it's about the only thing that binds us Tanners all together. The only thing we have in common. We shouldn't throw that away. We just *shouldn't*."

"I realize that, Gail. But Matt needs money and the town needs help and Curt just wants to be rid of it all, apparently."

"Matt will always need money, Marsh. And the town will always need help. Now that Billy's dead I doubt that Curt cares one way or the other what we do."

"And you will always want to help your kids, Gail, and pretend that the Tanners are all for one and one for all."

"Is there something wrong with that? We *are* a family, after all."

"We just barely qualify, Gail. Don't pretend we're something we're not."

"Don't say that, Marsh."

"Okay. But it's true."

"Karen and Paul will be here soon, Marsh. Will you stay and meet them? So you can see how much they . . ."

"Deserve our help?"

"I guess so. Yes. Promise you'll stay?"

I promised.

Gail went back toward the kitchen as despairing as I had ever seen her. When he saw her leave, Matt came over to me and slapped an arm across my shoulder. "Bet you're anxious to get back to Frisco, huh, little brother?"

"I guess so."

"Hell of a town. Full of queers now, though, huh?"

"Some."

"Takes all kinds, I guess." Matt paused, then squeezed my shoulder. "*You're* not light on your feet, are you, Marsh? I mean, you never got married; makes a man think."

"I'm okay, Matt. How about you?"

"Me? With a broad like Pilar? Are you kidding?"

"Could be compensation, Matt. Old man with a young woman? Makes you think, you know?"

Matt's face clouded and he took away his arm. "Let's hunker down here, Marsh," he said, his voice suddenly husky and conspiratorial. "I been asking around, and the way to go is with the oil boys. No question about it."

"I thought you needed big money up front."

"Well, I do. But not so bad I can afford to toss away the long term. You realize what it would mean if they hit oil or gas out there, Marsh?"

"You don't really think there's oil out on that farm, do you, Matt?"

"Why not? Hell, they've hit in Illinois, and North Dakota. Kansas and Nebraska, too. Why not here?"

"How much money do you need up front, Matt? To keep your mobile home deal alive?"

"Ten grand. They're calling my share at the end of the month. I don't come up with the ten, I forfeit the ten I put up at the first offering."

"Any more commitments after that?"

"Not if the cash flow runs the way it's supposed to."

"And if it doesn't?"

"If it doesn't we're all in the bankruptcy courts anyway.

Take a bath and start again. But no way that's going to happen. You thinking about coming in with me after all, Marsh?"

I didn't answer his question.

"What made you change your mind on the oil thing, Matt?"

"Nothing special. I just been talking to people."

"What people?"

"Some English guy. Field rep for Cosmos. Stopped me on the street and ran some data by me. Pretty damned convincing." Matt slapped my shoulder again. "So, you're in, Marsh? We go with the oil boys?"

"Not yet, I'm not."

"What the hell's holding you back? Shit, what you need is to grow up, Marsh. This is business, not a fucking *ball* game. You take the best deal you can get and go." Matt squeezed my arm again, and this time there was nothing comradely about it. This time he was the older brother, passing on advice that approached a threat.

"I'm leaving town in the morning," Matt went on. "I got some other deals to look after and Pilar's had all of this cornbread stuff she can take. You better let me know by then which way you're going to jump. If you're not with me, though, I'll find some way to get you. Believe me, I will. This ain't a game, young brother. This is *life*." And Matt stomped off, as estranged from me as he had ever been, following a path I didn't know or want to. The clomp of his heels on the stiff linoleum was finally muffled by the doorbell's chime.

The pair that entered were as young as puppies and as bursting with life. As they twitched with energy and flushed with embarrassment through the introductions, Gail passed them through the room like hors d'oeuvres, showing them off. They were Karen and Paul, and they wore designer jeans and ski sweaters that matched and they clasped hands and bumped smiles and bodies the way kids do when they're young and love every single thing about each other. To Gail's chagrin they'd left the baby behind. But it was the cutest thing there ever was, we could take Gail's word for that.

When my turn came they both said they were pleased to see me and I said likewise. Then Gail steered us all off to a private corner, which was heated by an iron radiator that reminded me of jail. "Paul's farming half his daddy's place,

Marsh," Gail said, after the preliminaries were behind us. "It's down by Exline, not too far from ours. He's been working it for a couple of years now. But they need to take on more land to make a go of it, right, Paul?"

Paul nodded on cue and rubbed his flaming skin where the razor had scraped him closer than it was meant to. I felt sorry for him. He'd been prepped and he was ready to play according to Gail's plan, but his heart wasn't in it because he sensed there was a bit of snake oil about it. For her part, Karen looked wiser and more capable than any of us, the way Midwestern girls can look after they live twenty years and never encounter anything they don't understand. "You have any college, Paul?" I asked, so he'd have something to do besides fidget.

"Two years ag school at Ames. Then Dad got sick and I had to come home."

"How many acres you think you need to make a living?"

"Well, I work close to a hundred now. Three hundred would do if prices get back up to where they were. If they don't, it won't matter how much land we got."

"Could you make it with two hundred?"

Paul smiled. "If we get luckier."

"You plan on sticking to grain?"

"Mostly. A few hogs, maybe; chickens. Maybe some sheep, depending on how much grass we got. No cattle, I don't guess. No money in cattle."

"What'll you do if you don't get the Tanner farm?"

Paul looked at Karen. She shrugged. "Keep on like we have, I reckon," he said. "Karen'll keep her job in town and I'll keep humping out on Dad's place, maybe get me some night work."

"Like what?"

"I don't know. Delivering pizza is about all there is since the box factory closed down. That or pumping gas."

"We'll make a go somehow," Karen chimed in.

"What job do you have, Karen?"

"I keep the books for Rascal Newsome. He's an auctioneer."

"You mean antiques or you mean pigs and cows?"

"Both. Fridays and Saturdays we work the sale barns and the rest of the week we do estate sales, farm auctions, like that."

"You like the job?"

She shrugged. "You meet a lot of people. And sometimes you can buy some nice things real cheap, though not as much since the dealers came to town. But Rascal can't pay much, especially lately, what with prices being so bad. And he gets frisky if you let him. But what's worse is that now we're mostly selling people out to pay their debts. That's no fun at all."

Paul frowned and Gail gazed sadly at her daughter, then looked at me. "Anything more you want to know, Marsh?"

"One thing. Are you two willing to pay rent for our land?"

Paul glanced at Karen. She nodded. "Sure," he said. "Shares."

"How does that work?" I asked.

"Half the costs, half the income, usually."

"What kinds of costs we talking about?"

"Seed. Fertilizer. Herbicide. Fence, maybe."

"Labor?"

Paul laughed. "Just me and Karen. We work cheap."

"Equipment?"

"Sure. We could figure something out. Amortize it, or whatever you call it."

"Who sells the crop?"

"We do. Sell it right along with what we harvest off Dad's place, I reckon."

"But who decides the timing? I mean, prices are better at some times than others, aren't they?"

"Sure. They drop at harvest time, but if you haven't got anyplace to store the grain it don't matter. Cost you more to rent storage than you'll get in higher prices anyway. Or can. Gets kind of tricky, sometimes."

"But you'll take care of that yourselves?"

"If you want. Whatever's right, Mr. Tanner."

"Okay," I said. "Thanks for your time."

Gail smiled. "Nice-looking kids, aren't they?"

"Sure are," I said.

"Mom," Karen warned, stretching the word.

"Well, we got to go," Paul interjected. "Promised to help Slick Hartwell get his corn in. Slick's always the last in the county to pick. Once he left it in the field all winter. Birds ate half his yield."

"Heck of a place to hunt quail, though," Karen said. "See you, Mom. Uncle . . . Mr. Tanner. Sorry about Billy."

"Did you know him very well, Karen?" I asked.

She shook her head. "Saw him around, is all. Never really talked to him since he came back."

"How about you, Paul?"

"Naw. Seemed kind of goofy to me. I gave him a wide berth. Most people did the same, seems like. He and Bruce were kind of tight for a while there, before Bruce left for the navy."

I looked at Gail for a comment but got only a puzzled shrug. Whatever Bruce found to like in Billy was not shared by his mother.

Paul and Karen sidled off, nodding their way out of the room. Gail and I waved good-bye. "They seem happy," I said.

"They are, I think," Gail answered. "You never know, though. Karen doesn't say much. Never did. But in this town you usually hear something if a marriage starts to go bad. Folks smell it, somehow, a bad marriage."

Gail paused for a moment and glanced over at her husband. Tom was talking to Pilar, making her laugh. I wondered what people smelled about Gail and Tom. "Well," Gail said, "what do you think?"

"About the farm? I still don't know. It seems there should be some way to compromise."

"Karen and Paul, Marsh. They're, I mean, with Billy gone and you and Matt not having kids, well, they're the only ones left to keep the family line going. We should help them."

"You're forgetting Starbright's baby."

"Oh. That, too, I guess. But still."

"But still. I'll let you know by tomorrow night."

I went into the living room to look for Curt but he wasn't there. I found him out back in the garage. He didn't hear me coming, and when I got to him he was cradling a deflated basketball in his hands like a chalice. I put a hand on his shoulder and he turned to me. "I don't know why I'm crying now," he said. "The boy who bounced this silly ball died a long time ago . . . It's just that I couldn't talk to him anymore. I couldn't get through to him. He didn't want me to, I don't think. Because of what he'd done in the war. I think he was ashamed, more than anything. Ashamed of both of us."

"You shouldn't blame yourself, Curt. Sometimes things just happen. We always try to blame someone for what goes wrong, but sometimes there's just no blame at all."

"But I quit trying, Marsh. I gave up on him. That's what I can't live with."

"There's one thing I have to tell you, Curt."

"What?"

"Billy was sick. I'm not positive, but I think he was poisoned by something called Agent Orange, a defoliant they used over in Vietnam."

"I think I read about that. Is that what made him hang himself, do you think?" There was a note of hope in Curt's voice, at the prospect of an easy explanation for what had happened.

"I don't think it had anything to do with his death," I said. "But it has something to do with his baby."

"What?"

"It may be deformed. There have been several instances of that happening to Vietnam veterans with exposure to Agent Orange."

"Do you know for sure?"

"No. Maybe there's no way to know till the baby's born, I'm not sure. But I thought you ought to know."

Curt uttered his Lord's name once again. "I'll keep a lookout for the girl, Marsh. If she or the baby need anything, I'll see they get it. You can tell her that."

"Maybe you should tell her yourself."

"I guess I should. Marsh?"

In the fading light Curt's face took on a symbolic, tortured look.

"This still doesn't mean I want to know why he died. I just feel it, somehow. It's something I'd best not hear."

"Okay," I said. "Maybe you don't need to know. But someone around here should. Before I leave I'll try to see to it that they do." And then I watched my brother closely. "Who's Rufus Pantley?"

Curt twitched like startled game. The ball went splat on the floor beside him. "How did you know?" he asked with an urgent rasp.

"He told me."

"Pantley?"

"Yes. He wants his money."

"But now there's no . . ." Curt paused, then a grim smile streaked slowly across his face. "He didn't do it, then. Thank the Lord. It wasn't him."

"Didn't do what?" I asked over Curt's heavy sigh.

"Didn't kill Billy. I was so afraid he had."

It was my turn to be startled. "Why would he do that?"

"Because of what I hired him to do," Curt said. "I was afraid he went too far, see? Oh, God, Marsh. You don't know what it's like to spend two days thinking you had your own boy killed."

"Is that what you needed money for, Curt? To give to Pantley?"

Curt nodded.

"What for? What was he going to do?"

Curt squatted down and rocked back on his heels. I sat on the floor beside him to hear his tale. "Pantley's one of those, what they call deprogrammers, Marsh. You heard of them?"

"You didn't, Curt."

"You're damned right I did. I hired him to get Billy away from Zedda and that WILD outfit, and the girl, and the drugs, and everything. To bring him back to his senses. Pantley said he'd do it for ten thousand dollars, half in advance. So you see, if he still wants his money he can't know Billy's dead. So that means he didn't do it."

"I suppose not," I said, less certain of that conclusion than Curt. The threat of hanging was just the sort of coercive device a deprogrammer might employ, and it was one that could easily go awry and result in death instead of intimidation. Still, when I left the garage I was thankful that I had finally brought something to my brother besides grief.

# Chapter
# 18

The Tall Corn Motel was new and surprisingly large for a town like Chaldea, which meant it must have catered to the only people in that part of the state who could afford such accommodations—the guys who spent four nights a week on the road, peddling wares and deducting the expenses. The thin young man behind the desk had already shoved a registration card and a room key my way before I had a chance to tell him I was just looking for one of his guests, a Mr. Rufus Pantley. After consulting his papers he told me Pantley was in room nineteen, first floor, new units in the rear. I bought a picture postcard of the Chaldea square, aerial view, then went on back.

I knocked on the door and heard a grunt and turned the knob. Pantley was lying on the bed, arms behind his head, his chest a thicket above his undershirt, his stumpy legs protruding like bandaged logs from his boxer shorts. The television was on, a rerun of "The Love Boat." A pint of bourbon was open on the table beside the bed, and a plastic glass still held the dregs of the last shot. Next to the glass was a tin of Spanish peanuts. The room smelled of ointment liberally applied, and the white sauce oozing from between Pantley's toes told me what it was.

"I thought you was someone else," Pantley growled when

he saw me. "Unless you got my money you can get the fuck out."

"You've got it wrong, Pantley. You're the one who's getting out."

"Don't make me laugh."

"I don't know anything legal that would."

Pantley ignored the barb. "You give your brother my message?"

"Not exactly."

"Why the hell not?"

"Because it's like I said. You're leaving town."

"Not till I get my money, I'm not."

I sat in the chair beside the door. "Where do you come from, Pantley?"

"California. Why?"

"North or south?"

"Gardena. Why? What's the difference?"

I opened my wallet. "Here's two hundred bucks. That'll get you back to LA on the next flight. Your business here is finished."

"What do you know about my business, fuck-face?"

"I know what my brother told me," I said. "I know he hired you to come here and deprogram his son."

"I call it countercondition." Pantley's smile was as sour as the smell of his room.

"Whatever."

"And you don't think he needs it, huh?" Pantley challenged, rising off the bed like the recipient of a miracle. "I bet you think what I do is barbaric, criminal, unconstitutional, huh? The whole smear."

"Something like that."

"You know anything about the cults in this country, friend? You one of those thinks Jonestown was an accident? Huh? Wise up, friend. They're all prisoners and the only way to get them back is to jerk them out of their brainwashing environment and stash them away for a few weeks and toss some counterconditioning at them till they get back some sense. Sometimes it's too late, sure, but I never give up till I've taken my best shot. Now, I come here to take care of the Tanner kid and I ain't leaving till I do. You don't have my money, you can hit the door."

Pantley's face flooded with his speech. He drained the plastic glass to quench his thirst, then splintered the glass and tossed it to the floor to punctuate his point. "Someone's already taken care of the Tanner kid," I said.

"Who? Schmidt? Did they bring that creep in on this?"

"Not Schmidt. Someone killed Billy. Person or persons unknown. I'm wondering if it could have been you."

Pantley thought it over while I listened to a commercial for something called Weedban. It apparently killed weeds and farmers, too, if they weren't careful. "So the kid's dead, huh? What'd he do, try to make a break and they stopped him? Made it look like an OD? That's their usual trick, types like that."

"Types like what?"

"This WILD cult he was into."

"Where were you two nights ago, Pantley?"

Pantley made a fist and hit the wall. "I don't have to tell that to you or anyone."

"You will if I tell the sheriff who you are and why you're in his town."

"Hey. I got a schedule to meet. Three days from now I'm supposed to be in Philly to snatch a kid from the Church of the Perpetual Rise. Know it?"

I shook my head.

"Drink steers' blood and eat cabbage. Pray lying on their backs with their feet in the air. Had this kid for six years. Six feet tall, weighs a hundred and twelve pounds."

Pantley shook his head at the lunacy of it all. From the noise coming from the TV it sounded like the Love Boat was sinking. "You still haven't answered my question," I said to Pantley. "What I want to know is if you tried a little counterconditioning with a rope, maybe drugged Billy and slipped it around his neck and over a limb and tried to make him see the light with the aid of a little terror. Maybe things got out of hand. You stretched the rope too tight and crushed his throat, then tried to make it look like suicide to cover up. Is that the way it went down, Pantley? You don't answer me, I go to the cops."

Pantley rubbed his lips, then scratched his balls. "Hey. Why would I be here if that's what happened? You want to know where I was two nights ago, ask the waitress at that hotel uptown there, the blonde. Named Darlene, I think. She and me spent the night right here watching a Kenny Rogers movie on the tube. Desk clerk out there probably knows it, too. Gave me a fishy look this morning, the fucking fag. In fact, when you come in here I thought it was her. Supposed to come by after work."

I sighed. I hadn't really thought Pantley was the one, and now I thought it even less. "Okay, Pantley," I said. "I'm going to check back here tomorrow. You'd better be gone, to the Perpetual Rise or wherever."

"Not till I get my money, friend. The deal was half in advance. Five grand. It's not my fault the kid is dead. I showed up on schedule and I want my bread."

"The two hundred's all you get."

"Fuck you, buster. Use the door. Tell your brother I'll see him real soon."

"I better not hear you've said one word to Curt, Pantley. Not one word."

"Yeah? Or what?" Pantley rolled to his side and drank deeply from the bourbon bottle, emptying the pint.

"Here's what," I said. "I'm from California, too. A member of the bar of the state. A lawyer. And the minute I hear you've been harassing Curt for money or anything else, the next person you see will be a process-server. I'll slap you with a civil suit, ask for fifty grand in actuals and a million punitives, then haul you into a lawyer's office somewhere in Van Nuys and take your deposition for about ten days, then serve about three hundred interrogatories and a subpoena *duces tecum* for your documents, and one by one I'll drag out of you every single little deprogramming adventure you've ever had, chapter and verse. It'll be real interesting to me, and I bet even more interesting to some law enforcement agencies around the country. And all the while it'll be costing you a hundred bucks an hour in fees to the lucky lawyer you pick to defend you. Now, you want to go through all that or you want to catch the next plane to Gardena courtesy of my two hundred bucks?"

Pantley frowned and swore and thought it over. Then he raised his hand from his crotch and smiled peaceably. "You win, friend. This time. Business is good and getting better so I don't need the aggravation. But maybe we'll meet again."

"I'll look for you the next time I genuflect," I said, and

opened the door to leave. The face in front of me belonged to the waitress who had worried about my buckwheats. She was startled, then confused, then embarrassed. She flopped inside her uniform like bait in a bucket. I patted her shoulder and told her to have a good time. She was still searching for a word when I rounded the corner at the end of the building.

I was halfway to my car when I noticed a man get out of a blue Fairmont and walk up the steps to the level above me. The look of the man and the car he drove convinced me it was the guy who had been following me around town the day after I arrived in Chaldea. I waited to see which room he entered, then climbed the stairs and knocked on the door. He opened the door himself, and raised his brows when he saw me. The brows were thin and gray, the lips full and red and feminine. "Yes?"

"I'm Marsh Tanner."

"Yes?"

I was certain he knew me, but he gave no sign of it. And he was far more at ease than I was. "Who are you?" I asked.

"What business can that possibly be of yours?" He started to close the door, still bland, still unperturbed. I began to wonder if I'd made a mistake.

"You were following me all over town the other day." I said quickly, and put my foot in the door. "I want to know why."

He gave the situation some thought. "I suppose I should explain," he said a few seconds later. "Why don't you come inside?"

The man stepped back and I entered a room identical to Pantley's except for the odor and array. This one was neat as a new car. I finally spotted a two-suiter and a toilet kit and an historical novel that indicated someone was actually staying there, but otherwise it was all motel.

The man walked to the octagonal table in the corner beneath the swag light and sat in one of the orange chairs. His clothes didn't seem to wrinkle even when he sat in them. I took the chair across from him. "My name is Kinsey Beech, Mr. Tanner, and you're quite correct, I *was* shadowing you the other day."

"Why?"

"Just to see what you were doing. To see whom you saw, more precisely."

"Why would you want to do that?"

"I'm a vice president of Cosmos Petroleum, Mr. Tanner. Does that explain my interest?" Beech smiled with tasteful extravagance.

"Are you still in the bidding for the farm?" I asked.

"Very much so. Perhaps I can ask what your inclinations are in that regard? Our understanding is that yours is the key vote in the matter."

"You English, Mr. Beech?"

"Cornwall. Shed everything but the accent."

"How much did you pay my brother Matt to change his mind?" I asked quickly, over the gleam of his sunny smile.

"I beg your pardon?"

"I said, how much did it cost you to change Matt's mind? Two days ago he was all in favor of selling out to an agribusiness consortium for as much front money as he could get. Now he's a human dipstick. The only thing that could have changed Matt's mind that fast is cash. And the only place it could have come from is you."

Beech's smile remained fixed. "Are you proposing a similar arrangement for yourself, Mr. Tanner? Assuming you have assessed the situation correctly?"

"You don't know me at all, Mr. Beech. Has the cash been paid?"

"I don't think it's in my interest to disclose that."

"Which means it hasn't. Contingent on signing the lease, I'd guess. So if I were you I wouldn't count on getting more than one vote, Mr. Beech. I don't think the others are going to be too thrilled that Matt tried to cut himself a private deal."

Beech nodded and clasped and unclasped his hands. "Perhaps I was precipitous. Your brother talks an exceedingly good game. If I didn't know better, I'd suspect Australian ancestry. But no matter. Cosmos does offer a potentially enormous profit to you and your siblings, Mr. Tanner. Perhaps you'd care to listen to my proposal."

I shrugged. "Why not?"

"Indeed. Basically we offer thirty dollars an acre as a signing bonus plus a four percent royalty per barrel. In exchange for all surface and subsurface rights over a ninety-nine-year lease."

"Both surface and subsurface?"

"That is correct."

"Which means you can block any other use of the property that's a potential obstacle to your rights. Which could include almost anything."

"My understanding is that the law is not precise on the rights of the underlying fee interest as against the grantee of surface mineral rights, so your analysis may be incorrect. But we have no desire to engage in litigation, Mr. Tanner. I'm sure you'd find Cosmos quite reasonable as to a parallel usage of the plot."

"So you say."

"Indeed."

"Why not just take the petroleum rights and leave the surface out of it?"

"Because of the potential for interference with our drilling program, Mr. Tanner. Drilling costs are enormous already; they approach seventy dollars a foot in some regions. We've found that unrestricted access to the surface is essential in instances such as this in which the geology is not at all precise. There are indications of a stratigraphic trap below the little creek bed, and sufficient millardarcies, but the soundings are quite ambiguous. It's one of the reasons so little drilling has been done in this part of the country."

"Let me ask you something, Mr. Beech. Has one drop of oil ever been pumped anywhere in this entire state?"

Beech smiled his drowsy smile again. "I don't believe so."

"But you're convinced it's down there?"

"Hardly convinced. One is never convinced. But with the price of oil at thirty dollars we can afford to drill much further down than ever before, to twenty thousand feet or more. Also, this part of the state is substantially different geologically from the areas further north. This region is similar to areas of downstate Illinois in which commercial quantities of oil and gas have been found. That's encouraging."

"Why Cosmos? Why not Exxon or Mobil or some such?"

"That's the oil business, Mr. Tanner. The big companies have always found it more profitable to allow the independents to take the risks. Fully ninety percent of wildcat drilling is undertaken by companies like Cosmos. Bravery does not flourish in teak-paneled boardrooms occupied by men with stock options."

"Anything else you'd like to tell me, Mr. Beech?"

"Just to urge you to employ some calculations. At thirty dollars per barrel, and figuring a conservative pumping rate of two hundred barrels a day, you can easily learn what a four percent royalty will mean to you and your family. It is not a negligible sum. There are once-poor families in Louisiana today receiving royalty checks of twenty thousand dollars or more every month. The same in the Dakotas, or almost. The same could be true for you."

"If there's oil."

"Of course."

"And if there isn't?"

"We both lose, but Cosmos loses a great deal more than the Tanners."

"Maybe. Money's always relative, Mr. Beech. Depends on what you've got and what you need." I stood up. "I'll let you know."

Beech stood as well and presented me his hand. "I'll be here through the end of the week. I've found your sister charming, by the way. A most attractive and intelligent woman."

"I'll tell her you said so."

I started for the door and then turned back. "One thing puzzles me, Mr. Beech."

"What's that?"

"When the family met to decide what to do with the farm, my brother Curt seemed absolutely convinced there wasn't any oil on our farm. Why do you think he'd seem so sure of it?"

"I haven't the faintest idea," Beech said calmly.

"I can think of one reason," I said.

"Yes?"

"His son might have told him. The son that lived out on the farm. The son that was murdered two days ago. You happen to know anything about that, Mr. Beech?"

"Don't be ridiculous, Mr. Tanner."

That was all he said or did. I wasn't sure what I expected that was different. In the end it was me and not him who looked away. I left the motel and went back to my room.

It was almost nine, which meant it was the dinner hour back in San Francisco, a good time to catch Clay Oerter and find out what he knew about some of the players in the game.

Clay was still chewing as he spoke. "Hey, Marsh. You back in town?"

"Nope. Still in corn country."

"How is it?"

"Looks like a bin-buster this year."

"Humm. Maybe I'll get into fructose futures with an option hedge."

"If you're looking for an intelligent comment, you're talking to the wrong man."

"No one's intelligent when it comes to commodities, Marsh," Clay said with a chuckle.

"So how's business?"

"Great. People buying left and right for no good reason whatsoever except blind faith."

"Faith in what?"

"Who knows? Ronald Reagan, maybe."

I held back a quip. "Did you check on the companies Peggy asked you about?" I asked.

"Sure. You want it now?"

"If you can."

"Well, Black Diamond Coal is no problem. Old-line company, been around for years, mining coal and nothing else. Started out in the Midwest; then in the fifties when the shaft mines shut down they got in on some new Wyoming fields out around Rock Springs. Nothing exciting, but they're hanging on, hoping higher oil prices will make everyone look to coal. Was a flurry in their stock back in seventy-four when the first oil crisis hit and everyone thought coal was going to be our way out, but it calmed down after no one quite figured out how to convert to coal and comply with the Clean Air Act at the same time."

"So nothing fishy in their picture?"

"Norman Rockwell all the way. Why? You know something?"

"No. How about the other? Cosmos Petroleum."

"There you get a different picture. Abstract expressionism, maybe pop. One of those where you don't know if it's art or just a crack in the plaster."

"How so?"

"Hard to get much of a line on Cosmos, for one thing. Not very big, privately owned, so not much financial reporting required. Headed by a guy named Jones and his right hand, an English type named Beech who does most of the fieldwork. They don't do much if any drilling themselves, farm most of their leases out on a turnkey deal. Operate something like a tax shelter, but it's all their own funds. They're selling leases on both private and government lands, hoping to hit it big. Look toward new technology, too. Synfuels. Played with some lignite fields in Texas awhile, that type of thing. Looking for the big strike like everyone else."

"Have they hit anything at all, yet?"

"Nothing spectacular. They pumped commercially on some of their properties in Idaho on the overthrust belt a few years back, enough to finance their wheeling and dealing till now, I guess. No one knows that much about them, is the main thing."

"Are you saying they're shady, Clay?"

"No, but I'm not saying they're not, either. You know the oil business, Marsh. You talk to one guy and he'll tell you the independents are what made America great and you talk to another and he'll tell you they're all snakes and to go into any deal with them with a firm grip on your wallet, an open line to your lawyer, and a Bible on your knee. My advice would be to go slow and get a second opinion."

"About coal, Clay. It's all surface mining now, right?"

"Right."

"Do they have to clean up afterward? Make the land usable again?"

"Well, there's a law that says so, the Surface Mining Reclamation and Control Act, but some people say it's honored more in the breach than the observance. It's not going to look like Golden Gate Park when they're through, that's for sure."

"About Cosmos. There's some technology trying to get oil from coal, isn't there?"

"Yeah. Several different processes, none of them commercial as yet. But getting closer."

"So Cosmos might really be after coal rights and not oil, and trying to hide the fact so they avoid environmental pressures and also pay less of a bonus up front than a coal outfit would pay?"

"Anything's possible, Marsh. Wildcat drilling's way down now, so maybe that is what's happening. Just watch your step."

"You watch your step around here and you see a lot of cow shit, Clay. Kind of ruins the day."

I thanked Clay and said good-bye and left for my next appointment, my mind cluttered with the traces of motive and intent.

# Chapter
# 19

The house was small and square, its slick white siding scored to mimic wood. The lawn was a hash of leaves and twigs, the ashen sidewalk was pitted from winter salts. A sugar maple grew in the front yard and a row of poplars at the side. A television tower rose from behind the house to a point just below the stars.

The little front stoop was wrapped with a wrought-iron rail and the mailbox was emblazoned with the name Hasburg in gold stick-on letters. An old newspaper, soggy and black, slanted from the stoop to the ground. A single light burned at the rear of the house, its rays barely virile enough to pierce the filmy blue curtains that draped the front windows. I pressed the bell and waited while the cold night air made my breath a cloud.

A sheet of plastic was stapled over the screen door for warmth, and behind it Carol Hasburg suddenly appeared, her features waxed dull by the synthetic barrier between us. She stayed behind the plastic for a moment, then pushed open the screen and beckoned me inside. I bent and kissed her on the cheek. She smiled wryly and pressed my arm between her narrow hands. The screen sucked shut behind me and I followed Carol into the living room.

She was wearing a blue plaid hostess gown cut low above her breasts. Two fuzzy white slippers had gobbled up her feet.

A gold chain suspended a gold coin at the crown of her cleavage. By the time I was in the center of the house there was a highball in her hand and she was offering to put one in mine.

While she was in the kitchen I snooped around the room. The television was huge and new and remote-controlled, ensconced in a cabinet reminiscent of the vault they buried Billy in. The rest of the furnishings were well-worn and graceless, as though their charm had been pledged to pay for the gaudy television. The décor was halfheartedly Colonial, but the three coordinated pieces made way for a lumpy beanbag, two metal TV trays, and a reclining chair that was half the size of Houston. The magazine on the tray was *TV Guide* and the book next to it was Danielle Steel. Along one wall was an empty space, where something had been once but wasn't anymore, a familiar scar of divorce. The carpet beneath it all was gold and oddly flowered and stained in spots by something black.

I looked for signs of Billy but there weren't any, unless the opened jars of rouge and face cream littering the second TV tray fell into that category. Chuck wasn't in evidence either, except in the features of a brown-haired girl whose photographs gave the room its only bits of cheer. When Carol came back I had one of the snapshots in my hand. "Your daughter?" I asked.

Carol nodded.

"What's her name?"

"Chambra."

"Pretty."

"It was taken a long time ago."

I remembered Gail's story of the Hasburgs' retarded child. The snapshot grew warm in my hand and I put it down. Carol looked at me. "You heard," she said.

"Yes. It's too bad. I'm sorry."

"It's bad in some ways. In other ways it's the best thing that could have happened. She's still glad to see me, Marsh. In spite of everything." Carol's eyes filled with the heavy water of tears. "Shit," she said, then handed me my drink and sat on the couch and dabbed at her eyes with a cocktail napkin.

I took the recliner across from Carol and struggled to find

an equilibrium in its mechanics, not knowing what to think or say.

Carol's face, no longer veiled by her funeral costume, was surprisingly unlined, as though age had skipped her name. There were streaks of gray in her hair, and the slightest pucker at the point of her chin and along her neck, but otherwise she seemed unchanged from the days when we had cruised Chaldea like jackals, scavenging fun. Carol wasn't stunning, but she was firmly handsome, with a touch of the aristocrat about her. She had always been more in control than anyone else in our foursome, more certain of her likes and dislikes, far braver. If anything, I sensed that the years had made her braver yet. It was one of the things that would account for her relationship with Billy, whatever it had been.

"It's really good to see you, Marsh," Carol said calmly, after sipping her drink. A hint of amusement lifted her eyes and the crest of her lips. "I used to wonder if our paths would ever cross again."

"Me, too."

"We saw each other almost every day for, what, twelve years?"

"At least."

"Then, nothing. You went to the army and I went to Chuck. Funny, isn't it?"

"What?"

"How life can change so fast. How one day you do one thing, the same thing you've been doing for years and years, and then the next day it's all different." Carol closed her eyes for a moment, then opened them.

We looked at each other, our thoughts scrambling past and present, making something that was neither. Carol curled her legs under her and draped an arm across the back of the couch, striking a blatant pose. I smiled and she smiled, too. "You weigh a little more, Marsh."

"A lot more."

"You don't look fat, though. Just big. No. Tough. You look tough, Marsh. Are you? Did you turn into one of those hard-boiled detectives I read about?" Carol's smile was sloppy, the drink in her hand not her first.

"I'm pretty soft-boiled, Carol, if I'm boiled at all. How

about you? Are you still tough? You used to be tougher than any of us."

"Actually I am. I'm pretty damned tough. A tough old broad, isn't that what they call them in those books?"

"Something like that."

"You know what I've discovered, though?"

"What?"

"Being tough's not quite enough to be." Carol eyed her glass and drained it. "You want another drink, Marsh?"

"Sure."

"Good." She went away again, moving a bit unsteadily above her fuzzy slippers, then came back quickly with our drinks. Before she sat down she put a record on the little stereo console that was hidden within the coffin cabinet. In a minute Johnny Mathis joined us. Carol sat down, curled her legs again, and sipped her freshened drink. "Ever get laid to Johnny Mathis, Marsh?"

"Didn't everyone?"

"I did, for sure. About a thousand times, down in Chuck's basement. God, it was cold down there. I think I married him mostly to get a warm place to fuck."

Carol giggled briefly, then quit. It still jars me when women of my age swear. I don't like it, and don't know any men who do, but I guess that's why some women do it.

"You know, Marsh," Carol began again, "no one really knew whether you and Sally were making it or not. I mean, Chuck told the *world* the night he got in my pants the first time, but you never talked much. I kind of liked that about you."

"And you never seemed to mind that Chuck kissed and told. I mean, you seemed to accept what you were and what you did, come what may. I kind of liked that, too."

"Why, hell, Marsh. Maybe I should have married you instead of old Chuck. Then maybe I could get through the night without waking up in a cold sweat."

"It was that bad?"

Carol chuckled bitterly. "I could tell you things that would make you go looking for Chuck with a gun. Or maybe not. Maybe men think it's their right to do what he did." Carol waved a hand in the air. "But Chuck's got his problems, too. Nowdays the main one is what kind of disease he's going to get from those hippie chicks he sleeps with. But live and let live, huh, Marsh? He fucked Sally once, did you know that? Your best friend Chuck screwed your girl." Carol's smile was on the far side of mischief, the side toward cruelty.

"Sally told me about that last night."

"A little late."

"A little."

"The whole school knew about it, you know."

"Great."

"Gets to you even now, doesn't it, Marsh?" Carol taunted. "You should see your face. You still hate to be laughed at, don't you?"

"Not really."

"Sure you do. Your face is red right now." Carol finished off her drink. "So. Now that we're more or less on the same level of shame, we can talk about Billy."

There were no tears, no false sentiment at the mention of his name, only a continuation of the brazen, sexy pose. Tough. I asked Carol how it got started with Billy.

"He tracked me," she said simply. "I mean, he followed me around till he knew my routine, then made sure he showed up where I'd be. Grocery. Liquor store. Tennis court. Places like that."

"Then what?"

"Just talk, at first. Married women are suckers for men who take them seriously, you know, and that's what Billy did. Asked questions Chuck never asked, told me personal things Chuck never did. But no pass, not at first. Platonic, I guess you'd say. People talked some, even then, but I didn't care. I didn't see anything wrong and I got so I looked forward to bumping into Billy, started thinking of things to tell him that would make him laugh. He looked like he needed real bad to laugh."

"Then what?"

"He showed up at the house one night a little over a year ago, when Chuck was up in Canada fishing. All planned, of course, though I didn't realize it at the time. And Chuck, well, we'd been having problems. Sex problems, booze problems, violence problems, money problems. We'd drifted into one of those marriages that is so deadening, no one has the strength to do anything, even end it. Billy saw that right away, and moved in."

I thought over my next question so long that Carol read my mind. "Why me? Is that what you're thinking, Marsh? Why a tough old broad like Carol Kline Hasburg?"

I smiled and Carol smiled, too, making it easy for me. "Something like that," I said.

"Well, I may not be much in San Francisco terms, Tanner, but in Chaldea I'm about as prime as it gets. I think I'm the only woman over thirty in town who still likes it and admits it, if you know what I mean. Experience and enthusiasm, Marsh. Not a bad combination, if I do say so myself."

The boast was only half humorous. I didn't say anything to dispute it, but Carol saw something on my face that made her yield a bit. "Okay, Marsh. Okay. Billy was using me, is what was really happening. After a while I knew it, but by then I didn't give a damn."

"Using you for what?"

"To get to Chuck."

"Why?"

"I don't know for sure. It wasn't exactly the kind of thing I could ask him about. Besides, in a way I was using Billy to get to Chuck, too. More than anything, Billy was my ticket out of my marriage. Tit for tat, excuse the expression." Carol plucked the coin from between her breasts and swung it idly, as though to daze me.

"Was there any connection between Chuck and Billy? I mean before you and Billy got together?"

"None I know of."

"Did either of them talk about the other at all?"

"Well, Chuck didn't say anything at all about Billy until he found out Billy was fucking me. Then it was the usual outrage, then drunken apologies for things I didn't even know he'd done, then finally he moved out. But Billy always asked about Chuck, from the very beginning. Whether Chuck would be mad if he knew, whether he suspected anything, what he did when he learned about us, that type of thing."

"How did Chuck learn about you and Billy?"

"I don't know for sure, but I'll tell you what I think."

"What?"

"I think Billy called him up and told him. Nice, huh? You got that same mean streak in *you*, Marsh? Like Billy's?"

I had no answer. Carol finished off her drink and I followed suit. We listened to the final strains of "Chances Are," then to the tinny racket of the stereo shutting down. Carol went to the kitchen and returned with new drinks. When she handed me mine, I smiled. She asked me what I thought was funny.

"I was just thinking how hard Chuck and I used to try to get you and Sally drunk."

"And now look at me? Is that it?"

"I suppose."

Carol's eyes turned hard as bearings. "Values change, Marsh. Staying sober doesn't seem very important anymore. In fact at my age sobriety and celibacy are as fatal as the plague. Does that shock you?"

"A little."

The hard eyes softened. "It shocks me, too, sometimes. I can't quite figure out how I got here, you know what I mean?"

I nodded.

"Remember in high school when we used to hear all those stories about certain women in town, how they supposedly seduced young boys? Mrs. Shuttleworth? Rebecca Fine? Women like that? Well, when I got to be forty I took a long look at my life and I decided it wouldn't be too bad to *be* one of those women. On balance, you know? I mean, people pretended to be shocked at Billy and me, but deep down there was some envy there. I started being asked to lots of parties. I became kind of a celebrity, in a way. Not many women in this town are doing the things they really want to do, but I was, or so people assumed. It got me through a lot of doors."

"Carol Hasburg, Lover of Lost Boys."

"Fuck you, Marsh," Carol snapped. "I knew you wouldn't understand. You always were a puritan."

Carol left the room in a huff. She was gone long enough for me to get up and pace and wonder if I should leave. On my third lap I noticed a copy of our high school yearbook on a shelf behind the TV set and I went over and pulled it out.

The cover was an etched rendering of the school building. Inside came the standard photos of the school grounds, followed by a tribute to a retired principal that no one, including the teachers, could abide. Then came teachers perched on desks or poised before blackboards, then the misanthropic faces of the boys, the brazen faces of the girls, and then the clubs and teams, singers and players and scholars. I thumbed through the book quickly, then went back to the Senior section, where my classmates and I stared from the pages in polished, formal poses that were unlike what any of us had ever been.

While I was looking at a long-forgotten name and face Carol came back. She was wearing slacks and a tight blouse. I raised my brows in a question.

"I'm going out to Mickey's," she said. "I need a little action tonight. You really brought me down, Marsh."

"I didn't mean to."

"Yeah, well, next time you're in town don't bother to call. I don't need what you bring me."

"Which is what?"

"You tell me."

I didn't say anything, but when Carol saw what I was doing her mood altered and she pulled me over to the couch and sat beside me and looked with me. "Conrad Abbott. Remember him?"

"Picked his teeth with a sheath knife and brought snakes to school. What's he doing now?"

"Has a body shop out on the highway. Married Rhonda Bleeker. Remember her?"

"No."

"Sure you do. She had ringworm in sixth grade. Remember those little white hats?"

"God, yes. The hell of hells. I mortgaged my soul not to get ringworm."

"How about her?" Carol covered some words with her hand.

"Weird name. What was it?"

"Porrison Sodden."

"What's she doing now?"

"A lawyer in Chicago. You know what she did when we were freshman?"

"What?"

"Bought an ID bracelet and put your name on it and wore it for two years. Pretended you and she were going steady. I bet you never spoke to her twice in your life."

"Nope. Hey, there you are. Looking good enough to eat, as they say."

"Looking knocked up, is what I was. I had an abortion ten days after that picture was taken."

"You're kidding."

She shook her head. "Daddy took me to some dog-faced man in Kansas City. Might have been a doctor, might have been a plumber."

"Did Chuck know?"

"Not then; not now."

"But your folks. They're Catholic. I mean, *real* Catholic." I thought of what Sally had said about Carol's father and the high school girl.

"It was shame before God or shame before the town, and Daddy made his choice. That's another thing that brightens my day, the fact that three blocks away from here he's still asking God for forgiveness for what I made him do."

I resisted the temptation to tell Carol what I knew about her father. "It's amazing you went through all that without any of us knowing," I said instead.

"I wasn't the only one. Your thumb's covering another of the inconveniently fertile right now."

I moved my thumb. "Really?"

"You bet."

"Who was the father?"

"I don't know and she didn't either. Last time I talked to her she'd narrowed it down to three. She had the baby and kept it. Now she lives like a hermit out by the water tower. The baby's grown and gone, no one knows where, not even her."

I was silent, making mental pictures.

"The Fabulous Fifties," Carol said gaily. "Now I'm going to Mickey's and forget all about you *and* this stupid yearbook."

I grabbed her wrist to keep her on the couch. "Just one thing, Carol. Did you see Billy the night he died?"

"No."

"Come on, Carol. I won't tell anyone. I'm just trying to figure out what happened to him. At this stage nothing much makes sense."

She thought it over, fingering the collar of her blouse all the while, looking not at me but at the pictures in the book that lay between us. "Okay," she said. "It doesn't matter anyway, I guess. He was here. I hadn't seen him for several weeks. He just showed up about nine, out of the blue."

"Did you have sex?"

"Come on, Marsh."

"It's important, Carol. There was semen on the body. If it wasn't you, then I have to find out who it was."

Carol sighed. "We had sex. Yes. That's just what we had."

"Was it rough? I mean, energetic or whatever you call it."

"No, Marsh," Carol said with exasperation. "It was not rough. Billy wasn't that way at all. What are you trying to prove?"

"I'm just trying to find out who left their handprints all over his body," I said. What I didn't say was that the only other possibility was Zedda's girl, Tamara. Maybe Billy had been kinky with her or vice versa. The more I thought about it the more likely it seemed.

"Can I go now?" Carol asked.

"Did Billy say anything about where he was going when he left you?" I asked.

"No. He was real strange. Talked a lot about the baby. Said he was sorry, but I wasn't quite sure what he was sorry for."

"Was he frightened?"

"No, actually he seemed quite calm. Serene, almost."

"Can you think of anything at all that might indicate why he was killed?"

"No. Nothing besides Chuck."

"Did he ever talk about drugs?"

"We did some, if that's what you mean. Marijuana, mostly. I prefer booze, myself. Booze takes it *all* away."

"I mean drug deals. Buys and sells, big money operations."

"Nothing like that."

"Do you really think Chuck could have done it?"

"Hell, I don't know," Carol said. "He was just my husband; he was *your* best friend. What do you think?"

I didn't say anything, but I knew murder was always possible, given the right circumstance, and screwing a man's wife had been the right circumstance for centuries. Carol flipped idly through the yearbook while I thought of things to ask her.

"Was Billy the only one, Carol?" I asked finally.

"Why, Marsh? You writing a book?"

"If there were others, one of them might have wanted to make you his exclusive."

"There were others, but none that wanted me that way. Most of them were horny business types who'd meet me behind the bowling alley after Women's League on Wednesday nights and then pretend they'd never seen me before when I bumped into them on the square the next morning. I don't think there's anything there."

"You said Billy had money. What if he was blackmailing one of these friends of yours? What if the guy decided to get Billy off his back for good?"

Carol thought that one over for a time. "It's possible, Marsh, I have to admit that. But no one person comes to mind. I mean, over the years there have been a lot of guys. A whole lot. You'd have to move back here permanently to check them all out."

"If someone does come to mind, will you call me?"

"Sure. But no one will. An hour at Mickey's will see to that."

Carol flipped another page. "Well, here we are. John Marshall Tanner. Football, basketball, track. Band. C-Club. Student Council. FBLA. What the hell was FBLA?"

"Future Business Leaders."

"Ah. Is that what you are? A business leader?"

"The same way you're a nurse."

"The ideals of youth; the cesspool of age." Carol swore and closed the book and tossed it on the floor.

"I've got to go, Carol."

"You don't if you don't want to. I'm not mad at you anymore."

"Thanks, but I'd better take off."

Carol changed position and her blouse somehow flapped open above a braless breast. "You know," she said, "after Chuck slept with Sally that time I tried to let you know that you could do the same with me if you wanted, but you never seemed to get it. I mean, I spent about three months giving you peeks down the front of my dress, like I'm doing now, but it never took. Well, I'm a lot better at giving hints these days. Better at other things, too. Interested?"

"Yes. But I'm not going to take you up on it."

"Chicken?"

"I guess," I said. "Can I ask you one more thing?"

"What?"

"I want to know if you ever heard anything ʼ ˑ t my mother and Arnie Keene."

"Jesus." Carol shook her head. "Are you sure you want to know?"

"Yes."

"Okay. I heard some talk, is all."

"What talk?"

"That your mom and Keene were seeing each other."

"When did you hear that? How long before they died?"

"Jesus, Marsh, take it easy. I don't know. Not long, I guess."

"But why? Why did she do it?"

Carol shrugged. "No one ever knows that for sure, Marsh. Not even the person who does it."

"But what did people think?"

"They thought she and Keene had loved each other for a long time. And after seeing each other every day for twenty years they finally had to do something about it. I think it's kind of sweet, actually."

"Sweet and sour."

"It was a long time ago, Marsh."

"Not to me. To me it happened yesterday. I didn't know a damned thing about it."

Carol started to say something else but the doorbell rang. We both jumped, then looked at each other and then at the clock on the wall. It was close to midnight. "Who?" I asked.

Carol shrugged. "Maybe the guy I've been seeing, but he was supposed to play pitch with the boys tonight. It could be some kids, they've been doing that lately, usually when a man's here. That's what a certain reputation gets you."

Carol went to the door. When she opened it Chuck Hasburg burst into the room, his eyes slashing wildly till they sliced toward me. "Get out of here, Tanner. Now. I've taken all of this shit I can take."

"Relax, Chuck," I said, and stood up and made sure I knew where the things around me were.

"You son of a bitch. One Tanner has already crawled into my bed; you're not going to make it two." Chuck coughed, strangling on his rage.

"I know I'm not. So just take it easy."

"I ought to smash your face, you cocksucker. I've wanted to for thirty years."

"Why?"

"Because you had it fucking made, that's why. Big jock, big brain, always got anything you wanted. Well, I was as good as you. I even fucked your girl."

"Why don't you leave it at that?"

Chuck's hands made fists and he beat them on his thighs. "Yeah, well, maybe I'm not ready to."

"What do you want from me?"

"To start with, you can get out of here and don't come back."

"Let's both get out."

"You first."

"Okay. Come on, Chuck."

I walked to the door, my eyes still on his hands. "Thanks for the drink, Carol," I said, without looking at her.

"Come back anytime, Marsh." It was a taunt that rebounded off me and headed straight at Chuck.

"You cunt," he said, and took a step toward her.

I grabbed his arm. "Let's go, Chuck. Let's get out of here. I'll buy you a beer."

"I'm not going anywhere with you, goddamnit. I'm going back to Mickey's. I'll see *you* later," he said to Carol.

"Okay," I said, and pulled him out the door. Carol watched us stumble off the stoop. "Hey, Chuck," she said, "you still fucking Zedda's girls?"

Chuck swore again at her and she closed the door, her face a streak of triumph. The screen door closed with the mocking hiss of laughter. I asked Chuck if I could take him home.

"Fuck you," he said, and stumbled out of my grasp.

"Okay, Chuck. I'm leaving town in a day or two. I don't think I'll be back. Let me ask you one thing. What did Billy Tanner have against you? Why did he want to break up your marriage?"

"Fuck you, Tanner. Fuck you and the horse you rode in on."

"Come on, Chuck. What was happening there?"

"He was screwing my wife, asshole. You want pictures?"

"I mean between you and Billy."

"I know, but I'm not going to tell you."

"Why not?"

"Because I hate your guts, hotshot. Always have."

"Why?"

"Because that time I caught the pass against Mount Pleasant? The one that beat their ass?"

"Yeah."

"That's as good as it ever got for me. And folks around here never let me forget it."

# Chapter 20

Chuck Hasburg staggered down the street under the burden of his liquor and his torment, the light high above the corner making his hair a thatch of fairy-tale straw. I waited until he climbed into a battered Plymouth, then got in my own car and drove off slowly, my eyes on the rearview mirror. After I'd gone two blocks Chuck's car lights came on and he drove away as well. The headlights swayed to and fro, twin dancers lit by black light, then exited stage left.

I meandered through the town again, my mind fuzzed with drink and with memories of night, of the sex or thrill or violence that dark begets. Cafés and bars and gas stations, Elks and Eagles and the Legion, the night places glowed with warmth and light and music, the rest were dark and cold and quiet. And in their cars like me, the kids.

Eventually I drove past Carol's house again. The lights were out and her car was gone. Chuck's car wasn't in sight, either. Perhaps they met at Mickey's to continue their struggle. Perhaps not. It was not my problem. So the old lamplighter, having completed his appointed rounds, headed for the square.

For old times' sake I took a couple of laps. After the first I was followed by a kid in a jazzed-up pickup with roll bar and fog lights and extenders, a kid with a thick neck and muscled arms and a face that would turn from silly to savage in a second because if you're a strong young lad in a town like Chaldea there's not all that much in your way. The sticker on his bumper said FARMERS DO IT IN THE FIELD. The traffic over his CB radio suggested a new definition of hell. I pulled to the side and let him go around me and he waved his thanks and his pity and resumed his quest.

I parked in the hotel lot and started up to my room. But the sense of it drove me away. Halfway up the stairs I did an about-face and went outside and walked to the nearest bar, a place called the Fencepost. I was lonesome, in a town where once that would have been unlikely.

It was almost one, and the bar was almost empty. An empty bar is the loneliest place there is next to a foxhole on Christmas, but I went in anyway. I slipped onto a stool and ordered a Scotch I didn't need. The bartender was my age or better, with a puffy, florid face that suggested familiar contours beneath the excess flesh. Like me he needed someone to talk to. The only other singles in the place had drifted as far beyond speech as booze will take you. When he slid me my Scotch I thanked him and the word was enough to get him started.

"You sell?" he asked idly.

I shook my head. "Just visiting."

The bartender chuckled. "What's to visit?"

"Just some of my people."

"Who?"

He was pushing now and he knew it, but it was late and what the hell.

"The Tanners," I told him. "Curt and Laurel. Also the Nottings. Gail and Curt are my siblings."

"Are what?"

"My brother and sister."

"Oh. Yeah. So where you from, then?"

"San Francisco."

The big man nodded his heavy head. "Laid over there during the war. Wild place. Beatniks took over after that; guess the fruits got it now."

"Not quite."

"Yeah? Well, I only know what I hear. You're a Tanner, too, ain't you?"

"Marsh."

"Sure. I remember you. The Bloomfield game."

I nodded. "Who're you?"

"Joe Vilardi."

"Sure. I remember. You've been around here a long time, Joe."

"All my life. Old man worked the mines. Died in them, too. The black damp."

"A tough life."

"The toughest." Joe pushed his sweatshirt over his elbows and poured me a second drink.

"You have a sister named Violet?" I asked him.

"Yeah. Know her?"

"She was a class behind me, I think."

"Violet's in the Quad Cities, now. Moline. Got six kids. All assholes, just like her husband. Thinks his shit don't stink 'cause he's a shop steward at Deere." Joe shook his head at the invisible hauteur of his brother-in-law. "Town changed much, you think?" he asked.

"Not much."

"Not enough, is what you mean."

"I guess."

"Many kids in your grade still around town?"

"Not many. No one I knew very well." I could have mentioned Sally but I didn't want to.

Joe nodded. "That's the way it was in those days. Tied the old graduation tassel to the mirror and left town the same day. Getting that way again, too. Got a shirt they sell over at Penney's, says on it HAPPINESS IS CHALDEA IN YOUR REARVIEW MIRROR. Every kid in town's got one."

"Too bad."

"There's places worse. Take Abla. Know what they did to get themselves a new business over in Abla?"

"What?"

"Brought in this turkey-processing plant. You know, pluck 'em and gut 'em and grind 'em up to make those, what do you call, pressed turkey rolls. Ever eat one?"

"Nope."

"Like cardboard, only not as sweet. Anyways, know who they got to do the work?"

"Who?"

"Bunch of retards from Texas. Bring them all the way up here in a yellow school bus, stick them in a big old house out on the edge of town, bus them to the plant in the mornings and back to the house at night and put them to bed, day by day by day. Poor bastards stand there all day, ass deep in turkey guts, drooling down their chins into the gizzards, all for a couple of bucks an hour they never see anyway. Done under some program run by the state, is what they say. Texas, that is. Anyhow, that's what passes for progress over in Abla."

"I never did like Abla," I said.

Joe did some business beneath the bar, then straightened up again. "Hey," Joe said suddenly. "Sally Stillings. You used to run with her, didn't you? Back in the old days?"

"Yep."

"She's back, you know."

"I know."

"Comes in a lot, lately. Seen her since you got back?"

"Once. Yeah."

Joe looked closely, to see what Sally was to me, but if he found out, he knew more than I did. "Out to have fun if it kills her, is the way it looks," he said slowly.

"That's about it," I agreed.

"The boys fool with her a little."

"How?"

"Oh, get a little raunchy, dance with her crotch-to-crotch, talk dirty to see how much she'll take before she leaves. That kind of thing. She takes a lot, I'll say that. Still, this town's no place for a woman like her, on her own and everything. She keeps on the way she's been, it'll turn her into something she don't need to be. Like old Vivian Klippit. Remember her? Used to earn her beer money hauling her tits out and letting the boys fiddle with 'em for a buck."

I didn't want to hear any more about Vivian Klippit so I motioned for another drink. Joe brought it to me quickly. Down at the end of the bar two young men were arguing loudly about Limousins and Charolais. I asked Joe what they were. "Cows," he said simply. "Imported."

"What happened to Herefords and Angus?"

"Old-fashioned. Everyone's got to try the newest thing. Hell, though, it's like everything else. New one ain't nothing much but new." Joe smiled. "Hear about the fire department last night?"

"Nope."

"Elmo Frates' place went up. Elmo lives about three miles

outside the city limits, so there's no water line out there or nothing and they soon pumped the pumper dry. So old Buck Looftis got the bright idea of dipping the hose down Elmo's septic tank and pumping water out of there. Well, they got the fire put out all right, but when they was done old Elmo didn't want the place. Tried to set it back afire for the insurance. Smelled like a hog barn after a rainstorm, is what they say. Old Buck ain't too swift."

My laugh was eclipsed by a crash. Down at the end of the room one of the boys had broken off a beer bottle on the edge of the bar and was waving the jagged edge in the face of his buddy, taunting him with jeers and curses, egging him toward the sharp brown blades of glass. The other boy backed off slowly, making sure he didn't fall, his hands outstretched in a plea for peace. Joe swore under his breath and reached down under the bar and brought out a pistol, a big one. "Lloyd," he said quietly. "Put her down and back on out the door. Right now. You know I'll use this if I have to, Lloyd. You don't believe it, you can ask Fats Kinell. Gun-shot him a year ago New Year's."

Lloyd looked at Joe and then at the pistol and then at his buddy. Then he shrugged and put the broken bottle on the bar. It rolled slowly toward the edge, then shimmered, then died. "I'll see you sometime without your piece," Lloyd said to Joe. "Then we'll see who gives the orders."

Lloyd and his buddy walked out of the bar. By the time they reached the door they were arm in arm and laughing. "Shitty way to make a living sometimes," Joe said to me, and filled my glass on the house.

"You bartend a long time?" I asked him.

"Five years. Worked construction before that. Non-union. Worked Morrell's in Ottumwa before that. Union. The best money I ever made, but they closed her down. Flunked out of junior college before that. What's your trade?"

"Private investigator."

"No shit?"

"No shit."

"Say." Joe snapped his fingers and the solitary drinker down the bar jumped like he'd touched a hot wire. "You here to find out who killed, what's his name . . . Billy? He's your kin, right?"

"Right. That's not why I came to town, but I've been looking around a little. You hear anything about it?"

"Not much. Lots of folks glad he's out of their hair, though. No offense. Had this ear he used to pull on people. Gross as hell."

"I've heard that before, that Billy made people mad. Why do you think that was?"

Joe sipped a clear liquid from a glass, then put it back on the shelf behind him. "You live in a place like this, the only way to survive is to play a role. Like in the school play or something. Me, I'm the tough old bastard behind the bar who's good for a free drink once in a while if you behave yourself. I mean, I raise rabbits, English Lops, those ones with the long droopy ears, and I know a hell of a lot about it, win prizes in Chicago and everything, but that don't make no difference. I'm the barkeep, pure and simple. And we got our upright citizens and loving wives and political powers and the wheeler-dealers, bums, drunks, and what else have you. Everybody's got a part, only Billy, he wouldn't let folks play the game, and that didn't sit real well with some."

"Like who?"

"Well, your brother-in-law, for one. Suppose you heard about that. And Clark Jaspers, the lawyer, for another. And Chuck Hasburg, but that was different. Woman trouble."

"You know anything else about Billy, Joe? I mean, that he was into something that might get him killed?"

"Nothing besides that WILD bunch."

"What's the story on them?"

"Well, they're supposed to do all this environment stuff, and I guess they do, some, but word lately is you want to score some dope in big quantities that's not a bad door to knock on. Zedda's the guy you talk to, he's the boss down there."

"What kind of drugs?"

"Marijuana, mostly. But coke, too, if you got the money, which most don't. Even heroin, they say, though that may just be bragging. Not much call for heroin around here. Farm folks are dumb but they ain't that dumb. Gettin' there, I admit."

"Tell me about Chuck Hasburg."

"Chuck? Good man, or would be if they let him."

"How do you mean?"

"Oh, just that life up and kicked Chuck right in the gonads

a few years back, then hauled off and did it again for good measure. Lost his job, then lost his woman six months later. With most folks that's about all there is to lose. Chuck's on edge, like a lot of guys around here, nothing left for him to do but drink and whore. It's okay for a while, but after too long you get so deep in shit you can't climb out. Then either your liver rots or your dick does and either way you got a world of hurt."

"Is Chuck that far along?"

"Close. Comes in just after we open up, most days. Stays all day some days, too."

"What time do you open?"

"Seven A.M."

"Jesus."

"Jesus don't have nothing to do with it, Marsh. He ain't stopped in here for years."

Someone down the bar made a noise that meant nothing to me but did to Joe, and he went off to fill another glass. When he came back I had a question for him. "You know of any relationship between Chuck Hasburg and Billy Tanner? I mean, something before Billy moved in on Chuck's wife?"

"Well, now," Joe mused. "Let me chew on it a minute. Meantime, you want to kick the mule again?"

"I shouldn't but I will."

"You just sang the story of my life," Joe said, and went off and came back with a drink out of a bottle he pulled out from under the bar. "That bar Scotch'll turn your toenails green," he said. "This here's twelve going on a hundred."

"Thanks. But at this point you could serve some aftershave and I wouldn't know the difference."

"Welcome home," Joe said, and toasted me with an imaginary glass.

"Be happy to buy you one of the same," I said.

Joe shook his head. "Haven't had a drink in eight years," he said, then left me alone to imagine the reason.

Some more people came into the bar, a young couple looking like they were slumming and a drifter in a cowboy hat and a sparkling shirt trying to kill some more of a life that wouldn't stay dead. Joe went off to serve them and I sat where I was, drunk as a skunk, and toyed with the image of Chuck Hasburg, my old pal, with Billy's blood on his hands.

Chuck. The blood on his hands had once been mine, the day he'd helped me to the hospital when I'd been cut to the bone by a skate in a pickup hockey game back when we were about twelve. Now it turned out that Chuck had not only cuckolded me in a fashion, he had bitterly resented me for thirty years. Nothing is ever the way it seems, not even friendship. I finished off my drink and spun on my stool to leave and looked into the smiling countenance of Sheriff Rex Eason. Joe slid the sheriff a Bud in a bottle without being asked.

"Mr. Tanner," the sheriff boomed, rattling even the drunk at the end of the bar. "You still in town?"

"Last I looked," I said, the booze rendering me as silly as a vaudevillian at the bottom of the bill. "You find who killed my nephew yet, Sheriff?" I asked, the words long and thick.

"Don't think there's anyone to find. Pretty sure it's suicide."

"Oh?"

"That's right. Got no reason to call it murder. None at all."

"What the hell, Sheriff? I thought you said Billy wasn't the type to kill himself."

"Well, Billy was peculiar enough, plus I hear he was real sick. Sick people do things they wouldn't normally do, is how I see it. It's how you'd best see it, too. Save you a bunch of grief."

"Who got to you, Sheriff? Gladbrook? Mary Martha Whoever, the newspaper lady? The mayor? Who?" I didn't recognize the voice as mine.

"Don't know what you're talking about, Mr. Tanner."

"I'm talking cover-up, Sheriff. I'm talking 'let's let Billy die a suicide so the business folks who're thinking about coming here won't get all excited by some scary talk of murder.' I'm talking about a sacrifice, Sheriff. Billy Tanner's name for this town's future."

"You got no reason to talk that way, Mr. Tanner."

"Don't I?" I teetered on my stool.

"You appear to be a bit inebriated, so I'll take that into account. But I'd advise you to get on home now, and to think real hard about leaving town in the morning."

"Are you telling me the investigation is off, Sheriff? That you're not even looking for a killer anymore?"

"Oh, I'm checking some."

"Checking how?"

"I visited the people out at WILD today, for one."

"And?"

"Nothing much. Toilet in the back flushed a bunch of times while I was there, is about all."

"Who'd you talk to?"

"Zedda."

"How about his girl? Tamara?"

The sheriff shrugged. "Don't know the lady. What's she got to do with it?"

"Damned if I know," I admitted. "She might have had an affair with Billy at some time. Which means she might have seen him the night he died."

The sheriff swore. "If I look up every woman the boy slept with I'll be working till retirement," he said with a sad grin. He killed his Bud and moved a step away.

"So what else are you going to do?" I challenged, more belligerent than I had a right to be.

The sheriff seemed not to notice. "You going to keep on going around asking folks about Billy?" the sheriff asked me, his voice so smooth I had trouble holding the words in an intelligible order.

"Till I come across something that makes sense," I said.

"Sometimes death don't make no sense at all," the sheriff said. "You got some kind of client in this?"

"I do. A client of sterling character, I might add."

"Who?"

"Me." My gesture was as grand as my boast.

"You best get on to where you sleep, Mr. Tanner, before you fall off your stool and Joe has to put you up in the back."

"Well said, constable," I said.

"And you be careful," the sheriff added. "Some people might not want you sniffing too close in their affairs. Lots of folks in this part of the country, they hear someone sniffing around the barn lot, they just pull the old Remington off the wall and fire away. Know what I mean, Mr. Tanner?"

"You got anyone specific in mind that's so sensitive, Sheriff?"

"Not a one," the sheriff said. "Joe. Thanks for the beer. Mr. Tanner, you take it easy. I'll get them if they're there to get, but I'll do it my way. I got to live in this town after we get this all straightened out, and you'll just be moving on. So we got different ways of traveling to get to where we want to get."

The sheriff went out the door before my besotted mind could frame an objection to his counsel. Joe came over and asked if I wanted another belt. I shook my head, which taxed my motor skills to their limits. "I been thinking about what you asked," Joe said.

"What was that?"

"About what there was between Chuck Hasburg and Billy."

"Oh. That. What have you got?"

"Well, only one thing comes to mind."

"What is it?"

"You'll have to check at the courthouse to make sure, but I think old Chuck was on the draft board some years back. I think he was the one sent Billy Tanner off to war."

# Chapter
## 21

In my dreams I was surrounded and attacked by creatures with turned-up collars and pimpled faces, wearing white socks and angora sweaters, with hair in ponytails or flattops with wings. Above them all Chuck Hasburg threatened me with a bomb in the shape of a football. When I got to the Laundromat I was dulled and pained from lack of sleep and from the hot sour residue of booze and smoke. The spinning dryers and sudsy washers didn't do a thing for me.

There was only one person in the place, a girl standing way in the back. The mounds of clothes in plastic baskets that surrounded her looked like outsized scoops of pistachio in sugar cones. She was an unreconstructed flower child, with straight blond hair, bare feet, feathered headband, love beads, granny dress and glasses, and rings on every digit but the thumb. Behind the glasses her blue eyes were baked enamel, impervious to whatever enemy had surrounded her. When I walked up to her she raised a hand to wave me away. "I got no change, mister," she said, already angry, perhaps perpetually so. "No spare soap, either."

"I'm not here to wash clothes," I said. "Just cleaning up the past a little."

"Is that supposed to mean something rational?" Her mouth twisted with the acid taste of disdain.

"I'm Marsh Tanner. Are you Tamara?"

"What if I am?" Suspicion tugged down her brow and made her ugly, the way suspicion always does to anyone.

"If you are, I'd like to talk to you about Billy. Billy Tanner, my nephew."

The baked eyes widened. She checked the clothes in the spinning dryer, then looked at me through tiny glass discs that made her eyes seem jeweled. "I'm Tamara. You the guy came to see Zedda the other night?"

"Right."

"And took Starbright to see them bury Billy's bones?"

"Right again."

"She says you're mellow."

"Why don't we assume she's right?" I smiled a great big smile. It bounced back at me off a flat board of boredom.

"Starbright thinks Reagan is mellow," Tamara said brusquely. "Zedda know you're here?"

"No."

"You tell him you were going to check me out?"

"Nope."

"You going to tell him anything I say?"

"Still no."

She glanced around the room and saw nothing but mildew and machines. "My load has ten minutes left in the cycle, then I got to get back. We could go next door till then."

"What's next door?"

"Head shop."

"In Chaldea?"

"Why not?"

"I didn't realize there were that many dopers in this part of the country."

"There's dopers where there's dope." Tamara led me into the shop next door.

The establishment was named Head Case, and it contained a rather uninspired collection of drug paraphernalia and an odor of incense heavy enough to stun anything olfactory. There was a girl behind a counter with a tulip tattooed on her cheek. A WILD poster on the wall featured poisoned fish and empty barrels of pesticide. My guess was the place was an offshoot of the group, another of Zedda's integrated enterprises. My next guess was that there was a cop permanently stationed nearby, on the alert for reefer madness.

Tamara mumbled something to the girl behind the counter and she left the room as though she were walking on clouds, taking her tattoo and her incense with her. The speakers in the corner squirted heavy metal, the sound as thick and numbing as the acrid smoke that soured the room.

"What about him?" Tamara asked as she lowered herself to a pillow on the floor. I didn't want to sit down there with her—there's something perverse about sitting on the floor while wearing a necktie—but I did.

"Billy was killed," I said, when our heads were on the same plane.

Tamara frowned. "Zedda said suicide."

"Zedda was wrong."

"Says who?"

"Says me."

Tamara squirmed on the satin pillow, then reached into her bag for a cigarette and added to the haze that billowed about us. "Who wasted him, then?" she asked, after she'd waxed her lungs with tar.

"I don't know that. It's why I'm here."

"Well, *I* don't know anything about it."

"Do you want to?"

"Not really." The words were elaborately casual. "I've got enough friction in my life already. Billy's karma was bad and I don't need any of it laid on me. I mean, I'm thinking about splitting this scene anyway. I can't afford to get involved in any pig trip."

"What if Zedda killed him?" I asked harshly. I was mad at her dismissal of Billy, at her easy ability to deprive him of significance.

The question startled her for a minute, seemed even to confirm a fear, but then she relaxed. "He didn't," she said, and seemed certain of it.

"Were you with Zedda that night?"

"It was Monday, right?"

"Right."

"I was with him."

"Doing what?"

"Massage. We gave him his massage that night."

"You and who?"

"Me and the chick who just left."

"Did you see Billy at all?"

"No."

"What time did things with Zedda start?"

"Eleven or so."

"And you were all together till when?"

"Morning. I mean, we smoked a little weed and got it on and bagged out right after. Anyway, why would Zedda kill Billy?"

"Maybe because Billy was sleeping with you."

She frowned and checked the door. "That's garbage, man. Who told you that?" There was even more fear behind the little glasses now, and it spread electrically to her fingers, which crushed a fold of her skirt.

"Come on, Tamara. Don't play games. I can get it from you here or we can bring in the cops and let them sweat it out of you. I don't think you want that."

She closed her eyes and said nothing. She looked older, suddenly, too old and wise to be who and where she was. When she opened her eyes the jewels within them had vanished. "Zedda can't know about this," she said in a whisper. "I'm trying to get out of here and the only way is for him to give me the bread. If he flashes on me and Billy he won't dole."

"How much money do you need?"

She thought. "A hundred will get me to Tucson. I got friends in Tucson."

"I can give that to you. If you tell me all you know."

"When?"

"Now. I've got the money with me. It's yours when we're through talking."

She released her skirt and looked despondently at the wrinkles she had made in the thin, flowered fabric. "What do you want to know?"

"Just about you and Billy. What was the arrangement?"

"We got it on, is all."

"How often?"

"Once a month, maybe. Not that often, really."

"Where? At WILD?"

"Are you crazy?"

"Then where? Billy's cabin?"

"Not there. Starbright was there. *There*."

She grinned and pointed out the window of the shop, at the building across the street. "The church?" I asked, my voice cracking with amazement.

"You got it, Jack."

"How?"

"Billy knew about this little room in the basement. Said it used to be his Sunday school room. Billy knew the Apostle's Creed, can you dig it? They use it for storage now, I guess. Has an old couch, a rug, and the door was never locked. Churches still don't lock things. Comes in handy sometimes."

"So you and Billy just crept in there and did your thing once or twice a month. That's all there was to it?"

"That's it."

"Why? I mean, you each had other partners, why go to each other?"

Tamara laughed bitterly. "Kicks. The only reason there is for anything. Plus who knows? Maybe I owed Zedda some things and this was one way to pay him back. And maybe I felt sorry for Billy."

"Sorry why?"

"The sores and everything. You know about them?"

I nodded.

"Starbright wouldn't go down on him anymore, so I did. Made me feel righteous." Her look challenged me to be dismayed.

"Did Billy ever mention being afraid of someone?" I asked. "That someone was out to get him?"

"Plenty of dudes were out to get Billy. He stoked a lot of fear around here. But *he* wasn't afraid. He wasn't even afraid of Zedda."

"Why would he be afraid of Zedda?"

"Because I'm Zedda's old lady. And because of what Zedda was in the war."

"What was that?"

"An assassin."

I laughed. "Zedda wasn't the assassin; Billy was."

"You sure?" Tamara asked, her frown a puzzled wrinkle.

I told her I was sure but I wasn't, quite. Zedda could have been playing head games with me, transposing his and Billy's relationship for purposes known only to him. Still, Billy's overall behavior squared more with the version Zedda had given me than with Tamara's. "What did Starbright think about you and Billy?" I asked.

"She didn't care. Sex isn't a big deal to us the way it is to you. It makes people feel good, so whoever needs it gets it, not counting creeps. Besides, all Starbright cares about is the baby in her belly."

I let her carnal communism pass. "You're pregnant, too, aren't you?"

"Who the fuck told you that?"

I didn't say anything.

"Was it Zedda? Come on. I have to know."

I shook my head.

"Okay. So it was Starbright, the stupid bitch. I'm pregnant all right, but Zedda's not supposed to know. If he did, he wouldn't let me split. Or he'd come after me if I did."

"Is Zedda the father?"

"Who else?"

"Billy?"

"Not Billy. You can't get pregnant sucking cock."

The statement drove me away from her relationship with Billy on to something else. "How about a woman named Carol Hasburg?" I asked. "You ever hear of her?"

"Not from Billy."

"From whom?"

"Zedda."

"What did he say?"

"He said Billy was fucking her."

"Did he say why?"

She shrugged. "I don't know, but Zedda was pissed about it."

"Why? Was he screwing her, too?"

"I don't think so. But Zedda knew this Hasburg guy, the husband. He came around a lot, lately."

"Why?"

"Looking for young chicks, I think. But who knows? I flamed out on Zedda and his trip months ago. I'm just looking for a way out of town. And here you are."

She held out her hand. I took out my wallet and gave her the hundred. She thanked me and we stood up. "You know anything else that might help?" I asked Tamara.

"Like what?"

"I don't know. Was Billy dealing drugs, for example?"

"I don't know anything about drugs," Tamara said quickly and falsely, and turned for the door.

"I know about the marijuana out at the farm. What did Billy have to do with it?"

She looked at the money in her hand and then at me. I added to the total. "He was just the guard. Scared people off. Zedda handled all the deals. Billy just made one rule."

"What?"

"Zedda couldn't deal with anyone local. He had to deal to Chicago or KC or St. Louis, someplace like that."

"Did Zedda go along?"

"As far as I know."

"How much did Zedda get for the dope?"

"I don't know. Lots. He always had bread, until lately."

"What happened lately?"

"I don't know for sure. I think he got ripped off, maybe. He's bent out of shape about something, that's for sure."

"I hear Zedda got in some trouble with the law a year ago."

"Yeah. So?"

"Tell me about it."

Tamara looked at her watch. "I got to go."

"What was he charged with?"

"Rape." She said the word as though speaking a foreign tongue.

"What happened?"

"This high school honey came around WILD, wanted to join the group, then when it was too late decided she didn't like the games we played. A political farce. Zedda got off."

"Who was his lawyer?"

"Some guy on crutches."

"Is there anything else? Anything at all that struck you as strange? Anything Billy said or did?"

She thought for a moment. "Come to think of it, there is something. But you know, I don't think this amount's going to be enough to get me all the way to Tucson. I'd hate to end up short, you know what I mean? Lot of desert out there." A grin as greedy as Fagin's spread across her face.

"How much do you think it will take?"

"Another hundred?"

I gave it to her. "Now, what was it you remembered?"

"Well, a few nights ago, last week, maybe, Billy and I were uptown. Just wandering around, you know. He'd been in getting some soybean milk for Starbright. Anyway, all of a sudden I noticed Billy looking at something real hard. He stopped walking and everything."

"What was it?"

"I don't know. I looked but I couldn't see anything. It was dark by then. But it must have been something weird, from the way he looked. Spacemen or something."

"What did he say?"

"He just said, 'They've finally come.' Or something like that. I don't know what the hell it meant, but that's what he said."

"Did he seem frightened?"

"Not really. I think he kind of smiled, even. I can't say for sure." Tamara looked again at her watch. "Now I got to go. Zedda's a fiend for clean underwear." She stuffed the money into her bag. "Don't bother looking for me again. I'll be gone."

She went out the door of the head shop and I followed after, heading for the law office of Clark Jaspers.

Clark was a lawyer and he used crutches, which meant he was both the man who had defended Zedda in his rape trial and the man representing the agribusiness consortium that Matt had originally wanted to buy our farm. I went inside and gave the receptionist my name and asked to see her boss.

"Do you have an appointment, Mr. Tanner?"

"It's a personal matter."

"Well, I'll just see. Wait here a moment."

The woman left me for a minute. I spent it thumbing through the current *Farm Journal*. Then she came back, with Clark Jaspers trailing along behind, his large mouth smiling, his dead legs scraping across the floor between the gleaming shafts of his crutches. "Marsh. How the hell are you?" His voice was as sonorous as rolling barrels.

He released a crutch and gave me a muscled hand to squeeze, then motioned me back toward his office. It was tastefully done in reds and browns and golds, tweeds and leathers and woods and glazes. With a fabulous grace Clark moved to his chair and descended into it, his crutches suddenly vanishing, his legs hidden beneath the desk, only his massive arms and shoulders hinting of his handicaps. "Been a long time, Marsh," he said.

"Too long."

"Good to have you back."

"Good to be here. Or was."

Clark nodded solemnly. "Sorry about Billy."

"Kind of ruined the homecoming."

Clark started to say something else, then changed his mind. "Hear you're not a lawyer anymore."

"Nope."

"Lots of reasons to get out of the practice. Which one was yours?"

"Time, I guess," I said. "Not enough of it." That wasn't the whole truth, but it was a part of it.

Clark rubbed a hand across his heavy jaw. Above the hand his dark eyes brooded and burned, the way they always had, hatching thoughts beyond the ken of healthy men. "Know what you mean," he said. "Don't know whether I'm coming or going half the time myself. Sometimes I think my bum legs are a blessing, otherwise I'd run myself right into the ground."

Clark laughed easily, likeable and self-deprecating as always. "You went to Harvard, didn't you, Clark?" I asked.

"Yep."

"*Law Review* and Coif and all that?"

"Afraid so."

"Which means you got an engraved invitation to Wall Street. Why'd you come back here?"

The affable smile left his face. "I've been asked that a lot, Marsh. Usually I lie, because everyone in town's a potential client. But you of all people should be able to understand the truth. If you really want to hear it."

"Sure."

"You're one of the ones I wished I was in those days, you know. I mean, that's what I did a lot, pick out people I wished I was. But I was the opposite from you. You left town a hero, a champion. Jock and all that. I left town a cripple who was ignored on his best days and taunted on his worst, and tossed a few awards for citizenship or school spirit or whatever as a sop to people's guilt for leaving me out of everything that counted. So I *had* to come back. To show them that in anything that mattered it was me who was the champion. Does that make sense to you?"

I nodded because it did. "Are you happy you did come back?"

Clark shrugged. "Mostly, but not entirely. The practice is a bit routine. The money was only fair for a long time, and I made a few mistakes trying to get rich quick. But things are real good now. I've exorcised my devils. You have something in mind, Marsh, or is this just social?"

"Both," I said. "The business part is about the farm. I hear you're interested."

"True. I'm part of a group that's been investing in farmland around the state over the past year. It's a tax deal, in part, but we're not just after a capital gain. We'll work the farm. I hope you'll take our offer seriously, Marsh. I doubt anyone else in the picture will let you realize as much cash up front as we will."

"Let's say for a minute your group is out of it, Clark. Could you represent me in structuring a deal with someone else?"

He frowned and tapped a tooth, and said what I knew he'd say. "I think that would be a conflict, Marsh. You'd have to go to someone else."

"Who do you recommend?"

"Ed Buckles would be good. Young kid, smart, hardworking, which is more important. Most of the rest in town are well into retirement. Or you could go elsewhere. A couple of men in Oskaloosa are tops."

"I'll probably try Buckles."

"So you've made up your mind, Marsh?"

"Getting there."

"I take it we're not in the picture."

"I don't think so, Clark. Hope that doesn't cause you problems. I heard a little about that country club deal."

Clark brushed the intangible loss away. "I'm well again, Marsh. And there's plenty of other places for sale in the county. Don't worry about it."

"Okay, I won't," I said.

The phone beside Clark buzzed and he picked it up. I looked around, at his diplomas and awards and certificates of admission to various courts in the land, including the highest.

Whoever was on the end of the line was angry, the insistent buzz of his voice audible even to me. And Clark was getting angry as well. He grudgingly made an appointment to see the caller in two hours, then hung up. Just before the phone fell to its cradle I suddenly thought I knew who the caller had been.

"There's one other thing, Clark," I said when he looked at me again.

"What's that?"

"Billy."

Clark nodded slowly. "I couldn't believe it when I heard. That something could make a boy like Billy want to kill himself. I mean, I've considered suicide all my life, especially in the days when it seemed that nothing short of that would make my legs go away. But Billy was like you, Marsh. He had everything. Of course, he changed a lot."

"So I hear. Any idea why?"

"The war, I think. He had a rough time over there."

"I hear he made some charges against you, Clark. What was that all about?"

Clark shook his head with what seemed like sorrow. "It was part of the country club thing. The land the development was on was originally owned by an old woman named Jones. Her husband farmed it, then died and left it to her. I wrote her will, was executor of the estate when she died. The estate had to sell the farm to pay taxes and expenses of administration. Billy claimed it was unethical for me to be a shareholder in the corporation that bought the land. He claimed we paid less than top dollar, so that I profited from my fiduciary position as executor. All nonsense, of course, but to keep the bar association happy I had to bail out of the development at exactly the wrong time. I took a pretty good bath, but hell. Easy come, easy go."

Clark laughed easily. Money was clearly not a problem for him now. "Why do you think Billy went after you, Clark?" I asked him.

"Who knows?"

I found myself watching closely for a reaction, suspecting Clark, suspecting everyone, eager to stop asking the same questions and getting the same answers, eager to be gone. It occurred to me that I would probably never learn what I wanted to know, that I would leave town without avenging Billy. I wasn't as bothered by the idea as I had been the day before. "Did you have anything to do with the war, Clark?" I asked. "Most of Billy's targets seemed to."

"Well, I was with the U.S. Attorney until sixty-eight. Prosecuted several draft evasion cases toward the end. That's the only thing I can think of."

"It may be enough. How about Tom Notting? What did he do that had to do with Vietnam? Billy went after him the same way he went after you."

Clark laughed. "Yeah, poor Tom couldn't even retire in peace." He reached down and adjusted his leg. "There's only one thing I know of. Tom and the mayor have always been close, at least they were until the mayor and his buddies decided to run someone else for Tom's job. Anyway, the mayor has a son. About fifteen years ago he was playing basketball for Drake and about to become prime meat for the draft. Well, Tom knew this congressman from Michigan— they'd been college roommates or something—so Tom had this guy fix it up so the mayor's son spent his hitch at West Point teaching plebes how to shoot free throws or something. Pissed off a lot of people around town, Republicans mostly, but it blew over. God, that seems a long time ago. What an epoch."

"I hear you represented one of Billy's friends a while back," I said.

"Who's that?"

"Zedda."

"So?"

"Just wondering if he ever mentioned Billy to you."

"Maybe. In passing. Why?"

"Oh, I just think Billy's death may be connected with the WILD operation somehow."

"What do you mean, Marsh? It was suicide. The sheriff says so."

"The sheriff's wrong."

"You're saying murder?"

"I am. Do you know anything that might tell me who the killer was?"

"Of course not. You must be wrong, Marsh."

"I don't think so."

"I don't know what to say. Is there anything I can do? To help you, I mean."

"Tell me about the drug trade in Chaldea."

Clark frowned and rubbed the shadow of his beard. "Drugs? Why drugs?"

"I think Billy and his friend Zedda were dealing. Billy might have been killed because a drug buy went bad. Know anything about it?"

"Why would I?"

"You're Zedda's lawyer."

"True. And anything he might have told me would be privileged. But I'm in the dark on this one, Marsh. If I hear anything I'll let you know." Clark ended his lecture and glanced at the clock on the wall behind me. "I've got an appointment in a minute, Marsh. Maybe we can have lunch in a few days."

"Sure, Clark," I said. "Nice to see you again. One last thing. Who was the girl Zedda raped?"

"He didn't rape her, Marsh. He was acquitted."

"Who was she?"

"Norma Gladbrook. The daughter of the guy who runs a hardware store in town."

"Norm Gladbrook's daughter?"

"Yes."

"Where is she now?"

"I don't have the faintest idea."

# Chapter 22

I parked beside the crumbling farmhouse and crawled again through barbed wire, heading once more for Billy's underground domain. I took a roundabout path this time, to see if any more surprises were sprouting out of Tanner ground, to make a set with the marijuana crop. Along the way I found myself wondering whether, with so many people wanting Billy Tanner dead, it made any real difference which one of them had finally killed him.

At the top of the second ridge, the one beyond the creek, I did come across something strange. Over an area the size of an infield the grass was smashed flat, the dirt patterned by the crosshatch of Jeep tracks. Interspersed among the disturbance, at regular intervals, were holes, several of them, some dug to a depth I couldn't determine, others looking like the results of explosions. I wasn't certain, but I thought they had been made for seismic soundings, and my guess was that Cosmos had made real or bogus probes for oil in this spot, and that Billy had spied on them and somehow learned that there was no oil to be had, either because the results of the soundings weren't encouraging or because the search wasn't genuine in the first place. At some time Billy had probably told Curt what he had learned, to convince him to keep the farm, not sell it, which accounted for Curt's conviction that there was no oil on the property. If Billy's suspicions had eventually been learned by

Kinsey Beech, there was yet another reason for Billy to be dead, to keep the Cosmos scheme under wraps, whatever that scheme might be.

I scuffed around in the already well-scuffed dirt for a time, weaving a lanyard of my thoughts, then headed on for Billy's cavern. By the time I reached it I was sweating and itching and things were sticking to my clothes as though nature had tarred and feathered me.

I descended the hill with as much noise as I could muster, so as not to surprise anyone within the house. But there was nothing to surprise but bugs and grasshoppers and flies that looked like marbles with wings and fur. I called out and listened to my voice drift off across the rolling land, then pushed back the curtain across the doorway and entered the house, uneasy at being in something that in more than one respect resembled a grave.

The interior was a single room that smelled of rotting foods and dried plants and mystic oils. Other than the door, the only light came from a hole in the roof, which was the size of a plate and covered by a sheet of plastic. Like the front, the walls at the rear and sides, as well as the roof, were planks of rough-hewn cedar. The chinks were filled with something that resembled porridge. In a few places where the calk had fallen out I could see the shiny black of polyethylene, holding back the dirt and moisture. The floor underfoot was hard-packed clay.

Even with the curtain drawn back it was too dark to see things clearly in the rear of the house. A kerosene lantern sat on a low table near the center of the room, but I hesitated to use its unfamiliar system for fear of fire. I blundered about for another minute before I found a candle. The light sprayed the room, giving it the patina of spun flax. The smoke from the candle snaked toward an exit in the ceiling that was both invisible and disconcerting.

Someone had beaten me to the room. It was a mess, the result of a hurried, frantic search. Cans and bottles were tossed aside, books spilled from shelves, wood scattered randomly for me to stumble over. Since I wasn't sure exactly what I was looking for, I fumbled among it all, beginning with the flat pallet that was Billy and Starbright's bed.

The mattress was essentially a bag of dirt and sand, the

blankets a patchwork swatch of everything from flags to gunny sacks. Scattered among the bedding were some threadbare garments but nothing else. There was a second lamp beside the bed, and around it were books that chronicled supernatural occurrences and governmental crimes and nutritive miracles.

In the opposite corner I found some cookware, much of it hand-wrought from maple and walnut, the rest unmatched foundlings that were chipped and cracked and haphazardly repaired. Beside the kitchen corner was a work in progress—a bassinet being woven from strips of bark and leafless willow branches, its hickory frame complete but its sides only partly so. Beyond the baby bed were bottles that smelled of elixirs that I was sure would perform miracles that Starbright would swear to. I opened a small plastic bottle and sniffed and sneezed, then replaced the bottle and scratched the smell out of my nose as best I could.

Except for scattered items of clothing and some decoration in the form of dried weeds and bits of shell and glass and colored fabric, there was little else in the room. The wood-burning stove against one wall was cold and quiet, its ash only that, as far as I could see. I hadn't even found the placenta bowl, which probably meant that Starbright had taken it with her into town.

The lack of treasures of a personal nature in the cave suggested the existence of a hiding place. There didn't seem room for one in the ceiling or the floor, so I felt my way along the walls, alert for something false.

It didn't take long to find. In the back corner, over an area perhaps a yard square, there was a hollow echo behind the cedar when I tapped it. More by feel than sight I located the notch that allowed me to pull the hidden door away and find the nest that held a metal box and something more immediately arresting.

The first thing I pulled out was an M-16, army issue, with a full magazine locked in place and a dozen extra banana clips piled beside its resting place. Even more incredibly, a high pyramid of fragmentation grenades lay beside the rifle clips like a peaceful relic of Indian ritual. Behind the grenades was the stubby menace of a grenade launcher. A brass-topped round was already loaded in its chamber and two just like it lay on the floor. And around it all was a mysterious tangle of wires, heavily insulated, probably the project Starbright had said that Billy had been working on the last morning he'd been alive.

I smelled the muzzle of the rifle and absorbed the whiff of oil, but none of the fragrance was of recent use. I put the rifle back in its place. Was the arsenal the result of paranoia or was it a more reasonable precaution for someone who dealt in dope? I had no way of knowing anything but the vicarious fright that the guns gave off. I sat down on the floor and pulled out the metal box and opened it, suddenly conscious of the heavy earth above and around me on three sides.

The box was full of papers and pictures, of various shapes and sizes and significance. Some were snapshots of Starbright and of Billy, separately and together, Billy looking in each of them as though he had just been wronged. And there were newspaper clippings about Tom Notting and Clark Jaspers, detailing malfeasances I already knew of, one of them also featuring a photograph of a laughing Billy that had obviously been snapped without his knowledge. And then a letter from Seaman Bruce Notting, return address the Great Lakes Naval Training Center.

I started to open the envelope but stopped, because the next item in the box was a legal document, typed, complete with a blue backing stamped with the name and address of Clark Jaspers' law office. I flipped the cover page and read the standard legalisms of a grant deed.

This one transferred, for the consideration of one dollar, receipt of which was acknowledged, all right, title, and interest of the Grantor, Curtis Harold Tanner, in an undivided one-eighth interest in that certain parcel of real property situated in Appanoose County, commonly known as the Tanner plot, full legal description of which is recorded in Book 30, Page 45, of the Appanoose County Index, to William Lyle Tanner, the Grantee, his heirs and assigns, to their use and benefit forever. Dated July 1, 1976. Signed by Curt and Laurel. Legal as hell, or so it looked.

So Billy had owned half of Curt's share of the farm. I looked further into the box.

The rest was junk—notes, letters, pictures, poems, lists of prediction and revelation plucked from sources ranging from the *Book of Mormon* to the *National Enquirer*. But there was nothing to indicate a cause for Billy's murder. I picked up the letter from Bruce to Billy and opened it.

The note was handwritten on dime-store paper, the kind the PX sells. The message was brief: "You did the right thing. I only wish I'd done my part sooner. If it doesn't end, let me know and I'll find a way to stop him myself. Good luck with your plan. Let me know how it comes out. Kiss Starbright and the baby when it comes. You told me how it would be, and it's that way and worse, but better here than there. Sincerely, Bruce." I put the letter back in the box and replaced the panel in the wall and went outside the cave, breathing deeply, thankful to be no longer entombed.

There were a zillion more hiding places outside the house, and I burrowed through some of them as well, gathering a splinter and a scratch in the process, but not much else, my mind half on my random search and half on what if anything Billy's deed meant as to the ultimate disposition of the farm. Over hot humid minutes I probed the stack of hickory logs and the pile of sawdust and shavings beside it, tipped back buckets and rain barrels and peered behind spades and saws, looking for the headwaters of death, finding only creatures that lived beyond the reach of light.

High above me a chicken hawk circled, and above that the white ink of a commercial jet wrote west to east. I watched the invisible finger write and then move on, until it disappeared in the foliage of the tree that shaded Billy's lair. Had I not been attuned by the plane to streams of white I might never have seen it, and even when I stared at it I wasn't sure it was anything to bother with. But there seemed to be a white ring around the tree, a band of unnatural precision high above me, at the fork of two large branches, the left one dead, the right still leafed and fertile.

The tree was an oak, its lowest branch fat and well above my reach. I walked around to the other side. Two boards had been nailed to its trunk, clearly climbing-aids. I placed a foot on one, reached high for the other and pulled myself up. From the bottom step I could reach the lowest branch, and soon my pants were ripped in the seat and my palms were scratched by bark as sharp as ocean coral, but I was sitting in the tree, feet dangling, chest heaving, plotting my route up to the thin white rope that had caught my eye.

I caught my breath and set out for it, smiling as I climbed because of how much fun it was. When I reached my goal I yelled like Tarzan. Then a breeze came up and I held on tightly until it died.

The rope was made of nylon, and when it was at eye level I recognized its purpose. The dead branch in the fork was hollow, and one end of the rope was tied around it so that something on its other end could be lowered into the rotted void within the bark and thus secreted.

I pulled the rope. Whatever it secured was heavy, and partially wedged inside the hollow branch. I pulled again, and then again. The branch shuddered and exhaled dust. And then I had my prize.

It was a plastic bag, black, the size for lawns and leaves, its open end strangled by the rope I pulled to fish it out. Whatever it held was lumpy. I let out some slack, then swung the rope back and forth until the bundle cleared the branches down below, then I let it fall to the ground. I made my way to the bottom branch, locked my legs around it and swung to its underside, then dropped to the ground beside the sack. When I hit the ground I fell forward on my face, which caused the tree to absorb the shot instead of me.

# Chapter
23

The report came from somewhere on the hill to my left, near the trail between the house and the marijuana. As I reached for the bag the rifle cracked again, and a twig next to my foot exploded. I grabbed my booty and scurried behind the tree and took a careful peek.

Someone was moving down the hill toward me in short, jagged bursts of movement, using trees and brush for cover. He was holding his rifle high overhead so as not to snag it. From where I was it looked as big as a bazooka.

I assumed he was alone until I heard him call out to someone on the ridge behind him. I tried but failed to glimpse this or any other confederate the rifleman might have. In a reflex I felt for my revolver, the one I'd left behind in San Francisco, unable to imagine a need for it on the sleepy streets of my hometown.

The gunman moved closer. As long as he was moving I decided to move myself, toward the only weapons that were close at hand.

Another shot rang out as I scampered around the woodpile and into the house. Whatever it hit was left to die behind me. I tossed the bag on the ground and went to the back wall and removed the panel and grabbed the M-16 and checked the clip to be sure it was full, then locked and loaded a round. With its plastic stock and featherweight alloys the weapon felt like a toy in my hands. The house around me seemed part of juvenile antics as well, a cave, a place for hide-and-seek, cowboys and Indians. And with the only exit the filmy curtain across the only door, a trap as well. I picked up the plastic bag and peered around the curtain.

I sensed no further movement on the western slope, but I was conscious that armies could be massed on the ridge behind me without my knowing it. I had to get out of my buried box and the woodpile seemed the best bet. From there I could possibly work my way back up the ridge behind the house, keeping my foes in front of me, and once on the other side run like hell for the car. I let the curtain fall again, picked up three extra ammunition clips off the floor and stuck them in my pockets, then peeked outside again.

The shot nicked the rough wood beside my ear. Chips of cedar raked my cheek like claws. The sound created a vacuum that sucked my breath away. I dropped the bag to the floor and sat beside it, wondering who was out there, wondering what they wanted besides my life.

"Tanner? Hey. Tanner."

The voice was one I knew, the one I suspected it would be. "What do you want, Zedda?"

"I want the bag, man. Toss it out and we go away."

"And if I don't?"

"We take it from you, man. Dead or alive, we take it from you."

I looked at the slick sack on the floor beside me and decided to see what the game was all about. I unknotted the rope and reached through the plastic throat and pulled out money.

Cash. A bundle of it, tied haphazardly with a bit of ragged twine. I dumped the rest of it out, a score or more of money-bricks.

The denominations seemed to range from fives to hundreds, the thickness of the rectangles from one inch to three. There was no way to know how much I had without counting it all. I put the money back in the bag and cinched it up again and cradled my rifle like a child who craved a story, awaiting Zedda's next move, planning my own.

"How about it, Tanner?" The words seemed closer than they had been.

"This is Billy's money, not yours," I yelled back.

"The hell it is. He stole it from me, the bastard. I spent all day out here yesterday, looking for it."

"Where'd it come from?"

"Here and there," Zedda yelled. "What's it matter?"

"Drugs?"

Zedda paused. I heard scrambled sounds of movement. "What if it did?" he said finally.

"Then I think I'll keep it," I said. "I've got a use for it."

"You think I *don't*, man? Toss it out, Tanner. You don't have a chance and you know it."

"Did you kill Billy, Zedda? String him up to make him tell you where the money was?"

"Hell, no. I wish I had, the fucker, but shit. I was never fool enough to go up against *him*. No way."

I heard more noise of movement, the scratchy sounds of brush and weeds. Then I heard voices, indistinct: directions, orders, strategy. And I was in a bag as black and slick and vulnerable as the one that held the money.

"Toss out the bag, man. Now."

"Or what?"

"This."

He riddled the front of the house with bullets. I flattened on the floor, dirt coating my face and lips, tasting of the dry ash of death. Another string of shots rang out, measured, torturing, ambiguous, reminding me of the false volleys that had ended Billy's funeral.

From the sound of it Zedda had a hunting rifle, a thirty-aught-six or so, lever-action. The heavy boards across the face of the house weren't thick enough to stop the shells. They crossed the room above my head and lodged in the back wall in barely perceivable niches. Most of the shots had been high, but the last one had been low enough to knock the lantern off the table. The smell of kerosene erased the rest. I hurried to the iron stove and crouched behind it, trying to figure out what to do besides make a desperate dash for safety, hoping the holes in the wall behind me were not a sieve through which my life would leak.

Time swelled, becoming a physical bulk that pressed me toward the door. I crawled over to the cache of weapons and picked up a grenade and flipped it up and down. It felt like something I should start a game with rather than a war. Then

I put down the grenade and picked up the launcher and locked the brass-topped round inside the chamber. The sights on the stubby barrel seemed set for a close distance, but I could only guess how far. I remembered the shattered farmhouse and knew how Billy had sighted-in the piece. Then I wondered where Billy got the damned thing, and what he planned to do with it. Then I tried to figure out what I could do with it myself. None of the sounds I heard were comforting, including those I made.

"Hey, Tanner."

He was directly overhead now, his voice coming down through the vent in the ceiling, as clear as bird calls over lakes.

"Time's wasting, Tanner." His voice parachuted easily to my ears, under the weight of his confidence. "Make it easy on yourself, man. Toss out the cash and we'll be on our way. No need to make this bloody, man. No need at all."

I put down the launcher, considered whether the rifle could shoot through the roof, and decided it could. I considered whether a blind burst would have much chance of putting Zedda out of action and decided it wouldn't. I picked up the wires that were coiled behind the stack of grenades and tried to figure out if they could help me.

"How much, Tanner?"

"What?"

"How much you want? You found the bag, so I figure I owe you something. So how much?"

"How much is there?"

"Thirty grand, if it's still all there."

"Is anyone else looking for it?"

"You mean the buyer? Hell no. The bread's mine, man. All mine."

"I don't think so," I said. "I think Billy got the dope as well."

Zedda paused. "What if he did? The bread's still mine. I made delivery."

"I want it all," I said.

"What kind of shit is that?"

"I want it all. It was Billy's and he's dead and now it's mine."

"You're fucking up, man. You're half in the grave already down there. Don't make it something permanent."

"If I toss out the money, what happens?"

"You go on up the hill to your little car and we get the bread and go out the back way. Sayonara."

"What's to keep you from shooting me in the back?"

"Not a damned thing, man. But hey. Why would I? I'm a man of peace. Save the whales, you know?"

Zedda's laugh was curdling. I could think of a dozen reasons why he would shoot me down, reasons having to do with money and with the illegal and therefore profitable weed that grew on the next slope over.

I snuggled more securely into the iron womb of my fortified corner. As I shifted position my hand struck something I hadn't seen before, a square metal device of some kind. I looked more closely and saw that it went with the wires, was meant to be hooked to them and to act as a switch of some kind. I attached the bare ends of the wires to the terminals in the device. I had only to press a button to make happen whatever it was that Billy had rigged to happen just before he ran off up the hill, the last time Starbright saw him. Over the next few minutes I thought about everything I knew of Billy and made a guess about what that was.

"Zedda?" I yelled.

"You finally getting smart, man? Let's see the bag."

"How much grass do you have still on the stalk out there, Zedda?"

"Who knows, man. Enough."

"Worth a lot more than thirty grand, right?"

"Yeah. So?"

"So this. If you and your partner out there don't get away from here right now I'm going to destroy your crop."

"Bullshit. How you going to do that from where you are?"

"I've got ways. Now you and your buddy get back to the top of the ridge and climb that big walnut tree there, and when you're up in the top I'll take off and we'll all live happily ever after. Get moving."

"I got no time for bluffs, man. You toss the bag out or guess what."

"What?"

"Some of this."

A second later a fiery sprig of foxtail and thistle and dried twigs drifted down through the vent in the ceiling, trailing smoke behind it. I hurried to stamp out the flames and sneezed during the process, conscious all the while that I was putting all my eggs into a basket I couldn't see and hadn't made.

"Zedda?"

"Yeah."

"See the tree where I found the money?"

"Yeah."

"See the dead sapling about fifty yards beyond it?"

"Yeah."

"Watch."

I pulled the grenade launcher out of the hole in the wall and aimed it out the door and fired in the vicinity of the little tree. Three seconds later the arching shell fell to earth and the sapling vanished behind a roiling cloud of dust and smoke.

"What the fuck was that? Jesus fucking Christ, what you got down there?"

"Grenade launcher."

"Where'd it come from?"

"Right here."

"Billy's?"

"Right. Now, do I lob one of these babies at your weed or not?"

Zedda didn't answer me. When he spoke again the timbre of the words had changed, and he was in control again. "I been checking, Tanner. You ain't got the angle, man. The only way you can get a shot at the weed is to step outside the house. When you do that your ass is mine. So I figure I ain't got that much to worry about. How do you figure?"

"I figure you can kiss your weed good-bye."

I went back to the corner and picked up the little metal switch and pressed the button and blew up the world, or seemed to.

The ground shook and the air trembled from the blast. Since I wasn't sure what I had done, I peeked out the door. Beyond the ridge, above the spot where the marijuana had been growing, a gray-green pod of dust spread slowly toward the sky, its vaporous texture laced with solid bits of green and brown, its thick essence expanding as it rose.

"You fuck! What the hell did you do? Jesus Christ."

Zedda was off and running toward the cloud. From the field beyond the money tree another figure ran away from me as well, toward the salad that Billy's Claymore mines had made of Zedda's crop.

My guess was that just before he died Billy had mined the field, intending to blow it up himself. He obviously never got the chance, but when I triggered the firing mechanism the hundreds of thousands of steel pellets had reduced the weed to shredded dust. Justice, Tanner-style. I grabbed the bag of money and the M-16 and headed back toward my car. The last thing I heard before I topped the hill was Zedda's mournful curse.

# Chapter
# 24

I drove to the nearest town with a bank and deposited the money in a new account. The teller gave me and my horde of cash a wrinkled look until I told her I had recently auctioned off my great-aunt's place over in the next county, furniture and knick-knacks and farm machinery and all, even her set of china, and of course because of the times I had insisted all sales be cash only. I thought that was wisest, didn't she, even though I might have missed top dollar on a few items. She agreed with me completely. You couldn't be too careful, not these days, why she could tell me stories . . . And then she tuned me out and gave me some temporary checks in a folder with a picture of some amber waves of grain on the front and a pamphlet describing the many services the bank offered, which I would never use. On my way back to Chaldea I concocted a series of good deeds that would satisfy no one as much as me.

When I got to the hotel I called the airline and made a reservation for the next morning's flight to San Francisco. Then I packed up and checked out and drove to the old motel out on the highway east of town and registered under the name of Nick Carraway. When I was settled in I phoned Ed Buckles, the young lawyer Clark Jaspers had recommended. He told me he was pretty busy just now, and he thought we should have the conversation in person, but he listened silently to everything I had to say before he tried to tell me a better way to do it. It took almost an hour to get it all lined up, and I had to promise him I'd be at his office the first thing in the morning to look things over before I left town, and sign the papers and all, but when I hung up I felt confident that Buckles would structure the kind of arrangement I wanted, and that it would do the things I wanted it to do.

Then I telephoned Starbright at WILD. "I'm leaving town tomorrow," I told her. "I just wanted to remind you you can call me anytime you need anything. Anything at all."

"Okay. Thanks." Her voice was as placid as ever, the prospect of future difficulty as ominous as the next sunrise.

"And I think you'll be hearing from Curt, Billy's father. I mean, I think he'll offer to help you and the baby, if you need it. He's already done one thing, Starbright. He established a trust fund for the baby. The trustee is a man named Buckles, a lawyer here in town. He can pay you some of the income from the trust anytime you need it, to take care of the baby; food or clothes or toys or whatever. He can send the money to wherever you are. Depending on interest rates and things, it could amount to about twenty-five hundred dollars a year."

"Wow. That's heavy."

"And the principal and any income not previously distributed will be paid to your child when he turns eighteen. There should be at least twenty thousand dollars then. Maybe more. It can help pay for college, maybe."

"That's neat. Thanks."

"Thank Curt. He'll probably pretend he doesn't know anything about it, but don't you believe him. Okay?"

"Okay."

"Also, don't tell Zedda anything about the money. Don't even tell him you talked to me. Okay?"

"Okay. But why?"

"Zedda's a bit upset with me right now. He's going to be coming on some hard times, I think, and my advice is for you to get away from there as soon as you can. I'm not telling you what to do or anything, but I think you and the baby can do better elsewhere. Maybe even back in Dubuque."

"Not there."

"Well, somewhere. Will you think about it?"

"I guess. Zedda's been acting weird lately. I think he's hypoglycemic."

"Tamara is going to leave, I think. Maybe you could go with her."

"Maybe," Starbright said ambiguously.

"Just do me one favor, okay? Let Curt and Laurel know where you end up. And me, too. Okay?"

"Okay."

"I'll see you, Starbright."

"See you."

"Good luck."

"You, too."

"I think you're going to have a real nice baby."

"Yeah. Me, too. I can't wait." She paused. "Mr. Tanner?"

"Yes?"

"What about the name? I mean, do you think I have to name him Giap?"

"No."

"Good. I'm going to name him Billy. William Pisces Tanner. What do you think?"

"I think that's real nice."

"Bye, Mr. Tanner."

"Bye."

I listened to the buzz of a dead line for a moment, thinking of Billy and of babies, then made another call. "Marsh Tanner, Norm," I said when he answered.

"How are you, Marsh?"

"Good. Listen. I think we're about to reach a decision on the farm. And I think the city may get part of it for the industrial park. A long-term lease arrangement of some kind, probably."

"Hey. Great. That's just great."

"No guarantees yet, Norm. But there's one condition I want to impose, if that's the way it works out."

"Yeah? What's that?"

His words carried hints of kickbacks and side letters and double sets of books. I hurried to set him straight. "I want you to be sure they give Chuck Hasburg a job, whatever kind of business goes in there. A good job, too."

Gladbrook laughed. "Well, that's not what I expected you to say, I'll tell you that. Chuck, huh?"

"Right."

"Okay. No problem. Chuck'll shape up again when he gets something to do before dark."

"This is just between us, Norm."

"Right. Sure. No problem. You and Chuck were real buddies in the old days, weren't you?"

"Yes, we were."

"He'll hate your guts if he ever finds out about this," Gladbrook said.

"I know."

Gladbrook waited for me to say something else. "Is that it, then?" he asked after a minute. "Chaldea won't forget what you've done, Marsh. Thanks again."

"There is one more thing."

"What's that?"

"I heard about the problem between Zedda and your daughter, Norm. I'm sorry."

Gladbrook didn't say anything for a long time. I had opened an old wound and I was listening to its silent bleeding. "What's that got to do with anything?" Gladbrook asked finally, his anger like a noose around his throat.

"I was just wondering if you blamed my nephew Billy for any of that, Norm."

"Billy? Why would I do that?" His bemusement seemed genuine.

"I thought maybe because Billy used to hang out at WILD once in a while that you might think he was part of what happened."

"No." The word was hot. "Zedda was the one. And I'm not through with him yet, either. I'll get him out of Chaldea for good, one way or another. You can bet the ranch on it."

"I think he'll be a little easier to move right now," I said, my mind on the cloud of tattered plants I'd seen a few hours earlier. "Been nice talking to you, Norm."

"Yeah."

When I called Gail she told me Matt hadn't left town yet, but he planned to leave in about an hour. I asked her to try to get everyone together at her place in thirty minutes. She said she'd try, and asked me what was going on. I told her I was ready to vote. She asked me what I was going to do, but I evaded answering and told her good-bye and called Sally Stillings.

"I was hoping you'd call, Marsh," she said, her voice straining to be as gay as she thought I wanted her to be.

"This is just to say good-bye, Sally. I'm leaving in the morning."

"Oh."

"It was nice seeing you, Sally."

"Why do you have to go?"

"I've got a living to make, for one thing. Such as it is. And I think my business here is finished, or will be by the end of the day."

"Can I see you tonight?" Her voice was small, a whisper of loneliness.

"I don't think so, Sally. I've got some things to take care of."

"What kind of things?"

"Family things. Billy things."

"Oh." I heard her breathe or sigh. "Can I drive you to the airport tomorrow? Please? So we can talk?"

I sighed, too. "Okay. Pick me up at Gail's at nine."

"I'll be there. And I'll be *here* tonight, Marsh, if you want me."

"Don't count on me, Sally."

"Don't worry. I know you're not there, either." Sally replaced her phone. I steeled my mind against thoughts of her or us.

My next call took twenty minutes to complete. The Great Lakes Training Center might have been in Siberia for all the time it took. Finally a young man picked up a phone and said, "Seaman Notting speaking, sir."

"Bruce. This is Marsh Tanner. Your uncle. Maybe you remember when we met in San Francisco a few years back."

"Sure. How are you, sir?"

His voice was hesitant, anticipating calamity. As I considered how to proceed, Bruce spoke again. "Is anything wrong? Is it about Dad?"

"Nothing's wrong, Bruce," I said quickly. "I didn't mean to frighten you. Your dad and mom are fine."

"Good. I mean, I figured they were. I mean, well, long distance and everything. I get kind of scared."

"I know. Me, too. How's it going with the navy?"

"Okay. You know. Some good, some bad. Kind of depends on the people."

"I'm an old army man myself."

"Yeah? Well, my feet aren't so hot, so I thought I'd float my way through, but as it turns out I spend eight hours a day standing in a supply depot handing out dehydrated eggs and stuff."

"That's the military."

"I guess. I may get assigned to Japan next year. Sure hope so."

"Did you know Billy was dead, Bruce? Billy Tanner?"

He gasped. "Billy? Jesus. No."

"Your folks didn't tell you?"

"No. I . . . no."

"Didn't they know you and Billy were friends?"

"Not exactly."

"You *were* friends, weren't you?"

"Yeah. I mean, just before I joined up we were pretty close. I liked him a lot, despite some of the things he did. How did he die, Mr. Tanner?"

"It wasn't pretty."

"He was killed, wasn't he?"

"I think so. Why do you?"

"I was afraid that would happen. Damn it. I warned him, too. Was it Zedda?"

"I don't know for sure, but I don't think so."

"Then who was it?" He was clearly surprised at my exoneration of Zedda. I was kind of surprised myself.

"I think I'll know more by tonight," I said. "Meanwhile, what happened between you and your dad, Bruce? What caused the fight?"

"Who said there was a fight?"

"Come on, Bruce. I'm family. And I won't tell anyone what you say. Not even your parents."

"What difference does it make, though?"

"There are strange things going on here, Bruce. Billy's death is one, but there are other things, too. Such as the way Billy seemed to be out to get certain people lately. Such as what Zedda was doing behind the WILD front. I'm trying to sort through it all, to learn who killed Billy and why. I think your fight with your dad may have something to do with it."

"Why do you think that?"

"I don't know. I just do."

Bruce paused. I heard chatter and clatter in the background.

"I want you to get whoever killed Billy, Mr. Tanner," he said. "But my dad didn't have anything to do with it. I know that much. I mean, even if Billy . . . he just wouldn't. I know it."

"I don't think your dad killed Billy, Bruce. But he was up to something, and I think you found out about it, and confronted him with it, and that's what caused the fight. What was it?"

Bruce didn't say anything. The long minute twisted slowly around my mind, numbing it. "He's my dad, Mr. Tanner. I can't say anything bad about him. And anyway, I think he's stopped. He said he would."

"Stopped what?"

"Nothing. I can't talk anymore. This petty officer's giving me the evil eye. He already thinks I'm a goof-off."

"Okay, Bruce. Thanks anyway. And good luck. Maybe you'll be stationed near San Francisco someday and we can get together."

"I hope so. I sure liked it out there when we came to visit. They still rent roller skates in the park?"

"I think so."

"I'll see you, Mr. Tanner."

"Okay, Bruce. Sorry I asked those questions about your dad. You were right not to tell me."

Bruce said good-bye and went back to his powdered eggs. I felt dehydrated myself, and it would take more than water to get me whole. I found the pint in my suitcase and drained it from the bottle, then picked up the phone again. Arnie Keene sounded weary of mind and soul and body. I told him I needed to see him.

"When?"

"Now."

"Why? What about?" Arnie started to ask another question and then stopped.

"Is Ann there, Arnie?"

"Yes."

"Can we meet somewhere?"

"I suppose. If we have to."

"We do. How about the high school? You still live near there?"

"Same place."

"Okay. I'll see you under the north goalpost in ten minutes."

# Chapter 25

The field was crowned and freshly clipped, the yard lines striped with chalk as white and fluffy as a line of cocaine. Scarlet and black streamers flew from the tops of the goalposts, which had been wrapped like barber poles with similar strands as well. At the fifty-yard line the thrones for the Homecoming King and Queen had been set in place. Above the royal chairs a banner urged GO BIG REDS. I had an urge to take the field and look for someone to knock down.

Inside the auditorium beyond the field the band began the school song and the half-thousand voices at the pep rally sang it vigorously:

> Scarlet and Black, Hip, Hip, Hurray;
> Scarlet and Black flies high today.
> Everyone be on your guard,
> For the game is mighty hard.
> Fight, fight, fight, fight;
> Fight with all your might.

And after the song the throng voiced a familiar chant:

> We're from Chaldea, and we
> Couldn't be prouder.
> If you can't hear us,
> We'll yell a little louder.

I listened to it all with pleasure until Arnie Keene came up quietly behind me on turf that would soon cushion the fall of padded boys. His morose countenance was a perfect counter to my wistful mood.

"What's this all about, Marsh?" Arnie asked as I turned toward him. His eyes met mine, then jumped away to the school building, then jumped back. The wind snapped the streamers above us, mimicking the high quick pops of far-off weapons.

"The first thing it's about is that little song and dance you performed at my parents' grave," I said.

"What do you mean?" Fear congealed like gelatin in his eyes and clouded them. For a moment I felt sorry for him.

"You were trying to tell me something, weren't you, Arnie? You were trying to tell me that you and my mother were having an affair, weren't you?"

"I . . ."

"Weren't you?"

His eyes stayed fixed on the lush green grass. "Yes. I was. That is, we were. I . . . It didn't last long. Not actively. But we were. Yes. I was trying to find a way to tell you, but I wasn't brave enough."

"You were trying to tell me something else, too, weren't you? Something more than that."

"Yes."

"You were trying to tell me that this *argument* you speculated they were having—this distraction that caused my father to drive off the road and into a tree—this argument was about you. Isn't that right? You think they were arguing about you when they were killed."

"God help me. That's what I think. Yes." His voice held twenty-five years of horror.

"What happened? Did my mother tell you she was going to bring it out in the open? Confess all to my dad? Did you know that was the night for that little scene?"

He looked at the gilded thrones. "We'd been seen. She wanted to tell him before someone else in town did. But you have to know the rest. She told me she wasn't going to see me again. Not in that way. She was going to stay with your father. I wanted to marry her, you see, but she wouldn't. So it was over, really. That's what makes it so absurd."

I didn't say anything.

"What do you want from me, Marsh? I'm not sure I can add anything."

"Oh, I don't want you to add anything, Arnie. You've queered the past for me quite enough already."

"How do you mean?"

"You know damned well how I mean. I mean from now on every time I think of her I'll think of the two of you sneaking around behind my father's back, acting out your little appassionata while poor dumb Dad lived in ignorant bliss and all the town was laughing at him."

"It wasn't like that, Marsh. Not at all."

"So you say, Arnie. I'm sure I don't know what it was like, but I doubt if you do, either, by now. It was like whatever you want it to have been like. That's what memory does for you."

"No, Marsh. Please. It was good. It was, well, pure, if you will. At least till the very end. I thought you'd understand." Arnie's hand reached for me and I moved away.

"I didn't know either of you well enough back then to understand," I said. "But it's not important."

I thought I smiled, but from Arnie's reaction it must have been a sneer. "I'm going to return the favor now, Arnie. That's why I got you out here."

"What do you mean?"

"You gave me a little nugget to carry around inside my gut, so I'm going to give you one just like it. Or almost."

"I still don't understand," Arnie said, frowning. "Is it something about Grace?"

"No, it's not about Grace. Don't mention her name again."

He nodded rapidly.

I walked slowly around the goalpost, fingering the crepe paper that masked it, feeling the tug of youth and the urge to do it over, to make it right. Then I saw the thrones and the urge collapsed, because there's no way it can ever be right. I had thought that my return to Chaldea might reveal something that would explain or even excuse some of the things I was and unfortunately was not. But it hadn't done anything of the kind, of course. It had just reminded me that those days were worse than I remembered, not better, and that the search for excuses is endless and therefore worthless.

"This isn't my town anymore, Arnie," I began abruptly. "I

don't know what goes on, what the problems are and aren't. But you do, presumably. I mean, everyone always wondered why a smart guy like you stayed around Chaldea when you obviously could have done other things in other places. Though I guess now I know one reason why you stayed, don't I?"

"If you mean your mother, then yes."

"Okay. I've been nosing around the last few days, trying to find out who killed my nephew Billy. And the first thing I learned was that Billy had a lot of enemies in Chaldea."

"That's true," Arnie said. "At least, that's what I heard."

"But there was one group of men who especially had cause to resent Billy. He'd picked them out for special treatment for some reason, had tried his best to destroy them, or so it seemed."

"You mean like Tom."

"Right. And Chuck Hasburg, and Clark Jaspers, and maybe the extension man, too, whoever that is."

"I heard the stories. It did seem Billy was engaged in some sort of vendetta."

"Right. So after I learned what Billy had done to these men I tried to find a common link. And eventually I did."

"What was it?"

"The war. They all had something to do with Vietnam, at least all but the extension man. I didn't have time to find out much about him. But Chuck was on the draft board, and Clark prosecuted draft resisters, and Tom got the mayor's son out of combat duty by using political pull, and so forth. So I thought Billy's crusade was some kind of war protest. Revenge. But one thing bothered me."

"What?"

"Why did he wait so long? His attacks on these people started only within the last year or so, as near as I can figure. Ten years after Billy was in the war. So why did he wait so long?"

"I don't know. Why?" Arnie fidgeted, scraping at his hollowed cheeks with tapered fingers as gray and rigid as dead boughs.

"Because the link between those men didn't have anything to do with the war at all. That was just coincidental. Billy went after them for another reason entirely."

"What?"

I knelt in the end zone and ran my fingers through the grass, remembering the Bloomfield game and the gang of students who had pummeled me when I made the winning score. Maybe that was as good as it had gotten for me. Maybe I was like Chuck Hasburg and didn't know it. Maybe life was the same for everyone. I stood up and looked at Arnie Keene's haggard face. "Do you know anything about the drug problem in this town, Arnie? With kids, especially?"

He thought for a minute and shrugged. "Not much. It seems to have gotten worse lately, but no one really talks that much about it. There seem to be lots of kids just hanging around, dabbling in religious cults or the like, waiting for someone to tell them what to do with their lives, I know that much. Why?"

"You know a guy named Zedda?"

"He heads that nature group, doesn't he? WILD?"

"Right. Except it's not a nature group, it's a wholesale marijuana business. For several years Zedda has had several acres of marijuana under cultivation out on our farm. Billy was the guardian of the crop. He and his girlfriend lived out there near it."

"You must be kidding."

"No, I'm not. Now the rest of this is guesswork. I doubt if I could prove it in court without getting lucky and without spending a lot more time in Chaldea, which I definitely don't want to do. But I hope I won't *have* to prove it. That's where you come in."

Arnie rubbed his face again. I remembered how nervous he'd always gotten in school when kids had acted up. They'd called him Arnie the Twitch in those days, behind his back, but not very far behind. "I don't understand this, Marsh," he said slowly. "What do I have to do with it?"

"I don't know why Billy agreed to get involved with the dope, Arnie. I suppose he figured he owed Zedda something for opening his eyes about the war, and he probably didn't think marijuana was all that bad anyway, given the general state of inebriation of most of the adults around town. In any event, Billy agreed to keep the crop safe from intruders as long as Zedda sold only to outside buyers. Chicago. KC. St. Louis.

And I think that's the way it went for several years, in the beginning."

"Then what happened?"

"Then Zedda got busted on a rape charge and hired Clark Jaspers to defend him. Now, Clark by his own admission resented this town for a long time because of the way various people reacted to his handicap. He came back to town determined to show people what he could do, that he was just as good as any of us and maybe better. But for a long time it didn't work out that way. His practice wasn't all that rewarding financially, which is the usual measure of success in this town. So Clark was looking for a way to make a splash. Then there was Tom Notting. At about the same time Tom had just been dumped out of office by the city fathers, who had tapped some young Turk as their candidate for assessor instead of Tom. So Tom was mad. And there was Chuck Hasburg, who'd failed at a whole series of jobs and whose life had never measured up to his high school athletic exploits, at least in the eyes of other people. So you have those three men, plus maybe the extension man and some others, nursing resentments and needing money."

"I still don't understand, Marsh. What are you saying happened?"

"I think Clark and the others set up a local drug network. I think in exchange for getting Zedda off on the rape charge Clark got first shot at all the marijuana he could move. Chuck didn't have a job, so he had plenty of time to deal the dope. Tom worked with the Scouts, so he had access to the younger customers. I think Tom even faked an illness of his own so he could get tranquilizers and other drugs to deal along with the pot. I think these guys set up a sales organization, and sooner or later Billy found out about it and wanted them to stop and when they didn't he took out after them. That's the link. Not the war. The drugs."

"This is all fantastic, Marsh."

"I know."

"I can't really believe it."

"I can't either. But I'm pretty sure Tom and Gail's son Bruce found out about it, too. He and Tom had a fight before Bruce went off to the navy and I think that was the cause. But the point is, Arnie, you don't *have* to believe it. Not yet."

"What do you mean?"

"I destroyed Zedda's crop this morning. And we're going to lease out the farm so it will be hard for him or anyone to do anything out there in secret anymore. So I think Zedda will split pretty soon, and the drug scene will die down to normal. If that's what happens you can just forget everything I've said, pretend it never happened. But if the drug situation doesn't improve, if it's still a major problem in town, then you can talk to Tom and Chuck and Clark, tell them what you know, tell them they'd better cool it or you'll go to the sheriff."

"You mean I get to play God."

"Something like that."

"But if it all ends soon and Zedda leaves town?"

"You let bygones be bygones, and I do, too."

Arnie walked to the goalpost and leaned against it, his head cradled in his arm. "Are you saying this group killed Billy, Marsh? Zedda or one of the others? Tom? Or Chuck?"

"No. I thought so for a while, but I don't anymore."

"Why not?"

"Because of the way Billy died. Because they found him hanging from a goddamned tree."

# Chapter
# 26

When I pulled to a stop in front of Gail's house Matt's Lincoln was already in the drive. Pilar was sitting on the passenger's side, erect and motionless, a monument to impatience and disdain. I hurried past her rudeness and let myself into the house.

Curt was folded into the couch and Matt was pacing the floor, much as they had been the last time we met. Matt's outfit was by Bruce of Beverly Hills; Curt's by Oshkosh B'Gosh. "Let's get this show on the road," Matt said. "Pilar's booked into the Holiday Inn in Urbana tonight. She gets docked if she's late."

"This will only take a few minutes," I said, "if you all agree with my proposal. Then you can be on your way."

"I suppose you're going to tell us what to do with the farm," Matt said, his lips knotted in a practiced sneer.

"That's right. That's exactly what I'm going to do." I went over to the couch in the wake of Matt's grumble and sat beside Curt and asked him how he was doing.

"Okay, I guess. Laurel's feeling better."

"Great."

"She went up to Marshalltown to stay with her people for a while. Seemed like the best thing."

Curt's blue eyes seemed to have kindled overnight, the icy deadness melted by something known only to him, if anyone.

I patted his thick shoulder. "You listen to what I've got to say about the farm, Curt. If any of it bothers you, let me know."

"Sure, Marsh. Don't make much difference to me what we do. Not now."

"You hear anything from that deprogrammer character?"

"Him? No."

"Good. You let me know if he hassles you."

"Marsh, I can look out for myself. It's best you get that straight, I think."

The words were forged on the iron will I had always associated with my brother. Curt was Curt again. I smiled for what seemed like the first time since I'd hit Chaldea. "One more thing," I said to him. "I know about the deed you gave Billy. I know he owned half your interest in the farm."

Curt nodded. "I almost forgot I did that. Thought it would make him settle down. Like spit in the ocean, was what it amounted to."

Just then Gail entered from the kitchen, toting lemonade and cookies. As she passed them out I looked at my parents' furniture that occupied the room along with us more animate survivors. None of the others seemed at all interested, and I wondered if I would have been making the inspection had I not learned of our mother and Arnie Keene.

I ignored my father's things, which were uninteresting in any event. He was not an imaginative man, a trait he had passed on to me. He was merely a worker, tireless, intrepid, serene—traits he had passed on to Curt and Gail. There aren't many workers around anymore, perhaps because work is now as often ridiculed as praised.

It was my mother's sense I sought, and it was not in her collection of silver spoons or in the sprigs of flora and feathers she arranged. Perhaps it was in the fine line drawings she had done in college, the precise still lifes, the pencil portraits of smiling friends, the looser splash of rural landscapes. Or not in the drawings themselves so much as in the fact that as far as I knew she had drawn not another line after the day she married.

My eyes drifted from the drawings to the only photograph in the room, the one that had been the unofficial family portrait. The six of us were knee-deep in yellow grass, the Tetons looming like a dream behind us, our faces grinning self-consciously at the behest of the obliging stranger who had pressed the button on the Brownie. My mother's face was round and soft and white, from avoiding sun the way she avoided arguments. She had claimed at least once in my hearing to be the luckiest woman in the world. Now that seemed a lie, a mask for an ache to escape, for a resentment of many things, including me.

I looked away, remembering how she had surreptitiously comforted me after Dad had laid the quirt across my legs, remembering her kitchen treats and tortures, the cold tongue sandwiches and walnut brownies, the sauerkraut and lemon meringue pie. And her presence at Scouts and Sunday school and ball games. And how she looked when dressed for a party or an Elks Club dance, her hair and heels raised high, her dress wide and swishing above ridiculous mysterious garments, her eyes and voice eager to go to where the host of revelers would have included Arnie Keene.

"Hey." Matt's word broke my crystal reverie like a brick. "Come on. What's the great plan?"

I abandoned the role of son and took up the easier role of brother. "This is what I think we should do," I began, eyeing each of them in turn, receiving wary skepticism from all but Curt. "I've tried to take everything into account, and I'm sure none of you will be completely satisfied. But I think all of you will be satisfied at least a little."

"I'll bet," Matt mumbled, attracting a frown from Gail.

"First, the coal people. They're out. I don't think we should let a strip mine go in right on the edge of Chaldea. They say they'll put the land back into farm production when they're through, but if they don't, we'd have to sue them and it would cost more than it's worth even if we won. So coal's out."

"No problem," Matt said, and Curt nodded.

"Oil's out, too," I went on, looking at Matt.

"Shit."

"I've looked into Cosmos and they don't seem quite on the up and up. I think they want to sit on the mineral rights, not drill for oil. Wait for a technological breakthrough that will make it profitable to extract oil from coal. The Cosmos man told me they insist on getting all subsurface rights, not just petroleum, and they won't agree that we can farm the surface. They're wheeler-dealers, and I think we ought to keep away."

"Goddamnit it, Marsh," Matt said. "If they hit oil out there we'll be rich. I mean real money, not nickel-and-dime stuff. I mean—"

"There's no oil down there, Matt. Curt knows it and I know it."

Curt nodded silently.

"How the hell would *he* know?" Matt said. "Or you, either."

"Because Billy told him. Right?"

Curt nodded again. "He said he heard them talking. Told me not to sell out to them. Said they were crooks."

"The way I hear it, Billy was so stoned all the time he probably hallucinated the whole thing." Matt's laugh was cruel and was meant to be.

"Matt, goddamnit," I said. "If you don't shut up I'll go into the little side deal you tried to cut for yourself with Mr. Beech."

"You son of a bitch."

"Maybe so. But Cosmos is out."

"Let's hear the rest," he grumbled.

I looked at the others again. They seemed entranced, afraid to ask questions and afraid not to. I hurried on above my mounting eagerness to flee.

"Agribusiness is out, too, mostly because it means selling the land. I don't think we should sever that link, particularly the outsiders like Matt and me. And agribusiness wouldn't help the town that much. A couple of men and a bunch of big machines is the way they work, with all the profits going to Illinois."

"So what's left?" Matt asked. "I mean, now that you've made sure I'll take a bath on my mobile-home deal, what have you decided to do with the fucking place? Give it to UNICEF? Donate it to that crazy hippie outfit? WILD or whatever they call it?"

"You're not going to take a bath, Matt."

"Yeah, well, I got to come up with ten grand by next week. So far you've eliminated everyone with that kind of money."

"I've been talking to a lawyer in town named Ed Buckles. There's a thing called the Tanner Trust I've set up. Among other things the trust is going to acquire ten units of your

Caravan Towers at a thousand bucks apiece. So that should get you past the first call. Right, Matt?"

Matt frowned, unable to find pleasure in even this. "What the hell is this trust? I never heard of it."

"Just something I put together."

"So you were lying about having no bucks. I figured as much."

I turned to Gail. "What we're going to do with the farm is rent it out. No sale."

"Rent it to who?" she asked uneasily.

"Three people. First, the city. We enter a ninety-nine-year lease with them for the twenty acres nearest the road. We also give them a five-year option on another twenty contiguous acres. If they haven't attracted enough business to use the additional parcel in five years, then they forfeit it. The rent will depend on what they get from whatever business they get to go in there, plus maybe a flat fee to keep them humping to get off the hook. Buckles will negotiate the details for us. That's one part of it."

"What else?" Gail asked.

"The rest of the farm is split down the middle. We give the neighboring farmer, Waiters, a five-year share arrangement on the same basis he has now—half and half. After five years he has to make other arrangements. We get it in writing, so he knows that ultimately he has to leave, but he has time to do it. Then the other half goes to Karen and Paul. They farm it on the same basis—half and half. After five years they can farm it all. Waiters claims he's a good farmer. If he is, then Karen and Paul can learn from him. If he isn't, all the more reason to get him off after five years. And that's basically it."

No one said anything. Not a single thing. I got up and went over to the spoon collection and looked at one. It was engraved with the initial T and was badly tarnished on the bottom. The silence at my back pressed me like a winter wind. "There's one more thing," I said after a while.

"What?"

"The rents. Matt, I assume you want your share sent to you in Chicago."

"Damned right I do."

"Gail? How about you?"

"I don't know. Sent here to the house, I guess."

"Can I get even more pushy than I have already?"

"Sure. I guess."

"We're doing something for Karen by leasing out the farm to her and Paul. Maybe you should consider giving a portion of your share of the rents to Bruce. He's not exactly getting rich on seaman's pay. And you can give ten thousand a year to someone now without paying gift tax. So think it over."

"I will. I'll talk to Tom about it."

"Tom and Bruce aren't getting along so well just now. Maybe you should just decide what's fair and do it."

"I . . . maybe I will. Don't push me, Marsh."

I turned to Curt. "Curt gave Billy a half interest in his share. Billy and Starbright weren't married, but I think she could make a good claim that she's entitled to succeed to that share under the laws of intestate succession. She and the baby. The question is, are you going to make her sue you to get the share, or will you just give it to her?"

"She can have it," Curt said softly, his voice surprisingly firm. "Billy would want it to go to her."

"I've set it up so you can have your share paid to Buckles, the lawyer, and then he can send half to Starbright and half to you and Laurel. Be easier to do it that way, and it won't cost you anything. Buckles' expenses will come out of the trust."

"I don't get this trust business," Matt said. "Is it some kind of tax dodge or what?"

"Something like that. Dodging guilt, is more like it."

"Jesus. I haven't felt guilty since I stole all Marcy Stovall's valentines in the fourth grade."

I believed him. "So that's it," I said. "The land stays in the family, we help the town a little, we get a bit of money every year in rent and, if things change at a later date, we can always do something else. Any objections?"

"Sounds to me like you think you know what we need more than we do," Matt said. "Typical liberal crap."

"Are you voting no, Matt? Because if you are, that trust doesn't have any interest at all in making an investment in high-rise mobile-home parks."

"I'm not saying no," Matt said quickly. "I'm just saying I don't like being preached to by my younger brother."

"I took enough of it from you in the old days," I said. "You can stand a little now."

"I wish Karen and Paul could get it all, Marsh," Gail said

"They will in five years. All but the share the city has. We reserve an easement so the city has to give access to the rest of the farm, by the way, so there's no way Karen will be cut off from the road. I think there's some kind of back way in there anyway, so it's not a big problem."

"But times are so hard, Marsh. Five years may be too late."

"Times are hard for Waiters, too, Gail. He told me he almost doubled the yield out there since he took over. I don't think we should just throw him off overnight. Curt? How about you?"

"It sounds okay with me, Marsh."

"You sure?"

"Yep."

"Then I tell Buckles to go ahead and prepare the papers?"

Three heads nodded, one of them reluctantly. "When do get my money?" Matt asked.

"Middle of next week."

"Okay." Matt moved to the door. "I got to blow this pop stand. See you when I see you. It's been nice."

And he was gone.

"Curt?"

"Yeah, Marsh?"

"I'm leaving in the morning. It's been good to see you."

"You, too."

"I'm sorry about Billy."

"I know."

"I may find out something about his death before I leave If I do, do you want to know?"

"No. Not unless I have to. No."

"Okay." I hesitated, then asked Curt another question. "You know that psalm the minister read at the funeral? The one right before the rifle salute?"

"I guess so. Why?"

"Did you and Laurel pick it out or did the minister?"

Curt shrugged. "The minister, I guess. I don't know much about it. I didn't hear a word he said, to tell you the truth."

I nodded and slapped Curt on the shoulder once again and stood up. "Gail? Thanks for everything. I'll bring your car by in the morning early. Say good-bye to Tom for me."

"Don't you want me to take you to the airport, Marsh?"

"Sally said she'd do it. I guess she wants to talk."

"Oh. Well. Okay."

"Call me next week, Gail. Tell me how things are."

"Maybe I will."

"It'll all get better, Gail. Really, it will."

"If you say so, Marsh."

"There's no law that says you have to be unhappy, Gail. That says things have to stay the way they are. Try to keep that in mind, okay?"

"Okay."

I kissed my sister and left her house, feeling purer than I had a right to feel.

# Chapter
# 27

The church spire reached high toward a divinity that lay beyond the clouds. The stained-glass circle above the door portrayed the Son of God as teacher, shepherd, healer, priest. The wooden doors were open as Tamara had predicted. I swung them wide and entered the sanctuary.

The altar and pulpit were sheets of heavy walnut, the pews slick oak, the walls imperiled plaster, and the polished crucifix a golden source of awe and wonder above the silver altar candles. A current of cool air blew through the chapel, but my memory was of other days in another church, when heat had visited the room as mightily as the preacher's promise of God's own wrath. I closed my eyes and enjoyed the tranquil absence of the Lord's bureaucracy.

Long minutes of weightless time went by. I spent them imagining a sumptuous form of afterlife I didn't believe existed. As though on cue, I heard an organ's singing tones, played with an almost pagan passion. I went through a door near the rear of the sanctuary and entered the Sunday school room and saw the man I had come to see.

He sat like a frenzied conjurer at the small electric organ, hair flying, shoulders bobbing, his being inseparable from the pulsing rhythms of the music. His fingers pressed juice from the ivory keys, as though a thousand pipes lay subject to his chords. I listened with pleasure to the piece, as its familiar notes danced nimbly among the metal folding chairs that were the only witnesses besides myself.

After the final chord had fled, the minister slumped wearily on his bench as though he lacked the strength to move. Then he gulped a block of air, shook his blond head quickly, and stood. His bright eyes struck me like a spark. His smile was quick and real. "I didn't realize I had an audience," he said bashfully. "I hope it wasn't painful."

"I enjoyed it. You must play often."

The compliment pleased him and he showed it. "Not often enough to do justice to Bach, I'm afraid. But it picks me up. My drug of choice, you might say," he added with a boyish grin.

"Only Bach?"

"Oh, no. I've been known to wax positively ecstatic during a Springsteen album, but I try to confine that particular variety of religious experience to the manse."

"It is still the big place on Blaine Avenue?"

He nodded. "Do you know it?"

"I was there once, for some kind of youth meeting. At some point in the evening I snuck away. I hope the place has been painted since."

"Oh, yes. The congregation does the best it can. The heat bills are the killer. It's so large and drafty. Last February our utility bill was over three hundred dollars. Fortunately, it doesn't come out of my stipend." He smiled like a kid with a secret again, then peered closely at me with narrowed eyes. "You were at the funeral, weren't you?"

I nodded. "I'm Marsh Tanner. Billy's uncle. I should have introduced myself at the cemetery but . . ."

He waved a small pink hand. "It's all right. I don't feel comfortable myself exchanging pleasantries over an open grave." He smiled again, looking even younger than his years, which I guessed were thirty-five. "I'm Gary Vesselton. How can I help you?"

"I was struck by the psalm you read at the funeral. The last one."

"Yes? What about it?"

"Not a common choice."

"No."

"Select it yourself?"

"Yes."

I didn't say anything else and the Reverend Vesselton didn't volunteer. The traffic outside performed a raucous fugue of its own. The air in the church seemed suddenly to have lost the cool breeze of piety.

"What are we doing, Mr. Tanner?" the minister asked at last. "Has it something to do with Billy?"

"Billy was murdered, Reverend."

He registered no surprise, only interest. "The paper said suicide."

"The paper is run by Mary Martha Gormley. She happens to be very interested in seeing to it that nothing frightening happens in this town at the moment. So as not to scare off a potential employer."

The reverend nodded. "She *has* been known to sacrifice accuracy for her concept of the greater good. Are you the detective, Mr. Tanner?"

I admitted it.

"Billy told me about you once. He admired you, as much as he admired anyone. He saw you as an antiestablishment figure, I think."

"He must have thought that because I spent some time in jail. But the protest was strictly private. The only one it served was me."

The reverend only smiled, as though his case were private, too.

"I take it from the psalm and from what you just said that you knew Billy pretty well," I said.

"I knew him. Yes."

"Did he go to this church?"

"Not in the accepted sense."

"I didn't think so. That wouldn't have squared with the picture of him I've gotten from everyone else in town."

"Pictures are sometimes misleading, Mr. Tanner. There is frequently an element of trompe l'oeil about them, particularly when framed by a town like Chaldea. Billy was a very devout young man, in his own way."

"He and a girl he knew used to have trysts down in your basement, Reverend. Did you know that?"

"Generally, yes. Specifically, no. It didn't matter, if that's what you're asking."

I lifted my brows.

"One of the greatest mistakes people in my profession make is to apply the same standards to everyone. The Lord does not demand inflexibility, except perhaps when dispensing forgiveness and compassion. Were it otherwise we would not revere Saint Paul or Saint Augustine, among others."

The minister put his hands in his pockets and began to move among the scattered chairs as though he hoped to lose me in their maze. I just stood and watched him meander for a minute. "Why did Billy come to see you, Reverend?" I asked, as he was about to pirouette again.

"Just to talk."

"What about?"

He stopped walking and looked around, as though surprised to find himself in such a thicket. "The kinds of things you would expect us to talk about. And more. Billy was a thoughtful young man. More so than I, in many respects."

"You're not very forthcoming, Reverend."

"I seldom am when it comes to what people have told me within these walls."

"You're not a priest and Billy wasn't a penitent," I said with anger. "No legal privilege attaches to those conversations."

"That's hardly the issue," he replied placidly, and resumed walking. I moved to cut him off.

"I'm leaving town tomorrow," I said, when he had to stop to keep from stepping on me. "I'd like to know who killed Billy before I go. I think you can tell me, or point me in the right direction."

Vesselton closed his eyes and rubbed them. "Come into my office," he said finally, and walked around me toward the farthest door.

I followed him into a closet of a room that was lined with books and prints of modern art. Among the books were a surprising number of novels, as well as tracts by Eastern mystics. Among the art were reproductions of works by men as secular as Warhol, as ambiguous as Rauschenberg.

The reverend sat at a littered desk. The chair I sat in was soft and comfortable, making conversation or confession easy. Beside me on a stand was a King James Bible, heavy and black, as thick as sod. Beside the Bible was a typed text dated the following Sunday. Its title was "Nuclear War—The Hell of Man, Not God." When I was comfortable enough to suit him, Vesselton spoke. "Now, what makes you think I can help you, Mr. Tanner? I have no evidence that Billy was killed."

"I'm not suggesting you do. But I've been nosing around a lot the past couple of days. Virtually everyone in Chaldea disliked Billy, as I'm sure you know. But I can't match any of them with when and how he was killed. By the process of elimination I've reached the point where I think the key is something in Billy's past. And I have the feeling, based upon the psalm you read, that you know more about Billy's past than anyone else in Chaldea, his parents included."

The reverend considered my words for a long minute. A clock on the shelf behind him peppered the room with sound. The curtains across the little window behind me made the air seem scorched. I looked at the books again. Vesselton seemed equally enamored of Thomas Merton and Peter de Vries.

"Do you have anything specific in mind, Mr. Tanner? I mean, I'm reluctant to simply spew out everything Billy told me. He was an imaginative and an angry boy. A true skeptic. He challenged everything, in ways that many would find shocking, if not blasphemous. Perhaps even a sophisticated man such as yourself."

"I haven't been called sophisticated since I took a bottle of cognac and a foreign exchange student to a frat party, Reverend. But if you want me to be specific, I will. Vietnam. Talk to me about Billy and the war."

Vesselton nodded slowly. "It's where I would begin as well. The horror of what he went through is unimaginable, I think, even to me. And I was there myself for a time."

"As what?"

"A chaplain. America Division. At one time I intended to make it my life's work. I thought God should more than anywhere be present on the field of battle. I soon realized that war is a corruption of everything I believe, of everything that Jesus taught, and that many of the most corrupt enlist God in their enterprise. So I decided the deliverer of God's message can't wait till the trigger is pulled, he must speak before the gun is purchased."

"That tells me something about you," I said. "Now tell me something about Billy."

"But what?"

"Something he did that would make someone want to kill him."

"It's quite a long list."

"Tell me," I insisted.

Vesselton reached for the paraphernalia for lighting his pipe and scraped it to him. It was a ritual he enjoyed and performed with the precision of a watchmaker. I endured it, barely.

"Billy served as a special scout," he said, after the room was putrid with aromatic blends. "Essentially his assignment was to kill people. Specific people." The reverend looked at me to see if this was news. I indicated that it wasn't.

"Most of his victims were Viet Cong agents who had infiltrated otherwise friendly hamlets and were trying to subvert them. But at other times Billy killed friendlies, popular village leaders who were clearly on our side. The psywar types evidently felt that if some such leaders were killed in ways that made it appear to be the work of the VC, then the village would be more easily pacified. This was in the days when shaded maps were more important than human lives." The reverend's smile was spectral.

"What about Americans?" I asked. "Did any of our troops have any reason to want Billy out of the way?"

"Well, he turned adamantly against the war, as you know. He knew a lot of things about a lot of people who were doing the kinds of things he had done. Some of those people may be in vulnerable positions now, politics or what have you. Publicity about their wartime activities could possibly hurt."

"Or help."

"Possibly. Also, Billy was once ordered by an American colonel to kill an American artillery captain the colonel believed was undermining the morale of the unit."

"Did he do it?"

"I believe so."

"Do you know any names?"

"No."

I thought about it while the reverend perfected the draw in his pipe. "I saw some Orientals up on the square the other day. Who are they?"

"Boat people, the townspeople call them. This state has

taken in many Southeast Asian refugees. Thousands of them. Several have ended up here in Chaldea. One family has opened a restaurant just off the square. Some of the others have their own enterprises as well, tailoring and what have you."

"How many of them are there?"

"Here? About twenty, perhaps. The number seems to fluctuate, especially lately. There's a lot of movement among these people now, because of the pressures on them."

"So there may be some new arrivals in town?"

"It's possible. I don't really know. I do speak some Vietnamese and have gotten to know the family that owns the restaurant quite well. They're amazing people. Their daughter is a certified genius."

"What kinds of pressures are there?"

"Well, locally there have been incidents. When hard times hit the town some people started blaming the refugees for taking jobs that so-called Americans should have. But most of the things the refugees are doing in Chaldea aren't in conflict with the normal work force in any way."

"What kind of incidents?"

"Oh, someone, probably kids, painted a swastika on the restaurant door a few weeks ago. And one young man was mugged a few nights later, took a bad beating after a football game. And there's been some other trouble at the high school, I hear, mostly verbal. On top of the local problems, of course, a lot of tension is developing among the refugees, not just here but everywhere."

"Why?"

"First are the general things, the move to a strange land, the problem with the customs and the language. And of course the government in its wisdom has recently ended financial benefits for Asians who have been in this country for eighteen months or more, which most of them have by now. And then there are undercurrents I'm only dimly aware of."

"Like what?"

The reverend emptied his pipe into an ashtray shaped like an entreating hand. "There are hundreds of thousands of Southeast Asians in America now. Which means they've brought the kinds of problems that will be generated anywhere by a population of that number. In major cities a kind of mafia has developed in the refugee sectors. Extortion flourishes, along with other crimes. Then there are the tribal feuds that have simply been transported from Vietnam and Laos to America. Then recently there's been a movement afoot to recruit an army to go back to South Vietnam and retake the country from the Communists."

"You're kidding."

"Not at all. It's much like the anti-Castro force that was active in Florida and Guatemala a while back. My understanding is that some former ARVN officers are right now on the Laotian border trying to put together an army to move into Vietnam and begin guerrilla activities. Somewhat ironic, isn't it?"

"A bit."

"So there's pressure on these people from all sides. The kids become Americanized and shock the parents by their actions. Rumors of threats and dangers flourish. A recent one had it that the government was going to put all the Asians in concentration camps in Alaska. Another was that Viet Cong death squads have come to this country to eliminate everyone who collaborated with America during the war against the north. Perhaps you've heard of the sudden-death syndrome that strikes many Asian men. They just drop dead, from no apparent cause. I think it's stress myself. The strains are tremendous, and this on people who have lived with the stress of war for decades before they came over here. It's a sad chapter for a nation that already has a lot of sad chapters in its book."

"Do you know of any connection between the Vietnamese in Chaldea and Billy?"

"No."

"Do you know anything at all that might be helpful?"

"Only that Billy seemed very fatalistic the last time I saw him. He couched it in religious terms. Day of Judgment. Atonement. Mortal sin. He used these words when we spoke."

I shifted position and waited while the reverend sucked his pipe again. "Let's get down to it," I said. "What's the worst thing Billy did over there? The very worst."

"What do you mean?"

"I mean there must have been one thing that he thought was more horrible than the others, that messed with his mind more than all the rest. I want to know what it was."

The reverend smoked his pipe. His eyes were closed.

"Come on, goddamnit."

"Phuoc Binh," Vesselton said, and opened his eyes.

"What about Phuoc Binh?"

"That's a town. Billy went in one night to terminate a VC. When he was in the center of town he was surprised by a group of children. Three of them, about twelve or so, two boys and a girl who were out poking around for some excitement in the middle of the night when they were supposed to be in bed. Billy had no way out, he said. It was them or him."

"So he killed them."

The reverend nodded. "They started to run. He had a silenced weapon. He used it reflexively, virtually without thinking. He shot them all and he couldn't get the picture of it out of his mind—the blood, the choking sounds, the time it took the girl, particularly, to die while Billy held his hand over her mouth to keep her screams from being heard."

The reverend's words were agonized, his voice wrenched. I felt the pain myself, but stayed silent. Nothing I could say would deflate the cloud of sadness in the room.

"Billy was sick," I said finally. "Physically, I mean. Did he talk about it?"

"A little. It was Agent Orange, of course."

"Did he get treatment?"

"No. I tried to get him to go to the Veterans Hospital in the state capital but he refused. His only concern was that the baby might be damaged, but he knew of nothing that could be done about that save abortion, which he refused to accept."

"I'd like to talk to the Vietnamese who own the restaurant," I said. "Will you help me?"

"Of course. Up to a point."

"What point is that?"

"The point where I think you're taking the law into your own hands."

"Hell, Reverend. I've been doing that since the minute I hit town."

# Chapter
# 28

The restaurant was on North Tenth a half block off the square, the narrow storefront struggling for breath between a cobbler's shop and an insurance agency. I stopped the car at the end of the block. Vesselton looked at me. "What exactly is it you want to know?"

"Whether any of them knew Billy. Whether any of them felt threatened or wronged by him in any way. If they deny knowing him, I want to know whether any new refugees have arrived in town, men, within the past month or so. If so, I want to know who and where they are."

"You don't want much," Vesselton said, his sarcasm a bit of banter.

"I want what I have to have," I said, and got out of the car.

I followed Vesselton toward the restaurant. The sign over the door read "Qui Nhon Café—Vietnamese and American Specialties." The windows seemed glassless and were curtained with checked gingham. The door had a bell above it that made our arrival seem gay and exciting.

There was no one in the place except for three Vietnamese sitting at a table in the back, eating something that smelled like boiled fish. Vesselton walked toward them without pausing, smiling like a peddler. I hung back.

Two of the Vietnamese were old, a couple, their sienna skins shrunk tight across the sanded bones of their faces, their blinkless eyes not on the reverend but on me, eyes as hard as nuts from lives spent watching threats approach. The third was a girl, young and svelte, her hair a plank of black enamel, her eyes still liquid, not yet turned to stone by a life of jeopardy.

All of them rose as the reverend approached. He shook the man's hand and bowed to the woman and the girl. They exchanged some words I couldn't hear and the girl left through a door in the back that I assumed went to the kitchen. I decided not to approach unless invited.

A minute later Vesselton and the couple were seated at the table, talking rapidly. The girl emerged from the kitchen and served them tea in tiny cups. Then she came toward me. "Would you like a menu, sir?" she asked. Her voice was friendly in a practiced way. Her face was the kind that makes you cry because of what might someday happen to it.

"I'll just have coffee, if you have it," I said.

"Of course. Would you care for cream or sugar?"

"Black."

"Thank you."

She left me awestruck, her image as strong in my mind as though she were beside me in a bed. When she brought me my coffee I smiled and got friendly. For the first time her shiny features stiffened. She was already used to bullies and to braggarts and was steeling herself for what was to come from me. "I hear you're an excellent student," I said cheerily.

"I try to be."

"What subject do you like best?"

"History. World history."

"Why do you like it?"

"I want to know what happened," she said simply. "Do you care for anything else, sir?"

I wanted to pump her about Billy but I didn't have the heart. I told her I was fine and she left me gladly. I finished my coffee without tasting it, wondering if the Reverend Vesselton was doing my work for me, wondering if I any longer cared.

Ten minutes later Vesselton stood up, shook hands again and bowed, and came to where I was. "We may have something," he said.

"What?"

"A man came to town last month. A man named Tran Lam Duc. He'd been living in LA, at least that's what he said."

"Why did he come here?"

"Looking for relatives, he claimed. Apparently he didn't find any, so he was working here in the restaurant to earn enough money to move on."

"Where is he now?"

The reverend shrugged. "They don't know. They haven't seen him for three days."

"Where does he live?"

"No one knows. Or so they say. I pressed as much as I thought I could. I didn't want to frighten them."

I doubted that anything the reverend and I were capable of would frighten them. "Did Duc tell anyone he was leaving town?"

"No."

"Where was he from in Vietnam?"

"I don't know."

"Ask," I said.

Vesselton went back to the table and said some words and had some said to him. Then he came back. "Phuoc Binh," he said, as though reciting code

"Let's find him."

"Where?"

"I've got one guess," I said, and stood and headed for the door.

The sun had left Chaldea. I shoved my way through the dusty twilight like the invader that I was, my thoughts on death and vengeance. By the time I reached the edge of town I thought I knew what I was going to find, and what I was going to do when I found it. When I stopped the car the reverend asked me where we were.

"This is the Tanner plot," I told him. "The family farm. Billy lived out here, about a mile south of us. I was out here myself the other day. There's an old farmhouse on the other side of this field. A part of it looks lived in. Also, the farmer across the road has seen strangers around lately. I assumed it was probably Zedda or his people, checking up on Billy, but now I think this Tran Lam Duc was living here. I think he tracked Billy down and killed him for what he did in Phuoc Binh. My guess is when Billy turned against the war he told lots of people what he'd been doing, even before he left Vietnam. His name probably got linked to the Phuoc Binh killings. Word eventually got to Tran Lam Duc and he came here to get revenge. There were small hand prints all over Billy's body. Small, like an American woman or a Vietnamese man."

I got out of the car and Vesselton joined me on the weedy road into the farm. "The farmhouse is at the back edge of the field," I said to him. "Let's take it slow and easy, move along the hedgerow. Be ready to find cover. The guy could be armed. Of course, you don't have to come with me," I added.

"I think I do," Vesselton said. We moved out in the dim light of the reverend's worried smile.

We seemed to make enough noise to wake the dead, if the dead do sleep, but the wind was in our faces and the sounds were mostly muffled stumblings and bumblings. It took us long enough to work up a sweat, and the night air immediately cooled it to a frigid shawl. When we reached the farmhouse I told Vesselton to wait outside while I went in. He made a silent protest but I ignored it.

"Do you have a gun?" he whispered.

"I don't even have a flashlight," I said, then left him in the weeds.

In the next minute I crossed the creaky porch and slipped through the door, trying to see what might be lying in wait in the dim dark corners of the dilapidated rooms. Something small skittered across the floor in front of me, making sounds that scared me. The smell of feces and decay was as present in the house as I was. I closed my eyes to improve my night vision, then moved into the main room as far as I dared, leery of crashing through the remaining floorboards and even more leery of stumbling across something vile or deadly or both.

I stayed in the house for a long time, looking and listening, then went back outside. "Anything?" Vesselton asked.

"I don't think so," I said. "I'll take one more look."

I reached down and pulled a handful of dried weeds out of the dirt and twisted them into a scraggly rope and went back inside the farmhouse. When I was in the middle of the room I struck a match and lit the weeds. My torch burned briefly but brightly, enough to show me there was nothing human in the house but me. I went back outside and pointed to the barn and started to walk that way. Vesselton followed without encouragement or caution.

The manure-spreader guarded the entrance like a seedy

majordomo. Inside the barn the sweet smell of mown hay toyed with my nose, then made me sneeze, to win the game. Cobwebs brushed my face like the fingers of a practiced whore. A score of sparrows played a different game among the rafters. I told the reverend I'd check it out and left him behind me near the door.

The barn had once stalled milk cows, but was no longer used for anything but warehousing. A few broken tools hung from pegs in the walls and a ripped bag of seed spilled its kerneled guts onto the floor. I grabbed a pitchfork to keep me company, but there was light from the moon enough for me to see that there was nothing threatening on the ground level, at least nothing that wasn't hiding out. A pigeon flapped suddenly away and caused my heart to burp.

I came to a stop beside the ladder to the mow. I didn't want to go up there, but if what I thought I'd find was anywhere on the farm, that was where it was. I ran my hand across a rung, then flapped my fingers across my thumb like a high roller on the verge of crapping out. When the only thing I felt was flesh, I put a foot on the bottom rung and climbed.

Most of the hay was gone, eaten by beef long butchered and by holsteins long milked dry. At the end of the mow the loading door was open, and the square of sky behind it was the purplish color of gun barrels and festered wounds. The body that hung from the rafters was perfectly framed in the opening, as though the event had been staged entirely for my pleasure.

For a moment it looked simply like a branchless tree that rose out of the crumpled bales below it. Then it twisted in the wind and the broken neck threw the image off and it looked like only what it was. When I touched the yellow flesh it was as cold as mine, though not with sweat.

Below the body something glistened in the moonlight like a gem. I picked it up and read the printing pressed into the shiny metal:

TANNER,
WILLIAM L.
US 54928078
O
PROTESTANT

I put the dog tag in my pocket and backed down the listing ladder. When I reached the reverend he asked me what I'd found.

"Tran Lam Duc. Dead. By his own hand."

"How?"

"Just like Billy."

"My God."

"Yours. Mine. His. Billy's."

"What are you going to do?"

"Go back to California."

"I mean about the sheriff."

I walked out of the barn and toward the car, across a field cobbled with chopped stalks and heavy clods of dirt, lurching like a spastic. Halfway to the road I stopped and turned to face the trailing preacher. "Do you have any doubt about what happened?" I asked him.

"How do you mean?"

"I mean, do you have any doubt that Duc killed Billy for what he did at Phuoc Binh? Or that Billy let him do it? Or that Duc then hung himself?"

"I'm . . . I'm not sure."

"Sure you're sure. So am I."

"What if I am?"

"Do you think anyone will be better off for knowing what we know?"

"I don't know. Billy's parents, surely."

"Do they know about Phuoc Binh?"

"I don't know."

"Come on, Reverend. Billy didn't tell them and you know it."

"I suppose not. No. I'm certain they don't know."

"You think they want to?"

"No."

"Neither do I."

"So what do we do?" the reverend asked.

"Nothing."

"But . . ."

"The guy across the road will find the body someday. And the sheriff may make a pretty good guess about the link between Duc and Billy. But unless one of us talks, that's all it'll be. A guess. And they don't print guesses like that in the papers. Not in Mary Martha Gormley's paper, at least."

"So we just go home?"

"You go to the manse and I go to California. I'm not sure where my home is anymore."

We got into the car and I put it in gear and drove a ways down the bumpy road, then stopped again. At the crest of the field beyond us, beneath the ring of yellow moon, two lights swept slowly across the faint horizon, bobbing lightly just above the ground, moving always west. I couldn't make out what they were, those lights, and I tried not to imagine wild reasons for their presence. After a time I grew conscious of Vesselton's eyes on my face.

"It's only Waiters," he said. "Picking corn. They expect some rain tomorrow."

"Oh."

"What did you think it was anyway?"

"I don't know," I said. "Something from another world, I guess."

The next morning Sally drove me to the airport. Along the way we talked about a lot of things. Important things. She told me she'd decided not to move to San Francisco. At least not right then. When we said good-bye she asked if I would write. I said I would. We both knew I was lying.